Praise for *First Among Nations*

"Ira Mosen has written a coming of age story that will resound with readers everywhere. He captures the complexities of family, religion, love and strength of finding one's own identity through the game of football. He identifies the dreams of young men pitted against their religious and moral beliefs in the beautiful telling of a story which crosses the boundaries felt by so many, for so long. Country, faith, family collide as Zar and his teammates struggle to separate these from living their own lives. An uplifting story which ultimately leads us to the only conclusion it can: it does not matter your race, religion, colour, ethnicity, we all bleed the same colour red."

— Heather Morris, author of the *New York Times* #1 bestselling book *The Tattooist of Auschwitz*

"Novels that inspire us or warm our souls capture a deeper truth. *First Among Nations* succeeds in offering a deeper truth about the challenges of different communities in Israel. The story of Zar and Hajji reminds us of not just their struggles to hold onto their identities but also their common humanity. In doing so, *First Among Nations* also reminds us of the real story of Israel."

— Dennis Ross, Former American Peace Envoy to the Middle East

"Mosen's depictions of life in Israel are vivid and captivating. *First Among Nations* is an excellent, thought-provoking read."

— Senator Joseph Lieberman

"Ira Mosen's fabulous book, *First Among Nations*, not only brings the game of soccer to life in Israel but weaves the brilliant story of Zar's struggle as an Ultra Orthodox Jew in the modern day State of Israel. Leaving his family behind to become a 'Lone Soldier' in the Israel Defense Forces, Zar finds the love of his life, Tikvah, and his crew of friends as they take an unforgettable journey that leads to the championship game of the World Cup held in Germany. Mosen expertly tells the tale of the young Zionist country with its challenges in cliffhanging fashion with plenty of surprises. You won't want to put this book down!"

— Joshua Halickman, SportsRabbi.com,
and sports columnist, *The Jerusalem Post*

"*First Among Nations* delves into the hearts and desires of those living in modern Israel. This story of several young soccer players paints a vivid picture of the interaction between the diverse cultures and religions. The reader will come away with a much better understanding of the complexities of living in a true melting pot, the dangers of anti-Semitism, and the richness gained through understanding and appreciation for one another."

— Phil Markwardt, Executive Director, Operation Exodus USA

FIRST
AMONG
NATIONS

FIRST AMONG NATIONS

A Novel about Struggle
and Perseverance
in the Holy Land

IRA MOSEN

Olive Blossom Press

ISBN (paperback): 978-1-7353741-0-9
ISBN (ebook): 978-1-7353741-1-6

Cover and interior design by Constellation Book Services

Printed in the United States of America

To Juju,
you are my tikvah...

PROLOGUE

The Germans were heavily favored to win the match. Their 2022 team, featuring several of Europe's top players, was reputed to be one of the best ever to have represented Germany in the World Cup. They were the reigning champions, and they had already handily defeated the Israelis in the qualifying round. Also, they had home field advantage.

With time running out and overtime imminent, the game remained scoreless, and all the players were tiring physically and mentally. Every now and then, the crowd would erupt as one team or the other snuck a shot at goal, only to be deflected by the fingertips of the goalkeeper.

As the sun set and the floodlights came on, a gentle breeze caressed Zar and the other perspiring players. Zar felt transfixed, dissociated; he envisioned himself back in the alleyway where he'd practiced soccer as a child, imagining adoring fans chanting his name: "Luzar, Luzar, Luzar..." He saw himself playing in the schoolyard with the *traif* boys, imagining adoring fans chanting his name: "Zar, Zar, Zar..." He recalled the night he ran away from home and heard his father call his name: "Luzar, Luzar, Luzar..."

He imagined—as if the sound could carry over the thousands of miles—that he could hear the fans chanting his name in the streets of Jerusalem. He was above nature, invincible, the only man on the field: there were no opponents, no teammates, just Zar and a ball and a goal. And no force on Earth could stop Zar from reaching that goal.

PART ONE

CHAPTER 1

Until he was twelve years old, Elazar had never ventured more than a few miles from Mea She'arim, the insular Jerusalem neighborhood that was his childhood home. In his dreams, however, he had traveled the world, visiting the most exotic places, sailing the high seas and sojourning on tropical islands, traversing the desert on camelback and discovering hidden oases. But most of all, he dreamed about playing professional soccer, jetting around the globe and competing against teams from cities in Europe and beyond.

His mother had given birth to him, with the assistance of a midwife, in a small apartment overlooking the ancient stone walls of Jerusalem's Old City. She gazed at these walls as she endured her labor pains, reciting prayers in the hope that her son would be a pious Jew and a Torah scholar.

His father named him Elazar (pronounced "Eloozar" in the Hungarian dialect of Yiddish spoken in his Hasidic neighborhood) in memory of the boy's great-grandfather. Elazar was a *kohen*, a member of the family of priests, so the name also commemorated the biblical high priest Elazar. As a child, Elazar was known as Luzar—pronounced "loser," although he was utterly oblivious to the negative connotations of his nickname in English.

Elazar was playful, even charming, but seldom crossed the line from wittiness to outright *chutzpah*. He was an adorable child, with thick, black hair, shaved on top and grown into long sidelocks on either side of his cherubic face. His mother pampered Elazar, the youngest of her eleven children, curling up his sidelocks at night with a curling iron. Elazar often objected to this practice, complaining that long curly hair was for girls.

Elazar's father, however, was adamant in demanding that Elazar grow his sidelocks long. He had a near obsession with them, and would often subject Elazar to his diatribe about the Yemenite children, whose sidelocks had been cut off by the Zionists in the early days of the Jewish state. "The heretics cut off their *'peyos'* and swept them away, along with the rest of their ancient traditions!"

The outside world, his parents had taught him, was too dangerous, filled with too many temptations and too many pernicious influences. In Mea She'arim, his parents thought, he would be shielded from those influences. In Elazar's cloistered world, everything was divided into two categories: kosher and *traif*. Only food with the strictest rabbinical supervision was permitted. But kosher and *traif* also applied to every conceivable activity. Kosher activities included prayer, performance of good deeds and other ritual obligations, and, above all else, studying holy books. The list of *traif* activities included almost everything else: secular books and media, movies and television, the internet, and secular music. Even toys and games were divided into kosher and *traif*. Sports that were popular among secular Israelis were also considered *traif*, so on the seemingly endless list of *traif* activities was soccer.

Elazar didn't mind refraining from reading secular books or magazines; he didn't really enjoy reading anyway. Nor did he oppose the strictures against television, movies, or the internet; he had never experienced any of these alleged vices, so he didn't long for them. But Elazar resented the restriction on soccer. He had never even played a formal game of soccer, but he very much enjoyed kicking his only ball in the alleyway behind his apartment building. He loved to imagine that he was playing for a professional team. Every afternoon, after he came home from school, he practiced dribbling the ball with his imaginary team on an imaginary field in an imaginary stadium, imagining hordes of adoring fans chanting his name—"Luzar, Luzar, Luzar!"—as he kicked the ball into an imaginary goal.

Elazar's father was a tall and imposing figure. He too had black hair, shaved on top and grown into long curly sidelocks on the sides.

His black beard was peppered with specks of white, and his wardrobe consisted of only two colors: black and white. He wore a long black frock coat, black knickers, black slip-on shoes, a white shirt, and white stockings. Although he was fluent in Hebrew, he insisted on speaking only Yiddish at home. Modern Hebrew, he maintained, was invented by the Zionists, and the Hebrew of the Bible and other holy books—which he called *loshn koydesh*, "the holy tongue"—was reserved for prayer and study.

Elazar spent so much time practicing soccer that his grades suffered. As a punishment, his father confiscated his ball and scolded him for behaving like a *goy*. So Elazar improvised, using old rags tied into knots to form a makeshift ball. But his father soon confiscated the rag-ball as well, and scolded him again...and again.

So Elazar ran away. He had no real intention of leaving home permanently; he just needed a change of scenery. He walked up Mea She'arim Street, down winding staircases and narrow alleyways, until he saw a school building. It was a public school, with an Israeli flag flying from its roof. In the schoolyard were a bunch of boys, mostly bareheaded, but some wearing tiny knitted yarmulkes. And they were playing soccer! Elazar had never before seen an actual game of soccer. He watched with amazement, twirling his sidelocks with his fingers, spellbound, as the *traif* boys played their *traif* game with their *traif* ball.

When the game ended, the boys took the ball and left the schoolyard. Only then did Elazar realize how much time had elapsed. It was almost dark now; his parents would surely be looking for him. He hastily retraced his steps, up narrow staircases and alleyways, back to Mea She'arim Street, and back to his home. When he entered the apartment, his mother was crying and his father was pacing back and forth in their tiny kitchen. As punishment for his disobedience, Elazar received a smack on the backside and was grounded. For one week, he would have to come straight home after school, and he couldn't leave home until he went back to school the following morning.

For the next week, Elazar would go to school and dream all day about soccer. But now he dreamed of playing not with an imaginary team on an imaginary field, but with the *traif* boys and their *traif* ball in the *traif* yard of their *traif* school. After he came home from school, he would go straight to his bedroom and daydream some more about soccer, using laundry as an improvised soccer ball.

One night he overheard his mother pleading with his father to give him back the ball. "I want him to be happy!" she cried in Yiddish.

"Torah study and serving God are the only paths to happiness."

"But he's just a boy..."

CHAPTER 2

Elazar's *rebbe* was a diminutive, petulant man. He grew his fiery red beard and sidelocks extraordinarily long—perhaps to compensate for his short stature—and he carried a wooden stick, which he found to be a most versatile tool. He used it to point to the blackboard and to call upon boys who had raised their hands. He waved it over his head for emphasis when he was lecturing the children. But the stick also served as a silent display of his authority; periodically, he would strike an inattentive student with it. More often than not, that student was Elazar.

After his week of punishment was over, Elazar was warned not to leave the neighborhood. He was to walk straight home after school and play in the alley behind their apartment building. But the temptation to leave was too great. No force in nature could keep him away from that schoolyard. All day long, Elazar was preoccupied with his thoughts. He couldn't pay attention to his *rebbe* at all (and, consequently, he had to endure more than a few strikes from his *rebbe*'s stick). He planned the shortest route to the *traif* school and knew to remain cognizant of the time so he wouldn't come home too late.

The afternoon lesson was about the ritual sacrifice of the paschal lamb. The sun outside the classroom window cast a dark shadow on the *rebbe* as he described the details of the slaughter and disemboweling of the lamb. Elazar's thoughts were elsewhere. Jewish children, the *rebbe* explained, are the guardians of the faith; they must adhere to every detail of law and custom and strictly follow the instructions of their leaders. "You are the sheep," he told them, "who follow the shepherd without question or protest." Elazar, meanwhile, continued to daydream. "Repeat after me," said the rebbe, "We are sheep!"

The children complied, quietly at first: "We are sheep."

"Louder!" the rebbe demanded.

"We are sheep!"

"Again!"

"We are sheep!"

"*Again!*"

"*We are sheep! We are sheep! We are sheep!*" The children chanted over and over, in a frenzy, as the rebbe waved his stick over his head like an orchestra conductor. Some of the boys stood on their desks; others ran around the classroom. Soon the entire class—except Elazar—was dancing wildly. The tumult woke Elazar from his trance, and it gave him an opportunity to sneak out of the classroom.

Elazar ran out of school and through the back alley shortcut he'd devised. When he arrived at the schoolyard, he was dismayed. The schoolyard was empty. The soccer goals were still there, but there were no boys and no ball. Had it been a dream? An urban mirage? Elazar trudged home with his head lowered, disappointed and discouraged, but undeterred. He knew that he would return to the schoolyard one day. He had to! But for now, he could only dream about it.

CHAPTER 3

In Elazar's world, God was not an abstract concept; He pervaded every aspect of life. In casual conversation, phrases such as "Thank God" and "God willing" were commonplace. Stories about divine intervention in the affairs of men, especially pious men, were ubiquitous. And people, even ordinary people, would routinely speak with God. Elazar was accustomed to speaking with God too. When he was young, his requests tended to be juvenile and picayune. But as he matured, his requests and supplications became more sophisticated. After his disappointing return trip to the schoolyard, Elazar was angry at God. "Why did you send the *traif* boys away?" he asked. "Were you trying to send me a message?"

Elazar concluded that God *had*, in fact, sent him a message: he needed to improve his skills before returning to the schoolyard to play soccer with the *traif* boys. Every available minute, he would practice soccer in the alleyway. He created challenges for himself, aiming at a certain crack in the brick wall or at a plastic shopping bag that had somehow gotten stuck in a wire fence. One day, he took different-colored chalks and drew targets along the brick wall, some high and some low. He drew a series of concentric arcs on the pavement and created a point system, awarding himself points for accuracy and distance. He timed himself to see how many points he could accrue in one minute or five minutes.

He continued these drills, honing his skills day after day until his right foot was sore from kicking the ball. Out of desperation, he tried kicking with his left foot, and serendipitously discovered something that would forever change his life: to his great surprise and gratification, he found that his left-footed strikes were both forceful and accurate. His right hand was clearly his dominant hand, but when it came to his feet, he was ambidextrous. His left foot was not yet as effective as his right, but he had practiced a great deal with his right foot, and he knew that with enough training, he could improve his left-sided game to parallel the right. So for the next few weeks, he would use only his left foot for dribbling and kicking. He learned to step off the right side to set up his left for a kick, and he experimented, shifting his weight with his hips and shoulders to maximize the power and accuracy of his kicks. Eventually, his left foot also began to ache, but he reveled in the pain. And to make his drills even more challenging, he put obstacles on the pavement: a garbage can here, a cracked plastic chair over there, and a broken baby stroller, missing one wheel, in the middle.

But as much as he practiced, as much as he honed his skills, he knew that he needed coaching from someone who really knew how to play the game. And he needed teammates and opponents other than the ones he conjured in his fantasies.

Elazar had inherited his cherubic face from his mother. People often remarked that the two of them could be picked out from a crowd as mother and son. In his mother's more youthful days, she had been quite attractive. But with the passage of time, raising a large family and struggling with constant financial pressures, her previously pretty face had become creased, leaving her with a permanently worried appearance, as if she carried the weight of the world on her shoulders. She shaved her head regularly to preserve her modesty, as is the custom among some Hasidim. Her head was always covered with a cloth, stuffed with padding to disguise the curvature of her skull—if it were visible, that too would be deemed immodest.

Elazar's mother peered through the window, silently observing her son as he practiced his sport with great focus and dedication. "What will become of this boy?" she pondered. "Will he ever lose interest in this passion of his? When will he start to study and pray with even half of the devotion that he has for soccer?" She then tearfully recited a prayer, paraphrasing one that is usually said while lighting the Sabbath candles on Friday nights: "May I merit to raise sons who are wise and God-fearing and who enlighten the world with their Torah scholarship and good deeds and holy service." Elazar glanced up at his mother in the window and pretended not to have noticed her as she softly wept.

CHAPTER 4

Elazar's paternal grandfather was the patriarch of the family. He was known throughout their community as a pious and wise elder, offering sage advice to all who sought it. His hoary countenance was framed by curly white sidelocks and a dignified white beard flecked with streaks of silver. His face was adorned with a perpetual smile, in keeping with the Talmudic dictum to always greet people with a pleasant demeanor. He would share with young Elazar stories about all the pious rabbis who were his ancestors. Elazar especially enjoyed hearing the story of how his own paternal great-grandfather, the elder Elazar, had survived the war in Europe.

Elazar's great-grandfather was a Hasidic Jew from Budapest. While on a business trip to Munich in November 1938, he was apprehended during the Kristallnacht pogrom. He was beaten mercilessly, then detained in the Dachau concentration camp on the outskirts of the city. Ironically, it was his detention in Dachau that ultimately saved his life: after the war broke out, he escaped from Dachau while on a work detail and managed to reach Switzerland, crossing Lake Constance on a stolen rowboat in the middle of the night. For the next five years, he was unable to reunite with his family, who were eventually deported from Hungary to Auschwitz in the spring of 1944. They were all killed; he was the only member of his extended family to survive the Holocaust. Ultimately, he found his way to Jerusalem, where he started anew, found a new wife, and raised a family.

Elazar's grandfather never shared stories about his childhood. Elazar assumed that his grandfather had always been pious and righteous.

When Elazar was eleven years old, his grandfather died. Large black-and-white posters were pasted to the walls along Mea She'arim Street announcing the passing of the great, wise, and righteous elder and *kohen*. The funeral would be held that very day. He would be buried next to his father, Elazar's great-grandfather, in the ancient cemetery on the Mount of Olives in East Jerusalem.

In keeping with the Jerusalem tradition, Elazar's father and uncles—the sons of the deceased—did not participate in the funeral procession. And because a *kohen* is biblically commanded to avoid any contact with dead bodies, Elazar and his brothers were also forbidden from entering the cemetery.

Elazar found the eulogies monotonous. For the most part, they described his grandfather's wisdom, righteousness, and commitment to scrupulous observance of the commandments. There were occasional references to the father of the deceased, Elazar's great-grandfather, and his miraculous escape from Germany.

Over the next week, hundreds of people came to the small apartment where Elazar's family was sitting *shiva*. Many were rabbis, some of them famous rabbis accompanied by entourages. But some of the visitors were old childhood friends of his grandfather, and some of these men wore more colorful secular clothing and did not sport beards or long sidelocks. One of these men introduced himself to Elazar. His name was Simcha, and he told Elazar that he'd been friends with his grandfather since he was younger than Elazar. Simcha was a cheerful, elderly man who limped as he walked, one hand holding a cane and the other cradling his aching, arthritic hip. His playful smile ineffectually concealed a grimace as he spoke in a soft voice, almost whispering, as if he were sharing confidential information. He tantalized Elazar with fragments of sentences: "He was so mischievous as a youngster," "Your grandfather and I had so much fun dodging bullets from the Jordanian snipers," and "He was the best soccer player I knew...he could have played professionally, you know."

Elazar was enthralled. His pious old grandfather, always serious, with his long white beard and long black coat, was playful, even mischievous as a child—and he had played soccer! Twirling his sidelocks, Elazar asked for more details about his grandfather. But his father, who was always mindful to shield Elazar from pernicious outside influences, called out half-seriously, "Reb Simcha, leave the boy alone and stop poisoning his mind with foolishness." The two men spoke for a while, then Simcha got up and recited the traditional salutation for mourners: "May the Ever-Present console you among the rest of the mourners of Zion and Jerusalem." After that, Simcha said goodbye to everyone, and as he was leaving the room, he whispered to Elazar, "Come visit me at the nursing home on Zechariah Street sometime to hear more stories about the good old days."

Elazar had a newfound respect for his deceased grandfather, and he had a burning desire to learn more about his childhood. When he went to bed that night, he asked God if Simcha had been telling the truth: "Did my grandfather really play soccer? Was he really mischievous as a boy?"

CHAPTER 5

Elazar was now preoccupied with the need to find Simcha, who had known his grandfather and had information about him that Elazar's mother and father had never revealed. Why did they keep it secret? What were they hiding from him?

Fortunately, there was only one nursing home on Zechariah Street: Bais Avos. It had only male residents, and most, but not all, of them were Hasidic. In the lobby, Elazar saw several old Hasidic men in wheelchairs talking. There was no receptionist, so he decided to ask the old men if they knew a resident named Simcha. They answered affirmatively. Simcha liked to work in the garden behind the building, and he could often be found there. So Elazar walked along a narrow corridor until he saw a door leading to a backyard. Elazar was delighted when he entered the garden and saw Simcha there, holding onto his cane with one hand and pulling weeds from among the tomato plants with the other.

"Luzar, you came to visit. I can't tell you how happy I am to see you!" Simcha exclaimed, shifting his left hand from the weeds and resting it on his aching hip. Initially, Elazar was a bit shy. Simcha wasn't exactly *traif*, but he wasn't completely kosher either. Finally, Elazar said meekly, "You started telling me some stories when my father was sitting *shiva*... and I've been dying of curiosity since then."

The two of them sat down on a bench in the shade, underneath an aged, sinuous carob tree.

"Oh, do I have stories to tell you! Where should I start?"

"Soccer. You mentioned that my grandfather played soccer," Elazar said, twirling his sidelocks. "Did he really play soccer?"

"He didn't just *play* soccer. He was a *great* soccer player. You know, when we were growing up, things were different. It was right after the big wars—I mean the big war in Europe and the war here in Israel a few years later. The religious community wasn't as organized as it is today, and it wasn't as strict. People were just glad to have survived, glad to be alive. The children played together. Your grandfather and I were inseparable. We played hide-and-seek; we knew every secret hiding place in this neighborhood. And we played war: Jews versus Nazis, Jews versus Arabs. But more than anything else, we played soccer. And of all the kids in the neighborhood, no one was better than your grandfather." Elazar sat, wide-eyed, hanging on every word. "He was so quick. He could dribble the ball past any defender and kick it harder and straighter than any other kid."

"As we got older, there were more expectations for us. You know what I mean. In our community, the little boys play after school, but the older boys are supposed to be in the study halls, studying day and night. Not your grandfather. He kept on playing soccer. And when most of the kids lost interest in playing, he found other kids to play with, kids in other neighborhoods, from families that weren't so religious. When your great-grandfather and great-grandmother found out, they were furious. They forbade him from playing. But he disobeyed and kept on sneaking out of the study hall and onto the soccer field. He thought that he might even play professionally. He asked around and managed to meet some scouts for real soccer clubs."

"And then what happened?"

"Well, he was good, but not good enough. None of the professional teams were interested in him."

"So, what did he do?"

"At first he felt really rejected and angry. He thought that he really *was* good enough to play, and that the teams just didn't want him because of his background. I'm not sure who was right. But he became resentful of soccer and pretty much everything secular. He became very religious;

he put as much effort into Torah study as he had put into soccer. He became a real scholar. And then his marriage to your grandmother was arranged. They got married, and the rest is history."

Elazar was enthralled. His pious grandfather had played soccer, and he had almost played professionally!

"Tell me more! Tell me about his mischief. You said something about 'dodging bullets from Jordanian snipers.' What was that all about?"

Simcha burst out in laughter, forgetting momentarily about his arthritis. "Oh! We were crazy kids, without a fear in the world. Well, almost no fears. Back then, before the Six-Day War, the neighborhood ended at the bottom of Shmuel Hanavi Street."

"So you couldn't go to the Old City or visit the Western Wall?"

"No. The Old City was off-limits. It was on the other side of the border. There were walls and fences, and between us and them was no-man's-land."

"Who's 'them'?"

"The Jordanians. Our soldiers were on one side of the border and the Jordanian soldiers were on the other side. And between the two was a small strip of land that neither side controlled."

"Why? Why not just have a border?"

"Ah! Good question. When the War of Independence ended in 1949 — well, it didn't really end, there was just an armistice."

"What's that?"

"It's like a cease-fire. I suppose it's more than a cease-fire, but not a real end of the war. That's why there have been so many wars. The war never really ends; it just kind of pauses. Now, where was I?"

"You were telling me about the no-man's-land."

"Oh. That's right. So when there was the armistice, the two sides got together, took out a map, and marked down what the Israeli soldiers controlled and what the Jordanian soldiers controlled, and they basically just drew a line. They used a green marker, so the line was known as the Green Line. In fact, that border, between the land that was Israel before the Six-Day War and the land that Israel captured in the war, is still called the Green Line to this very day. The problem was that the marker was thick, and the green ink spread a bit as it was absorbed into the paper. So the green line on the paper took up some space, and that space became neither Jordan nor Israel. It became no-man's-land. Got it?"

"Yes. Now tell me about the snipers and the mischief."

"On the Jordanian side of the no-man's-land, there were soldiers—snipers, actually—stationed on top of buildings. We were warned to stay away, or else!"

"Or else what?"

"Or else they'd shoot."

"Did they shoot?"

"You bet they did!"

"Was anyone killed?"

"There were lots of rumors, but I don't know. It's been a long time, and I'm old now. Fact and fantasy start to get all mixed up in my mind. But I remember that day with your grandfather like it was yesterday..."

"Tell me already. I'm dying of curiosity!"

"We were playing soccer. Like I said before, we played a lot of soccer. We were playing in a vacant lot near the fence that separated us from no-man's-land. Your grandfather kicked a shot toward the goal. He kicked it so hard! This kid named Yanky was the goalkeeper; he blocked the shot and deflected it right over the fence and into no-man's-land. We all stood there with our mouths wide open, not knowing what to do. It was our only ball, and we could see it on the other side of the fence. There was a small hole in the fence, and we were skinny kids; we didn't get as much food as you kids get nowadays. But no one wanted to go through the fence to get the ball. We didn't want to disobey our mothers, who had warned us not to go into no-man's-land. We were scared of the snipers too, but I think most of us were probably more afraid of our mothers than we were of the snipers. In any case, nobody budged. Finally, your grandfather told me he would go, but only if I went with him. Somehow, if we went together, we'd feel safer, as if there was any way either one of us could protect the other from the snipers."

"So what happened?"

"We went in. He went first, then turned his head to look at me to remind me that it was my turn. Believe me, I didn't need to be reminded. I went through. Then we crawled through the grass on our bellies like snakes. We got the ball and crawled back. He went first, back through the hole in the fence to safety. It was like an unwritten rule: he'd gone in first, so he went out first. Actually, the ball went first. Then your grandfather, then me, and…"

Simcha started laughing again. He laughed so hard that his face turned red and tears started welling up in his eyes.

"Tell me already. I can't take the suspense!"

Finally, Simcha's laughter subsided enough that he was able to wheeze out a few more words.

"And then my pants got stuck on the fence!"

Simcha started laughing again, and so did Elazar. The two of them, the old man and the young boy, laughed together for nearly a full minute.

"So what happened next?"

"I was terrified, and everyone else was laughing. And we made so much noise that one of the snipers must have heard us. He started shooting. I'm sure he was just playing with us—he could easily have killed me. I was a sitting duck. My head and chest were on one side of the fence and my *tuchus* and legs were stuck on the other side. I couldn't move! The sniper shot to my left and he shot to my right. I bet he and his soldier friends thought it was the funniest thing ever. But I was so scared, I think I pished in my pants. Your grandfather and Yanky and a few other guys had to pull me out, and I tore a huge hole in my pants. Then we all ran to an alleyway behind a wall so the snipers couldn't see us, and we all burst out laughing. Boy, did I have some explaining to do when I got home and my mother saw the hole in my pants!"

"Tell me more stories about my grandfather."

"Luzar, I *so* enjoyed this visit. I haven't laughed so hard in years, probably not since that day I tore my pants. But it's getting late. They'll be serving dinner soon, and then I have to get ready for bed. I'm not as young as I used to be, and I run out of steam easily. So, good night, and thank you so much for visiting me. Please come again." Elazar thanked Simcha in return and walked home.

That night Elazar dreamed about his grandfather, not as a pious old man with a long white beard, but as a mischievous little boy, playing soccer in no-man's-land, dodging bullets from snipers.

CHAPTER 6

M ea She'arim has much beauty—spiritual beauty. The residents
are devout and pious and routinely perform acts of kindness for
neighbors in need. Tourists and other visitors routinely flock to this enclave to enjoy the sights and sounds, and they are generally welcomed.

But outsiders who visit Mea She'arim and fail to follow the rules and
social norms of the neighborhood are sometimes greeted with a most
unfriendly reception. Elazar had witnessed this phenomenon many
times in his childhood. He had seen people yell—and even spit—at
women who had meandered into Mea She'arim but had unwittingly
failed to conform to its strict ultra-Orthodox code of modesty. And
he had witnessed extremist elements, including boys his age, shouting
"*Shabbos! Shabbos!*" and throwing stones at cars that had dared to taint
the serenity of the Sabbath day by driving through the neighborhood.
The whole enterprise of throwing stones or yelling at strangers just
didn't seem right to Elazar, so he never participated in any of their
antics.

Israeli soldiers who entered the neighborhood were also sometimes
greeted with hostility. Like many boys in his neighborhood, Elazar had
been taught that Israeli soldiers were, by definition, *traif.* And religious
soldiers were even worse than their secular counterparts, since
they should have known better. He was told that the term "religious
soldier" was an oxymoron. His father would even profess that so-called
"religious" soldiers were agents of the devil, sent to snare spiritually
weak Jews.

Elazar was never comfortable with this doctrine. "Aren't they
protecting us?" he would think to himself. "We probably couldn't

live in this county without the army's protection," he reasoned. Only God protects us, and only in the merit of our Torah study and good deeds, he had been told, and he believed it. "But all of our schools and synagogues and houses of study would be destroyed if there was no army. Maybe the soldiers aren't agents of the devil, but agents of God. Maybe the army is *how* God protects us." So he secretly harbored a sense of gratitude and even pride whenever he saw soldiers, especially religious soldiers.

One Friday afternoon, a few months after his bar mitzvah, as he was walking home from school, Elazar had an experience that changed his life. Mea She'arim Street was congested with people: local residents buying food for the Sabbath, students streaming out of the yeshivas after a long week of Torah study, and tourists and other visitors shopping for souvenirs. One such visitor was a young religious soldier, with a black velvet yarmulke on his head, a short wispy beard, curly sidelocks, and fringes from his prayer shawl dangling from beneath his olive-green uniform. The soldier was perusing some newly published volumes of Talmudic discourse in the entryway of a bookstore. When Elazar saw the religious soldier with the beard and sidelocks, he was intrigued. The soldier didn't look *traif*, Elazar thought to himself. On the contrary, he looked studious, even pious.

A bossy kid named Pinchas and his gang of unruly juveniles were also marching down Mea She'arim Street that day. Pinchas spotted the soldier and proceeded to point him out to his friends. Suddenly, Pinchas started shouting, "*Goy! Shaygetz!*" (loosely translated, "Infidel! Disgusting one!"), and his gang responded on cue with their own shouts of "*Goy!*" and "*Shaygetz!*" Other bystanders, mostly teenagers and young adult men, soon came out of the woodwork to join in the revelry.

At first the young soldier didn't notice the scene unfolding around him. He was so engrossed in the book he was reading that he was oblivious to his surroundings. He was awoken from his trance when one of the young men at the front of the mob slapped the soldier's arms, causing him to stumble slightly and sending the holy book flying across the room and onto the floor. The soldier looked up and quickly understood that a lynching was underway. Elazar saw the look of fear on his face and instinctively felt that he had to do something to help the soldier, who was in real danger at this point. So he grabbed the soldier's arm and whispered to him, "Quick, come with me." Elazar led the soldier to the back of the store, into a dark corridor, through a narrow doorway, and into the alleyway behind the bookstore. Several members of the lynch mob followed behind. Elazar turned right and left, down hidden staircases and into other alleyways, past graffiti warning passersby to adhere to a strictly modest dress code, and past overflowing dumpsters, scurrying through the neighborhood like a rodent. Finally, they reached Strauss Street, a larger thoroughfare where several buses were waiting at a bus stop. "Get on a bus, any bus, quick!" Elazar shouted. The soldier obeyed Elazar's order and hopped onto a bus and out of danger. Elazar watched from the bus stop as the soldier walked down the aisle and settled into a seat with an open window facing Elazar. "Thank you," the soldier shouted. "Here! This is for you," he said, removing his shoulder tag and tossing it out the window. The badge gently floated to the ground—like a leaf, an olive leaf—as the bus, and the soldier, proceeded up Strauss Street and out of view.

Shoulder tags indicate a specific army unit. This soldier was from an army intelligence unit, and the badge he wore had a green-and-white circle with a Star of David in the center. Elazar picked up the badge and examined it. He didn't know what shoulder badges signified in general, and he certainly didn't understand the significance of this particular badge. To him, the circle with the star looked like a soccer ball. Maybe this was a medal he earned by winning a soccer tournament in the army...or maybe he plays soccer in the army, for a soccer battalion. "Thank you!" he shouted, although by then the soldier was far away. Instantly, the badge became Elazar's most prized possession. He raced home and hid his prize, since he knew his parents would certainly disapprove if they found it. When he was alone in his bedroom, he would often look at his prize, the army badge with the soccer ball, and dream...

CHAPTER 7

One morning in early May, Elazar wandered out of school during a short break between lessons, as he often did to escape the monotony of the classroom. Without any particular destination in mind, he walked all the way to Kikar Shabbat, a large intersection in the heart of the Mea She'arim neighborhood. He observed the familiar scene: mothers pushing strollers up and down the street and into and out of stores, adult men walking home from synagogue still carrying their prayer shawls and phylacteries in velvet bags, and some tourists shopping and conversing.

Suddenly, a loud siren pierced the routine of an otherwise ordinary day. Traffic halted as cars and buses stopped moving. Some of the drivers exited their vehicles and stood silently outside them. A few pedestrians likewise stood in silence, although most carried on with their routines, seemingly undisturbed by the siren. At first, Elazar was confused by the siren, but seeing the halted traffic and the people standing quietly, he remembered hearing that this "moment of silence" was how the Zionists remembered fallen soldiers on their Memorial Day. Although Elazar seldom paid attention in class, he vaguely remembered hearing his rebbe disparaging the practice that very morning. His father, too, often maligned soldiers, vehemently opposing any display of respect for them, dead or alive.

Should I stand silently, Elazar thought to himself, out of respect for the soldiers who died fighting to protect this country? Were they heroes, as the Zionists claimed, or villains, as he had been taught repeatedly by his teachers and his father? Certainly, the soldier he had saved from the lynch mob was no villain…

This brief internal deliberation was interrupted by the clamor of a small crowd of men shouting in the middle of the intersection, contributing to the halt in traffic against which they were ostensibly protesting. The men, and even some young boys, all dressed in ultra-Orthodox garb, marched in an unruly circle, chanting slogans and carrying signs decrying Zionism. Some of the men waved large flags emblazoned with three horizontal stripes of black, white and green, overlaid with a red triangle. Elazar recognized the Palestinian flag from graffiti spray-painted on the wall in an alleyway near his home. He didn't fully grasp the implications of waving that flag on this particular day, but he understood that it was meant to be provocative. The protesters were mostly members of the radical anti-Zionist Neturei Karta group, plus some like-minded sympathizers. After a minute, the siren waned, but the protesters continued demonstrating and blocking traffic. The drivers of the vehicles, now back in their seats, began honking impatiently.

A small cadre of police officers—including a few women in uniform—were waiting nearby, cautiously anticipating a possible confrontation. Through a megaphone, one of them ordered the group to clear the intersection and disperse, or at least move their demonstration to the sidewalk. The protesters didn't budge, so the policemen called for reinforcements, who arrived only moments later, dressed in riot gear. Again the police officer ordered the protesters to disperse and again they did not comply. On the contrary, more men and boys came and joined the demonstration, marching in the street and blocking the flow of traffic. The officer once again ordered them to disperse and threatened to use force if they did not obey the order. Predictably, the men did not disperse, and around twenty officers, one of them mounted on a horse, entered the intersection to confront the protesters directly. The men and boys responded by hurling anything and everything they had at their disposal: garbage, sticks, stones, even eggs, which they had been hiding in the pockets of their frocks. The police began physically removing the protesters and apprehending the ringleaders. Finally, the protesters disbanded, the police officers departed, and the flow of traffic resumed.

Instantly, the tense atmosphere dissipated, and the humdrum scene returned. Mothers pushed their strollers and pedestrians ambled on obliviously, as if there hadn't been a riot only moments earlier. The scattered trash and smashed eggs dripping down a wall were among the only remnants of the recent tumult. Life returned to normal. Or maybe, thought Elazar as he walked back to school, all of this *was* normal. Maybe life is an amalgam of calm and frenzy.

The entire episode had been filmed, and by the next day, large posters had been pasted on walls along Mea She'arim Street. The posters featured a photograph of a mounted policeman, holding a baton above his head threateningly. Cowering on the pavement, defenseless, with looks of fear on their faces, were an ultra-Othodox man and child. "*Know your enemy!*" the poster proclaimed in Yiddish.

Who were the heroes, Elazar wondered, and who were the villains? The protesters appeared pious. They prayed and studied Torah, and they defended the holiness of the land. The policemen, on the other hand, were bareheaded, *traif!* But the protesters were the ones blocking traffic and disrupting the peace. The policemen were the ones doing the responsible thing, restoring the peace. Perhaps, Elazar thought, his perspective had been too simplistic. Perhaps most people weren't complete heroes or complete villains, but a mixture of good and bad. At this point, Elazar wasn't even sure what a true hero or a true villain was supposed to look like.

CHAPTER 8

Shortly thereafter, Elazar began studying with a private tutor to review the lessons he had learned in school and prepare for the *farhers* (oral exams) he would have to take in order to get accepted to *yeshiva ketana* (high school). Elazar was not a diligent student, even under the best of circumstances. But now he was constantly distracted, always daydreaming about soccer, about the *traif* boys in the school-yard, about playing professionally someday. His performance at the *farhers* was mediocre, so he was not accepted into the top-tier yeshiva that his older brothers had attended. Eventually, he was accepted into a lower-tier—but still respectable—institution, and only due to pressure exerted by Elazar's father on the school administrators.

The school was in Bnei Brak, a suburb of Tel Aviv, around an hour's drive from Jerusalem. He lived in the dormitory and only came home for *Shabbos* every fourth weekend. The daily schedule consisted of many hours of Talmud study with little or no outlet for the unfortunate boy who was incapable of—or uninterested in—such intensive study. Somehow, Elazar and a few like-minded boys gravitated to one another and commiserated. He pooled together some loose change with three other boys, and they bought a soccer ball at a nearby shop. They managed to sneak out of the yeshiva and play soccer in a vacant lot a few blocks away. It didn't take long for the administration to find out about their disobedience, and all four of them soon found themselves in the office of the *rosh yeshiva* (dean). They were suspended and sent home by public transportation. They would be allowed back the next day on probation. One more infraction would result in expulsion. And so it was: one week later,

Elazar and another boy were spotted playing soccer in the empty lot, and they were expelled from the yeshiva.

CHAPTER 9

This story repeated itself, more or less, over the next several years. Elazar bounced from school to school, unable to conform to the routine of the yeshiva and unable to stop obsessing about soccer. At the age of sixteen, after having been kicked out of six schools, Elazar was enrolled in a local school with other Hasidic teenagers who couldn't "fit into the mold." In this new school, he would live at home and he'd have fewer hours of Talmud study.

For Elazar, being back in Jerusalem meant that he could go back to the *traif* schoolyard. At the end of his first day in the new school, he headed straight for the shortcut he'd devised a few years earlier, cutting through alleyways and down narrow staircases. To his delight, when he arrived at the *traif* school this time, some boys were there playing soccer! He wasn't sure if these were the same *traif* boys he had watched a few years earlier, but he was delighted nonetheless. He watched from the other side of the fence for twenty or thirty minutes, then raced home. When his mother asked him why he was late, he answered that he had been playing with some friends and had taken a circuitous route home. It was a white lie, the first of many he would have to tell to continue watching the *traif* boys. And so it continued, day after day, for several weeks. Elazar would race out of school, navigate the shortcut, and watch his "friends."

One day, as he was watching the boys playing, one of them kicked the ball over the fence. Elazar ran after the ball, skillfully dribbled it through the schoolyard gate, and kicked the ball around twenty meters, over the head of the goalkeeper and straight into the goal. The *traif* boys looked at him with amazement and wonder. Who was this religious boy with his long sidelocks and Hasidic clothing? Why had he been watching them every day? And how on earth did he get so good at soccer?

Finally, breaking the ice, one of the boys asked his name. "Luzar," he answered.

"Loser?" the boys asked.

"Luzar, short for Eloozar," he replied.

The boys started laughing, and Elazar turned bright red. After a few tense moments, one of the boys explained why they were laughing: "In English, 'loser' means a nobody, someone with bad luck and no friends." *Luzar*, then, would be truncated to *Zar*. In Hebrew, *zar* means "strange" or "stranger," as in the biblical verse "...and the stranger who comes too close [to holiness] will die." Elazar thought that *Zar* was an appropriate moniker for him. That's how he saw himself: a stranger who couldn't get too close to holiness, where he felt lifeless. Here, in the *traif* schoolyard, playing a *traif* sport with the *traif* boys, he felt alive!

That impromptu goal was a seminal moment for Zar. He was no longer an outsider watching the game from the other side of the fence. From now on, he would join the *traif* boys in their game. He quickly realized that he didn't just enjoy playing soccer—he *loved* it. And he wasn't just good at it—he was *very* good. And he knew that with time and lots of practice, he would someday be great!

CHAPTER 10

Day after day, Zar returned to the schoolyard to play soccer with his new friends. His mother began to wonder why he'd been coming home late from yeshiva every day. Zar revealed only that he'd been "playing with friends." His mother sensed instinctively that Zar was not being completely honest, but she was afraid to probe any deeper. He would come home drenched in sweat, and his shirts and pants, which had previously required laundering only every few days, now had to be washed every day. His shoes wore out quickly. When he came home one day with torn pants and a bloody knee, his mother interrogated him: "Who are these new friends of yours? Where do you meet them? What games are you playing?" Zar answered succinctly, but candidly, that he had been playing soccer with some boys from another neighborhood.

His mother feared the worst. Were these boys secular, or even worse, *goyim*? Had he been mingling with girls? He was a very handsome boy; if he had gotten involved with the wrong crowd, girls would certainly have been attracted to him. Had he been eating *traif* foods? Had he been using drugs? More probing questions followed when his father came home that night. His parents were concerned, but also somewhat relieved to learn that his new pastime was relatively innocuous. His new friends were Jewish, mostly from traditional—although not ultra-Orthodox—homes. No girls, *traif* foods, or drugs were involved. His only vice, it seemed, was soccer!

Surprisingly, his parents understood that they couldn't forbid him from playing with his new friends. Zar was too passionate about soccer. Forbidding it would be ineffective, since he would likely disobey, and counterproductive, because it would only further alienate him. Zar's father sought advice from his rabbi, who reassured him that Zar was only going through an adolescent phase. He needed some space and time; eventually, he would lose interest in soccer. A compromise was reached: Zar could continue playing soccer with his new friends as long as he maintained passing grades in school.

Zar was conflicted. On the one hand, he very much enjoyed playing with the *traif* boys; when he was with them, he felt accepted and unrestrained. But he also felt a sense of guilt. He had heard rumors of boys—and even some girls—in his neighborhood who had "gone off the path," leaving the strict, traditional patterns of dress and behavior. On occasion, he caught snippets of conversations, hushed whispers, regarding a neighbor or a distant cousin who had left the community. He couldn't help but think, "Are people now gossiping about me?" "Am I 'going off the path' and embarking on a different—even sinful—path?" But he still believed in, or at least practiced, the ways of his community. And he had no intention of leaving Orthodox Judaism. He just felt confined, almost imprisoned, in his current situation. He needed to break free, to experience new vistas. He needed to play soccer.

CHAPTER 11

Although Zar very much enjoyed his informal schoolyard games, he began to feel hampered in his ability to improve his skills. He didn't even have the right clothes for soccer. He mentioned these concerns to his new friends, and a few days later, they surprised him with some hand-me-down shorts and T-shirts and a new pair of soccer shoes. Zar sincerely appreciated these gifts, but still felt limited. He needed formal training and a higher level of competition. One of his new friends said he was planning on trying out for a youth soccer league and suggested that Zar join him. The tryouts were scheduled for the following Friday.

For the next week, Zar practiced basic skills: dribbling, passing, and scoring goals. On the day of the tryouts, Zar snuck out of yeshiva an hour early and met his friend in the schoolyard. He discreetly changed into his new soccer clothes, and the two of them took a bus to a large athletic facility in a mostly secular neighborhood in southern Jerusalem. Aside from traveling to and from school, this was Zar's first time on public transportation, and his first time venturing beyond walking distance from his home.

At the athletic facility were hundreds of kids of all ages. Most of the younger children were accompanied by one or two parents. The older kids were informally gathered in small groups. Some boys were passing soccer balls back and forth. Others were just horsing around. And some were sitting on the grass, seemingly bored or nervous or both. Only a handful of the boys were wearing yarmulkes, and only of the small knitted variety typically worn by the Modern Orthodox. No one else was wearing a large black yarmulke, and no one else had long sidelocks. Zar felt different and embarrassed. Some of the kids smirked at him; one even laughed at him. Most of the boys just ignored him.

A number of adults wore official-looking soccer jerseys and had whistles hanging around their necks. Zar correctly concluded that these men were in charge. Eventually, these coaches divided up the boys by age and started some basic soccer drills. In one of the drills, ten boys were arranged in two lines of five. The first boy in one line passed the ball to the first boy in the other line, then ran to the back of his own line. The ball would be passed back and forth, slowly working its way down the field. Finally, when the coach whistled, the boy who had the ball would have to kick it toward the goal. In another drill, a pair of boys would run up and down the field, quickly passing the ball back and forth.

The boys here were more talented than the boys in the schoolyard, but Zar held his own. He passed well, dribbled skillfully, and even scored a few goals. He stood out not only because of his large black yarmulke and curly sidelocks, but also in his determination—he was passionate and driven. When most of the boys sat down to rest and catch their breath, Zar continued playing. After about an hour, the coaches whistled and gathered all of the boys together. Only twenty boys in each of five age groups were selected to join the teams. The coaches had unanimously agreed that Zar had ample raw talent and determination. None of the boys were surprised to learn that Zar had been selected to join the senior division of the Jerusalem team in the Israeli National Youth Soccer League.

CHAPTER 12

The boys who had been selected were instructed to remain on the field while all of the other boys, including Zar's friend from the schoolyard, were dismissed. The coaches introduced themselves. Each of the five teams had two coaches: a senior coach and an assistant. The boys were asked to fill out some forms. Immediately, Zar encountered some challenges. First, he needed his pediatrician to fill out a form indicating that he was in good enough health to join the league. Also, his parents would have to sign a waiver permitting him to play. Finally, he looked at the schedule. Practice was to take place nearly every day for one to two hours, and the matches were sometimes held on Saturdays, the Jewish Sabbath.

Zar then became acutely aware of another, more immediate problem: it was Friday afternoon. The Sabbath would be starting within an hour. He was in an unfamiliar neighborhood far from home. The friend who had accompanied him there hadn't been selected and had already left. He had no money for a bus. He didn't even know which bus to take. Zar felt overwhelmed, despondent, scared, and alone. Suddenly, he saw a young man in Hasidic garb, with a beard and long, curly sidelocks. Zar ran up to him and briefly explained his predicament. Fortunately, the young Hasid had a car, and he offered to drive Zar to Mea She'arim Street. In his haste, Zar forgot to change back out of his soccer outfit. He ran home through his neighborhood in his soccer attire, passing by men in *shtreimels* walking hand in hand with young Hasidic boys dressed in their Sabbath finest.

Zar had much on his mind over the Sabbath. He had numerous hurdles to overcome, each seemingly insurmountable. There was no way he could even reveal to his parents that he had joined a soccer league, not to mention one that played matches on *Shabbos*. The following day, Zar and his friends reluctantly forged a doctor's form and parents' waiver for Zar. Only one hurdle remained: *Shabbos*. Technically, they rationalized, playing soccer on *Shabbos* didn't violate Jewish religious law. After all, many of the boys in the more modern neighborhoods, and even some in the ultra-Orthodox neighborhoods, played soccer on *Shabbos*. And taking the team bus to matches on *Shabbos* didn't technically violate any laws. After all, he reasoned, he wouldn't be *driving* the bus. He would simply be a passenger.

His friends pointed out that the public buses don't run on *Shabbos*. How would he get to the athletic center to catch the team bus? They concluded that he could walk to the athletic center, although even walking there briskly would take him more than two hours. And so the major issues had been addressed, if not completely resolved. He would still have to be absent for nearly the whole day on *Shabbos*. And two hours of practice nearly every day (plus time for commuting to and from practice) would certainly affect his grades at school. That would violate the deal he had made with his parents and jeopardize the entire enterprise. Nevertheless, Zar was determined to play on the team, and no deals or rules were going to stand in his way.

CHAPTER 13

On Sunday afternoon, Zar took the number 18 bus and arrived at practice a few minutes early. He met his coach again and gave him the two forms he had fraudulently signed. Even after changing into his new uniform, he still felt different from the other boys. More than anything else, his long, curly sidelocks made him stand out. He contemplated cutting them off, but decided to trim them and keep them. They would one day become his trademark, although he would keep them pinned up and tucked underneath his yarmulke.

The coaches asked the boys to introduce themselves. One by one, the boys gave their names, neighborhoods, schools, ages, and grades. The other boys were fascinated to learn about Zar's background. They inundated him with questions until the coach asked for some decorum. The coach then divided the boys into smaller groups and started some of the same drills they'd done at the tryouts a week earlier. Zar felt compelled to prove himself. He imagined that this practice exercise was actually a World Cup match. He ran faster and kicked harder than anyone else on the field. His coaches and teammates were impressed. Clearly, he had talent, a lot of talent. But he was unruly and lacked precision. He needed guidance and practice. His coaches and teammates sensed that, with time and perseverance, he could achieve greatness.

The first Saturday, there was no scheduled match. Still, they had a double practice. That Friday night, Zar could hardly sleep. He was overcome with guilt and angst about having to play matches on *Shabbos*. He had never violated the Sabbath in his life, and even though playing the game didn't technically involve any Sabbath violation, he worried about taking the team bus on *Shabbos*, and about new challenges he'd face that he couldn't even anticipate.

The next day, he left synagogue extra-early and told his father a white lie—that he would be meeting a friend for lunch. His father sensed that Zar was lying, but he didn't forbid him from going. In fact, Zar hadn't even asked for permission; he'd simply informed his father that he was leaving. He walked more than two hours to the athletic center, arriving a few minutes late.

The coach noticed that Zar was drenched in sweat and asked him what had happened. Zar revealed to his coach all of his fears and guilt about possibly violating the Sabbath by playing and traveling by bus. His coach, who himself came from a very traditional Sephardic family, and who also harbored feelings of guilt about his own laxity in Sabbath observance, empathized with Zar's predicament and promised to see if he could make any special arrangements. Zar would later find out that his coach was true to his word: Zar would still have to come to team practices and home games on the Sabbath, but all of the away games would be rescheduled until after sundown on Saturday or pushed off to another day.

The coaches had already assigned positions to everyone; Zar was a striker. The coaches started explaining some basic strategies and several offensive and defensive scenarios. By the end of the session, the boys had become more comfortable with each other, both on and off the field. They were playing more like a team.

Zar came home late that afternoon. His father and brothers were already at synagogue for the evening prayers. His mother greeted him at the apartment door. Although Zar had already changed back into his Sabbath clothes, his mother knew that he had been playing soccer. His face was flushed and his hair was still moist with perspiration. Little did she know that his appearance reflected the two-hour walk home as much as the soccer practice. She had hoped that Zar would lose interest in soccer, but his interest only seemed to be growing stronger.

CHAPTER 14

The following Saturday was their first real match; they were playing a team from Kiryat Shmona. The two teams practiced on opposite sides of the field, giving them time to stretch and warm up, and an opportunity to observe their opponents. The Kiryat Shmona team appeared to be skilled. Zar could tell from the names on the backs of their jerseys that it was a mixed team, with both Jewish and Arab players. The teams were fairly evenly matched. The team from Kiryat Shmona had an amazing goalkeeper and an excellent backfield, but Zar's team had a stronger offense and had possession of the ball for the majority of the match. Nonetheless, Zar's team lost 1–0. Zar attempted multiple shots, but simply couldn't get one past the lanky Arab goalkeeper.

Initially, Zar was reticent and reclusive. The other boys on the team were secular, and could at times be lewd. Zar feared their negative influence, but he was also embarrassed by his Hasidic clothing and sidelocks, and he was bashful when his rituals were on display—when he had to say grace after meals, for example, or the afternoon prayers. The other players, in turn, viewed Zar as eccentric and aloof. His appearance was foreign and backward, and his timidity only served to magnify his exclusion.

But no one could ignore his skills. He was exceptional during the practice sessions and invaluable during the games. With time, the others grew to respect him not only for his athletic prowess but also for his sincerity and commitment to tradition. When his teammates lifted him up on their shoulders after one particularly remarkable performance, he knew that he was finally accepted.

With each practice and each game, Zar and his team continued to improve, and Zar's reputation spread throughout the league. An article profiling Zar appeared in the magazine of the Israel Football Association:

> The youth soccer league has been taken by storm this year with the emergence of a previously unknown soccer prodigy! Elazar Cohen, popularly known in the league by his nickname, "Zar," leads the under-eighteen division with 22 goals and 11 assists, and has helped his Beitar Jerusalem team to an impressive start with an 8–1–0 record. But even more remarkable than his statistics is the trail he blazed to get where he is. Raised in the ultra-Orthodox enclave of Mea She'arim, Zar had no formal training in soccer before joining the league…

The article was accompanied by a photograph of Zar, curly sidelocks flapping in the wind as he kicked a soccer ball past two defenders and the goalkeeper and into the goal.

Other than that initial match with the team from Kiryat Shmona, Zar's team was undefeated. They were unstoppable in the playoffs and ultimately won the championship match against a team from Haifa. Zar was named MVP of the championship match and MVP of the Youth League.

At the end of the season, Zar and his teammates promised to keep in touch. All his teammates were getting drafted into the army. Zar hadn't even thought about army service. Almost no one from his neighborhood joined the army; they would all get deferments as soon as they enrolled in a post-high school yeshiva. But Zar didn't want to go to yeshiva anymore—he wanted to play soccer. And he'd heard that in the army he could play soccer. Hence, three weeks later, on his eighteenth birthday, Zar reported to the conscription office to enlist.

CHAPTER 15

Kibbutz Nahal Eitan is an oasis of orange orchards and cotton fields in the Jezreel Valley of northern Israel, nestled between the Jewish city of Afula and the Palestinian village of Jenin. It was founded in the early 1900s by German Jews who had purchased swampy marshland from Ottoman landowners. A second wave of German Jews, who had remained in Germany and were ultimately deported to the Dachau concentration camp, but were fortunate enough to have survived, joined their landsmen after World War II. These Jews of the second wave were hardy, courageous, and resourceful. They endured a perilous journey on the Mediterranean in a merchant ship, secretly disembarking on the beach at night and illegally bypassing the British blockade. When they arrived at Nahal Eitan, these brave immigrants were immediately put to work on the kibbutz. They performed backbreaking labor, tilling the hard soil, running irrigation pipes, and defending their new home from hostile Arabs who viewed their new neighbors as infidels and invaders.

These "stiff-necks," as they were known, later joined the nascent Haganah, the precursor of the Israel Defense Forces. Some of the stiff-necks died fighting in the Israeli War of Independence in 1948–1949, but most of them survived. Egel's great-grandparents were among this group of survivors.

Egel's grandparents were among the first generation of *sabras* born at Kibbutz Nahal Eitan. They too worked the land, defending it repeatedly—first in 1967 and again in 1973, when the kibbutz was nearly destroyed by an invading Syrian tank corps. Egel's paternal grandfather was lightly wounded fighting in the Golan Heights. In

October 1973, shortly after his return from the hospital, he married his childhood sweetheart from the kibbutz.

Egel's father was born less than a year later. His entire childhood revolved around the kibbutz. He grew up there and went to grade school and even high school on the kibbutz. He didn't really leave until he turned eighteen and was drafted into the army. He married a girl he met during his army service. The young couple began their new life together in an apartment in Tel Aviv, but eventually grew tired of the big city. They missed the open spaces and fresh air of the kibbutz, so they moved to Nahal Eitan. Several months later, their son was born. They named him Egel, "calf." Like a calf roaming freely through the pastures, their son would be free—free from war, free from antisemitism.

And so it was. Egel was carefree and independent. He was tall and handsome, with golden-blond hair and blue eyes. He was exceptionally athletic, and he had charisma, incredible charisma. He was kind and polite, and despite his popularity, even a bit shy. Egel was friends with everyone. Many of the girls on his kibbutz and even on some of the neighboring kibbutzim had secret crushes on him; some of them practically worshiped him. He had numerous girlfriends and ample opportunity for promiscuity.

Life for Egel on the kibbutz was placid and congenial. He and the other teens would often sit around the firepit, with Egel strumming the guitar, singing old Israeli folk songs and classic rock songs from the 1960s and 1970s. In particular, they enjoyed singing "Turn, Turn, Turn," the Pete Seeger classic popularized by the Byrds, which proclaims that life is both war and peace, stones cast away and stones gathered together. The song seemed to aptly describe their homeland.

CHAPTER 16

Although Egel was friends with nearly everyone on the kibbutz, both those his age and those much older, his closest confidant was his grandfather, who was also Egel's biggest fan, attending all of his soccer matches.

Above all else, Egel loved to go on long walks through the kibbutz with his grandfather. They would walk for hours, talking about philosophy, religion, history, and family. Egel learned from his grandfather that he was named for his great-grandfather: Egel was a shortened and Hebraized version of Engelbert. He learned that he resembled his namesake. Both had golden-blond hair and blue eyes. In fact, it was these Aryan features that allowed Egel's great-grandfather to evade detection by the Gestapo and survive the Second World War. Egel's grandfather shared numerous stories from his own youth, from the early days of the Jewish state. But he shared very little with Egel about his own father, Egel's namesake. Indeed, whenever the topic of World War II or the Holocaust came up in conversation, Egel's grandfather would steer the discussion to something else, something benign: the weather, that year's crops, or Egel's budding prowess in soccer. And on their walks through the kibbutz, Egel's grandfather would consistently avoid the small memorial to those family members of the founders of Nahal Eitan who had perished in the Holocaust. Apparently, the Holocaust and anything related to it was simply too painful a topic for his grandfather to contemplate. But his grandfather didn't *need* to discuss the Holocaust; it was the ever-present elephant in the room. In fact, Egel felt that he was living his whole life in the shadow of the Holocaust. As he'd heard countless times, the kibbutzniks were unlike the weak Jews of Europe, who had marched to their deaths like sheep to the slaughterhouse. The kibbutzniks were strong and knew how to defend themselves.

There was another place Egel's grandfather would avoid: the rear gate, which was guarded by a pair of dogs. Egel's grandfather had a near-pathological fear of dogs, which he called "wolves," and he transmitted this phobia to his descendants. On this topic too, his grandfather was oddly evasive, as if it were a secret he wasn't yet prepared to disclose.

It wasn't until Egel's grandfather was nearing the end of his life that he began to share some of these secrets. One day, Egel and his grandfather were walking around the kibbutz. They approached a junction in the path; Egel, by force of habit, began to turn left, the way they'd always walked, but his grandfather held onto Egel's arm and steered him to the right, toward the Holocaust memorial. Egel had been to the memorial dozens of times. He had read the names chiseled in stone so many times that he practically knew them by heart. But he had never before been there with his grandfather. They walked arm in arm to the memorial, and when they reached it, they stood there silently. Egel glanced at his grandfather and saw tears streaming down his face. He had never before seen his grandfather cry. His grandfather was a war hero; he had fought valiantly in two wars, and he was even wounded in battle in 1973. Now he was crying as he stood in front of a memorial to his own grandfather, who had died in Germany nearly three-quarters of a century earlier.

"Egel," he finally said, interrupting the silence, "you never met my father, your namesake. He died only a few months before you were born. And I never met my grandfather, my namesake. He died—he was killed—a few years before I was born. They had Aryan features, just like you and your father and I have. Those features, the blue eyes and blond hair, allowed them to evade the Gestapo for years. Just how they did it, I'll never know. But somehow, they managed to survive. Countless times during the war, they were stopped by police or soldiers, their papers were examined, and miraculously, they avoided detection every time. Until that day…" Egel's grandfather paused, and he began to cry again.

"What day?" Egel asked innocently.

"*That* day!" he yelled, pointing with his trembling finger at the date of his grandfather's death, chiseled in stone. "It was Christmas Eve, 1944. My father described that day to me in such detail that I felt as if I was there, witnessing the events. They had been living incognito as gentiles, with fake names and forged documents. That day, they were stopped by a group of German soldiers and asked to identify themselves, to present their papers, as they had done countless times before. One of the soldiers looked at my grandfather, looked at the papers, then looked at my grandfather again. And then he called him by his real name, his Jewish name, Elijah.

My grandfather had been a businessman back in Munich before the war. He'd owned a small grocery, and this soldier had been one of his employees. My grandfather recognized him too. He reminded him that he'd been a good employer, that he'd always treated his employees with respect and fairness. And it was true. He had been honest and kind; there was no disputing that. He begged for mercy, but the soldier showed no gratitude, no sympathy. His eyes revealed only malice and cruelty.

The soldier decided to give my father and grandfather a 'Christmas present.' He would give them a chance to escape. But he wanted to make a sport of it, to make it fun for him and for his fellow soldiers. He gave them five minutes to run for their lives, after which he and his fellow soldiers and their dogs would come searching for them. He blew a whistle and yelled, 'Jews! Run for your lives!' They ran and ran, but there really wasn't anywhere to hide. There were soldiers everywhere, all laughing at this spectacle. After five minutes, the soldiers and their dogs caught up with them. My father described the scene to me many times. The dogs were barking wildly. Wolves, he called them. And then they were beaten. My grandfather died that very day. My father was taken to Dachau, a concentration camp near the city. By some miracle—if you believe in such things—he survived Dachau and came here. That part of the story you've heard me tell many times."

That was the last time Egel and his grandfather walked together. It was as if his grandfather's mission had been to transmit that piece of history—the horrific events of Christmas Eve, 1944—and once he had completed that task, he could move on. After Egel's grandfather died, Egel told his father about his final walk with his grandfather to the Holocaust memorial. His father had heard the same story from his father and from his grandfather. But there was one detail left out in the version Egel heard, his father told him. Although Egel's great-great-grandfather had been beaten by the soldiers, that wasn't how he died.

"So how did he die?" Egel asked his father.

"He was mauled to death, devoured...by the wolves."

CHAPTER 17

Egel excelled on the soccer field. He was stronger and faster than any of the other children on the kibbutz, and he quickly earned a reputation as a phenomenal player. He was one of the youngest players ever to have joined the Israeli National Youth Soccer League, and he was named MVP of the junior division his first year in the league. By the time he was in high school, he had already been scouted by coaches for a number of professional Israeli soccer clubs.

Egel was fiercely competitive, but his sportsmanship was impeccable. As captain, he led his team to an undefeated regular season in his senior year. Ultimately, his team lost the championship match to a Jerusalem team with a superstar of its own: an ultra-Orthodox boy with a large black yarmulke and curly sidelocks and a most *un*orthodox playing style. In fact, it was his wild, somewhat unruly approach that made this strange boy unpredictable and nearly impossible to defend against. His name was Zar, meaning "strange," which Egel thought was a most fitting name for this boy who looked so strange and played so strangely.

After the game, when the two teams lined up to shake hands, Egel spoke briefly with Zar. They complimented each other on their impressive performances in the game and speculated that someday they might play together on the same team. Such a team, they imagined, would be amazing. "Maybe we'd win the National Championship," Egel suggested. "Why stop there?" quipped Zar. "Who knows? Maybe we could win the World Cup."

CHAPTER 18

Ibrahim Al-Salem and his wife had been warned by her doctor not to travel. All of her prior pregnancies had been complicated, and she was already in her third trimester. But they had been planning this trip—their pilgrimage to Mecca—for over a year. The arrangements had been logistically difficult. They had to obtain temporary Jordanian passports. (It would not otherwise have been feasible for Israelis—even Muslim Israelis—to travel to Saudi Arabia.) Furthermore, they would be performing the Hajj, one of the five pillars of Islam. Certainly, they reasoned, in the merit of such an act of faith, Allah would protect her. Against the advice of the doctor and despite the risks, they traveled to Mecca. But the Great Mosque was crowded, and the heat was oppressive; she fainted.

Ibrahim's wife was quickly assessed by paramedics and rushed by ambulance to a nearby hospital, where she was resuscitated. Ibrahim, who had been in the men's section of the Great Mosque, found out about his wife's illness several hours later. He raced to the hospital and asked them to discharge his wife so he could bring her back home, to the small Israeli-Arab village of Al'ard Alhamra in the southeastern Galilee. But the doctors at the hospital insisted that such a move would jeopardize the health of both his wife and the fetus. Her blood pressure was dangerously elevated, and she was already in premature labor. When her condition deteriorated, the decision was made to deliver the baby.

The baby was very large, however, and the labor would not progress. Then Ibrahim's wife started having seizures. An emergency cesarean section was performed. The baby was, thankfully, robust, but the

49

mother was in severe distress. She began hemorrhaging uncontrollably. Her liver failed, then her kidneys, and despite the valiant efforts of the medical staff, her life could not be saved.

Ibrahim returned to his village a broken man. He had to bury his wife and raise their children himself. He named the baby Hajji, "pilgrim," since he had been born in Mecca, fulfilling his obligation of Hajj. Ibrahim became fervently religious. Most of the older men in the village were clean-shaven and wore typical Western clothing, but Ibrahim refused to shave his beard and started wearing the customary ankle-length *thawb* robe and a black-and-white fishnet-pattern *keffiyeh* headdress. He prayed in the village mosque five times a day and studied the Koran frequently. Cigarettes, which he smoked compulsively, were his only vice. But he refused to smoke the Israeli brands; he would smoke only homemade Palestinian cigarettes that were smuggled into the village.

Hajji's father was a strict disciplinarian, and he often scolded and chastised young Hajji for perceived insubordination. But Hajji was mischievous, even disobedient. His teachers would frequently evict him from the classroom, telling him that he would never amount to anything in life, so he spent more time outside of the classroom than in it. He would go play soccer with the older boys. He was agile, and he was exceptionally tall for his age—taller than some of the big kids. He had dark brown hair, closely shaved on the sides and longer on top, forming a sort of Mohawk. His skin was tanned from the countless hours he spent playing soccer, and his arms and legs were lean and muscular. But he was still weaker than the older kids he played with, and the games were very physical. He couldn't compete with the older boys on the field, so he was relegated to playing goalkeeper. To prove himself to the big kids, he would try his hardest to block every shot at goal. In this role he could thrive, even excel. In fact, he got so good at goalkeeping that, despite his young age, he joined one of the youth teams in his village and even competed against other nearby villages. With time, he earned a reputation as one of the best goalkeepers in the region.

For Hajji, soccer was not merely an outlet for pent-up physical energy; it was his license to break free from the psychological bondage of his home and classroom. When he was playing soccer, his mind would soar. In his imagination, he would be lifted out of his village and into the heavens above.

Besides the soccer field, Hajji had another escape. When he wasn't in school or on the soccer field, Hajji would wander through the village and befriend the old men. He loved to exchange jokes with the shopkeepers, and he especially loved to ascend to the highest spot in the village, the mosque, follow the old muezzin up to the minaret, and listen to his call for prayer: *"Allahu akbar! God is great!"*

Young Hajji had exceptional eyesight. From his perch in the minaret he could see for miles in every direction. He could see the rolling hills of the Galilee, olive-green and bronze and auburn waves speckled with a barrage of stones and decorated here and there with patches of red wildflowers, like blood spots on the earth. In the late afternoon, as the sun was setting, its rays would ignite the earth into a brilliant blood-red crimson. He observed the lush Jordan River Valley, her verdant shores concealing the nourishing waters within.

When the skies were clear, he could discern, in the distance to the north, the blue Sea of Galilee, like a sapphire glimmering among waves of green and bronze and auburn. Beyond that, he observed the towering heights of the Galilee and Golan.

To the south, he could spy out the army checkpoint separating his village from nearby Palestinian villages and a refugee camp just over the border in the West Bank. He had numerous relatives in those villages and in the refugee camp—aunts, uncles, and cousins. They would attend each other's weddings and religious ceremonies. Before the intifada, he'd heard, when movement between the West Bank and the rest of Israel was unrestricted, there had been a lot more contact.

He had heard a lot of rumors about the Israeli soldiers at the checkpoint: "Don't go near them. They're monsters! They'll beat you, or worse, kidnap you, and you'll never see your family again." But looking at the soldiers from his perch in the minaret, they didn't seem like monsters. They looked like ordinary people. They too would tell each other jokes. He couldn't hear them, but he could tell from their body language. And he yearned to see them up close.

One day, when he was fourteen years old, Hajji was sent out of school for failing to do his homework. There was going to be a party that day for having finished studying a long *surah* (chapter) in the *Quran*, and one of the boys had brought a bottle of Coca-Cola for the party. Hajji seldom indulged in drinking Coca-Cola; his father considered it too Western and therefore tainted. But he longed to savor the sweet drink, and he was indignant at being denied this privilege for such a minor infraction.

He wandered through the streets to the village gate. When he thought no one would notice, he ran down the road and kept on running until he approached the checkpoint. There were three soldiers. They looked bored. One soldier, tall and thin, kept an eye on the road, waiting for any approaching vehicles. Another, a dark-skinned Ethiopian, was using his cellphone. The third soldier was smoking a cigarette. Hajji hid behind some bushes and observed silently.

After a few minutes, the smoking soldier noticed him.

"*Shalom!*" the soldier said.

"*Salaam!*" he answered, instinctively, in Arabic.

"What's up?" the soldier asked, as the other two soldiers perked up and observed.

Hajji was silent.

"Do you have a knife?" the soldier asked.

"No."

"Do you need something? Are you lost? Is everything okay?"

"Oh, I'm fine. I'm just watching," he answered, this time in Hebrew.

"Are you thirsty?" the tall soldier asked. "Here! Have a Coke," he said, taking a can of Coca-Cola out of a cooler and handing it to Hajji.

"Thank you."

"You're welcome."

"Why do you carry guns?" Hajji asked.

"We live in a dangerous place," answered the soldier with the cigarette. "People want to harm us. We're protecting the country. We're protecting *you!*"

"Protecting *me*? From who?"

"From them." the soldier replied, gesturing with his thumb toward the Palestinian villages in the distance.

"They are my cousins."

"All of them?"

"Some of them."

"Well, maybe you can tell your cousins to stop attacking us."

"But you're the ones with guns…"

Suddenly, Hajji heard a familiar sound: the evening call to prayer from the village mosque. He had been unaware of how much time had elapsed, and now he had to rush to get home in time for dinner. He quickly said goodbye to the three soldiers and thanked them for the Coke. As he ran back up the road to his village, he was accompanied by the soothing words of the muezzin: "*Allahu akbar*, God is great. *Allahu akbar*, God is great."

CHAPTER 19

During dinner, Hajji was quiet. He picked at his food and contemplated. Many questions flooded his mind. Why had he been told to avoid the soldiers? Why did people in his village call them monsters? Had he been fed lies all these years? What other falsehoods had he been told? What *could* he believe? One thing, however, was clear. There was no question in his mind. He would go back soon to visit the soldiers.

The very next day, after playing a few games of soccer, and blocking every attempted goal, he again snuck to the village entrance, and when he was confident that no one was looking, he ran down the road and continued running until he reached the checkpoint.

"Shalom!" he said, greeting the soldiers.

"Shalom!" they responded. "Do you want another Coke?"

Hajji laughed and accepted their offer.

"What's your name?" one of the soldiers asked.

"Hajji. Hajji Al-Salem," he answered.

The soldiers shared their names, and they all shook hands.

A truck pulled up to the checkpoint. The tall soldier went over to inspect the truck, which was laden with dozens of crates of fruits and vegetables. He exchanged a few words with the driver, who exited the truck and began unloading the crates for inspection. Each crate had to be unloaded, carefully inspected, and stacked beside the truck. When all of the crates had been removed, the soldier began to inspect the interior of the now-empty truck. The process was slow and tedious, and in the interim, several more vehicles pulled up to the checkpoint. A second soldier approached and scrutinized the imposing stack of crates. As the sun blazed down on the truck, the driver, the soldiers, the crates, and the growing line of cars impatiently waiting to cross through the checkpoint, Hajji observed the scene. He walked over to the soldiers and gestured to the crates. "Can I help reload them?" he asked. The tall soldier stopped to think, then radioed to his superior officer, and they exchanged a few words. He asked Hajji to lift his shirt, then his pant legs, to ensure that he wasn't concealing any weapons or contraband, then permitted Hajji to assist the driver. Within a few minutes, the crates were reloaded and the truck passed through the checkpoint, followed by the line of cars.

The tall soldier thanked Hajji, laughing. "Now you've earned your Coca-Cola."

Hajji went home that evening with a broad smile on his face. He felt a sense of accomplishment, like he had a purpose.

Day after day, Hajji kept going back to the checkpoint. Every so often, a truck would be stopped for inspection. After revealing his bare torso and legs, Hajji would assist with unloading and loading the truck.

When he was with the soldiers at the checkpoint, he felt important and unrestrained, while in his village he felt scorned and constrained. He was a failure in school and he was rejected at home. His father disapproved of his soccer compulsion. Hajji even speculated that his father resented him for causing his mother's death.

Internally, however, he felt conflicted. Am I helping the enemy, he thought to himself, by helping the soldiers at the checkpoint? My Palestinian cousins are suffering under the occupation. Am I just as guilty as the soldiers?

One day, a few curious kids followed Hajji on one of his excursions, and soon the whole village found out about his strange new habit. His father was furious. He forbade him from returning to the checkpoint and threatened to beat him if he disobeyed. But Hajji, who had never been one to follow the rules, ignored his father's prohibition. In fact, his father's acrimony only impelled Hajji to continue visiting the soldiers.

By and large, the villagers didn't disapprove of Hajji's new pastime.

Most of them worked with Jewish Israelis in one way or another. There were several nurses and a doctor in the village who worked in Israeli hospitals. There was a car mechanic with dozens of Jewish customers. The market was stocked with Israeli produce and manufactured products. How was Hajji's "job" loading and unloading trucks for the army any different? Actually, some people reasoned, he was making life easier for Palestinians; they would be able to get through the checkpoint more quickly and with less hassle.

And to the young people in the village, there was certainly no issue. As the best goalkeeper in the village, he was respected, even revered.

CHAPTER 20

When he was fifteen, Hajji became determined to play in the National Israeli Youth League, despite his father's vocal opposition. Some of the other youths from his village who excelled at soccer played for Bnei Sakhnin, traditionally an Arab club, so Hajji went with some friends for tryouts. Hajji played very well during the tryouts, blocking all but two attempts at goal, and was selected to join the team. But Bnei Sakhnin already had a goalkeeper, a pretentious kid named Hassan who also happened to be a nephew of the head coach. Hajji quickly realized that he would be relegated to backup goalkeeper, and he left the tryouts somewhat dispirited. When he got back to Al'ard Alhamra, he wandered the streets in contemplation. One of the older men in the village, a taxi driver Hajji always addressed formally as "Mr. Al-Nasri," spotted Hajji trudging along the street with his head lowered. "What's wrong, Hajji? Did you lose a match?" the man asked.

"No. I just came back from tryouts for the Bnei Sakhnin youth team."

"And you didn't make the cut?"

"I did, actually. They chose me to join the club."

"That's great! So why the long face?"

"They already have a goalkeeper. I'd just be the backup goalkeeper."

"I see. Well, you never know. Maybe the other guy will get sick or be injured. Or maybe the coaches will be so impressed with you that they'll let you play. Besides, you're young—stick with it for a year or two and you'll get to start!"

Hajji looked down at the ground and didn't answer.

"Why not try out for a different team?" suggested Mr. Al-Nasri.

"Like what?"

"Kiryat Shmona. I know some of the players on their professional team. I take them in my taxi sometimes. I could make a few phone calls and see if their youth team is offering tryouts."

"But isn't that a Jewish team? Why would I play for a Jewish team?"

"They don't bite. You might even grow from the experience. Besides, most of the teams are mixed. You wouldn't be the only Arab player on the team."

The next day Mr. Al-Nasri found Hajji outside the mosque.

"Hajji, I made a few phone calls for you. You're in luck! The Kiryat Shmona youth team already had their tryouts, but the coach for the under-sixteen division said that their goalkeeper is moving up to the under-seventeen division, so they're looking for another goalkeeper. He said they'd be interested in seeing you play!"

"Really? When can I go?"

"Today."

"Today? How? Where? How will I get there—"

"I'll take you in my taxi."

"But I can't afford to pay for a taxi all the way there and back."

"Don't worry about it. It's my treat!"

Hajji ran home to change into proper soccer attire, and half an hour later, he and Mr. Al-Nasri left the village for the drive to Kiryat Shmona. Mr. Al-Nasri was a middle-aged man who wore blue jeans and a gray T-shirt that matched his thinning gray hair and mustache. He chain-smoked Time—an Israeli brand—and listened to Western music on the car radio. The two spoke sparingly. Hajji gazed out of the car window; he saw signs for Nazareth, then spotted the glistening sapphire-blue waters of the Sea of Galilee.

Mr. Al-Nasri drove well above the speed limit, so they arrived at the sports complex in just over an hour. The team was already practicing. Mr. Al-Nasri introduced Hajji to the coaches, and they invited Hajji to join the practice session as goalkeeper. Hajji performed flawlessly, greatly impressing coaches and players alike. Unsurprisingly, he was invited to join the team, and he gladly accepted the invitation.

Playing on the youth league team was his first meaningful interaction with Jewish Israelis—his relationship with the soldiers at the checkpoint had always been superficial. Initially, he felt somewhat remorseful, like he was betraying his people by collaborating with the enemy. He was also concerned that his Jewish teammates would shun him as an Arab and a Muslim. But his burning desire to play soccer at a higher level of competition drove him to overcome his apprehensions. Hajji was pleasantly surprised to find that his Jewish teammates treated him and the four other Arabs on the team as equals. Indeed, a strong camaraderie soon developed between Hajji and the other players on the team.

PART TWO

CHAPTER 21

The burly officer at the conscription office took a liking to Zar and offered to help him choose a unit that fit his needs and interests. "So, what are you interested in?" the officer asked. "Tanks? Infantry? Artillery?"

"Soccer," Zar replied, twirling his sidelocks.

"Soccer?" asked the officer. "What kind of unit is that?"

"I don't care what unit I'm in, as long as I can play soccer. Which units play the most soccer?"

The officer laughed. "In all my years in the army, I've fielded plenty of questions—which units have the best food, the best-looking girls... but not this one! I'll tell you what. Give me a few minutes and I'll ask around." Zar sat down and waited as the officer called some colleagues. After a few minutes, he had his answer: "The 101st infantry."

"What?"

"The 101st infantry unit in the Nahal Brigade. They have a reputation for soccer. The commander of the unit is obsessed with soccer, apparently. He trains his soldiers to play soccer. He thinks it gives them cohesion and focus. Some of the best professional players in the league served in that unit. If you love soccer and you want to play a lot of it in the army, join the 101st infantry unit."

After a cursory physical exam and a psychiatric assessment, Zar was approved for conscription to the 101st infantry unit of the Nahal Brigade. He was instructed to show up one week later at a building in downtown Jerusalem. He had a week of downtime until his official conscription date, and he still hadn't informed his parents.

Later that evening, after his father returned from the study hall, Zar told his parents about his recent adventures: the soccer team, winning the championship, getting drafted into the army. His mother cried. His father sat speechless, his head resting in both hands. After nearly a minute of uncomfortable silence, his father fired off a barrage of questions: "How are you going to keep kosher? How will you pray regularly? Will you have to cut off your '*peyos*' and shave your beard? Don't you know that the army is filled with evil men and loose women and temptations that no man—young or old—should ever have to resist? How will you find time to study Torah? Do you know what this will do to your marriage prospects? Men in our community want their daughters to marry scholars, not soldiers! And what about your brothers and sisters? The whole family will be tainted!" With each question, his voice grew louder and louder; soon he was screaming, red in the face, veins bulging in his neck. His mother, who had been sobbing quietly, was now wailing.

Zar tried to defend himself: "The Israeli army only serves kosher food. Religious soldiers don't have to work on *Shabbos*, and they get time to pray three times a day, and—" But he couldn't out-shout his father, who by this point was nearly delirious, and wasn't listening to a word Zar said. Zar began to fear that his father might actually harm him physically, so he ran out of the apartment. His father followed him to the stairwell, but Zar was too quick and nimble. He raced down several flights of stairs and into the alleyway where he'd spent countless hours as a child, practicing soccer and dreaming of cheering crowds chanting his name. Standing in the alleyway, dimly lit by a single flickering lamp, Zar was entranced by memories of his youth and dreams of his future. His father's delirious screams of "Luzar, Luzar, Luzar!" mingled in his imagination with the adoring crowds shouting "Zar, Zar, Zar!" As he left the alley and approached Mea She'arim Street, he could still hear his father screaming: "Luzar, Luzar, Luzar…" He wondered if he would ever again see his parents or the alleyway or the neighborhood of his youth.

More acutely, he wondered where he would sleep that night and where he would spend the next week until his conscription date. He sat on a park bench, overwhelmed with all that had transpired that night and over the last few days and weeks, but also filled with a sense of relief, as if some massive burden had been lifted from his shoulders.

He leafed through the conscription papers and remembered that the burly officer had told him to call anytime with questions. Despite the late hour, he called the officer on his cellphone and was relieved to hear a friendly voice on the line. The officer informed Zar that since his parents had not given their consent to his conscription, he would be drafted as a "lone soldier." This provided him with some perks, including an apartment where he could stay when he was on leave, a slightly higher monthly stipend, and an adoptive family where he could occasionally get home-cooked meals and a warm environment to spend *Shabbat* off the base. The lone soldiers' apartment was only a few miles away, not far from the soccer field where his team had practiced and played their home matches.

An hour or so later, Zar knocked on the door to the apartment. A young man in jeans and a T-shirt answered the door. He introduced himself, and they spoke briefly. Six lone soldiers were assigned to share this apartment. Zar found an empty bed and some clean linens, and within a few minutes, he was in a deep sleep. He dreamed that he was in a huge stadium, playing soccer on the Israeli national team. Thousands of adoring fans were chanting his name and thousands of others were cursing him. As he dribbled past his opponents and scored the winning goal, he saw that the soccer ball was dripping with blood.

CHAPTER 22

The next morning, Zar woke up early, but he stayed in bed contemplating his situation. Ordinarily, he would ritually wash his hands as soon as he woke up, then put on his phylacteries and say his morning prayers. But he didn't even *have* his phylacteries; fleeing his home the night before, he'd had no time to take any of his belongings. But even if he did have them, he wasn't certain that he'd say his morning prayers or wear his phylacteries. Zar knew of other boys who had gone "off the path," rejecting the ways of his insular community. Most of those boys had acculturated into secular Israeli society. They didn't wear yarmulkes, they didn't adhere to kosher dietary restrictions, and they certainly didn't wear phylacteries or pray.

But Zar wasn't one of them. He hadn't rejected his traditions; he had no intention of abandoning the laws and customs. He'd left his community, where he felt restricted and confined, but he hadn't left his faith. He believed in God, desired to be close to God, perhaps now more than ever. He wanted to pray, *needed* to pray—but he also needed his phylacteries. He considered asking his new roommate to lend him a pair, but he was still fast asleep. Besides, he didn't even know him. He had no idea if he was Orthodox and would have phylacteries to lend him. Anyway, borrowing phylacteries every day would be impractical. He needed his own, and he couldn't possibly afford to buy new ones. Eventually, he'd have to go back home to retrieve his phylacteries, and with only a week left before his army service, he figured he'd better do it sooner rather than later.

In the morning, his father would be in the study hall and wouldn't come home for lunch until after the afternoon prayers. His mother would be home straightening up the apartment, but she usually left around nine to go shopping or to mingle with friends in a nearby courtyard. If he hurried, he could get back home at just the right time to sneak up to the apartment, grab a few things—including his phylacteries—and escape unnoticed. He got out of bed, went to the bathroom, ritually washed his hands, got dressed, and quietly left the apartment.

The nearest bus stop was a few blocks away from the lone soldiers' apartment. As he waited for the bus, he saw schoolchildren walking to school, wearing their knapsacks. Several young women sat at a café conversing as they smoked cigarettes and drank coffee. In a small park, two old men were playing chess. There were people jogging, bicycling, walking their dogs. Many others were walking briskly, presumably on their way to work. A young man in a knitted yarmulke carried a velvet bag as he walked either to or from synagogue. For all these people, it was an ordinary day, not significantly different from the day before. But for Zar, today was anything but ordinary. It was the first day of a new life, with new challenges and new opportunities.

Zar twirled his sidelocks and gazed out the window as the bus wound its way down Strauss Street and approached Kikar Shabbat, the intersection where he had witnessed the riot on Memorial Day years earlier. The scenery was familiar. He had seen it countless times, but always as an insider; now he felt like an outsider looking in. He got off the bus at the intersection and cautiously walked down Mea She'arim Street. He reached his apartment building a few minutes before nine and waited in the shadows, crouching behind a dumpster, his eyes fixed on the front entrance. Just as he had calculated, his mother exited the building a few minutes later, pushing an empty collapsible shopping cart. Even from a distance, she looked forlorn and worried. He briefly contemplated running to greet his mother and reassure her that he wasn't abandoning her, but he reconsidered. There would be time for reconciliation sometime in the future. He hoped so, anyway. For now, he had a dream to pursue.

As soon as his mother turned the corner, Zar sprinted to the building and ran up the stairwell to his apartment. He experienced a brief moment of panic when he couldn't find the key in his right pocket, then relief when he found it in his left pocket. He hurriedly fished the key out and opened the door. No one was home. He scurried to the dining room and grabbed his phylacteries from the shelf, then took a few pairs of socks and underwear and other necessities from his bedroom. He rushed to the front door, paused to look back longingly at the only home he'd ever known, then left, closing and locking the front door and kissing the mezuzah. He sprinted back down the stairs, out of the building, and back to Kikar Shabbat to catch the bus back to the lone soldiers' apartment. When his mother returned later that morning, she noticed the empty space on the shelf in the dining room, and she smiled.

CHAPTER 23

That week, Zar bought the odds and ends that he would need in the army: warm underwear and socks, deodorant and other toiletries. On his conscription day, Zar went to a large building near the central bus station in downtown Jerusalem along with hundreds of other new conscripts and more seasoned soldiers, men and women in uniform returning to their bases after a free weekend. Zar found the table for new conscripts and presented his papers to the officer seated there. He signed some forms and was directed to one of the many buses waiting outside. They drove for about an hour to Tel Hashomer, a large army base in Ramat Gan, an eastern suburb of Tel Aviv.

Arriving at Tel Hashomer, hundreds of new recruits from Jerusalem and throughout the country were directed to a cavernous building known by its Hebrew acronym, the *Bakum*. Inside, they watched a short video presentation formally introducing them to the army and summarizing the protocol for their first day of conscription. Each new soldier was fingerprinted, posed for photographs and dental X-rays, and received a series of vaccinations. They were each given a large olive-green duffel bag and instructed to proceed to numerous stations where they received their ID badges, dog tags, uniforms, two pairs of boots, a *dubon*—a padded winter jacket—and other essentials of army life.

When it was time for his first army haircut, Zar explained to the barber that, as a religious soldier, he was entitled to keep his beard and sidelocks. A brief argument erupted between the barber and two low-ranking officers, but a high-ranking officer ruled that Zar was, in fact, correct. He could keep his beard and sidelocks, but they would have to be trimmed significantly to conform to army standards, and these much shorter sidelocks had to be tucked behind his ears. Zar glanced to either side and watched as his curly sidelocks fell to the floor and were swept away. "Look at yourself now," the barber said, giving Zar a mirror. "With your good looks, the female soldiers are going to flock to you like bees to honey." This attempt at reassurance only made Zar more uncomfortable. To add insult to injury, Zar later learned that he was, in fact, entitled to keep his long sidelocks after all.

The new conscripts were then directed back to the parking lot to board their assigned buses. Hundreds of soldiers dispersed to the buses that would take them to their bases. In the ensuing chaos, Zar boarded a bus with signage indicating an infantry unit. A junior officer on the bus examined Zar's ID badge and berated him loudly for boarding the wrong bus. Zar disembarked and frantically searched the large parking lot for the right one. Eventually, he found the bus with a sign for the Nahal Brigade. Apparently, Zar wasn't the only new conscript to have made such an error; numerous soldiers could be seen disembarking from one bus and frantically running, with their personal bags and army-issued duffel bags, to another bus. When all of the soldiers found their units, the buses departed for bases throughout Israel.

After riding for several hours, through the urban sprawl of Greater Tel Aviv, then past less densely populated agricultural communities south of Ben Gurion Airport, and finally into the barren landscape of the Negev, they arrived at an enormous army base deep in the desert. There were dozens of tents of various sizes and a few administrative buildings. The base was surrounded by a barbed wire fence, and at the front gate was a guard booth. Several dogs barked wildly as the buses entered the base.

The soldiers disembarked, and they were ordered to pile all their belongings together. Zar wondered how everyone would find their bags in the large pile, and he was tempted to ask if it might be wiser to divide everyone into their units before dumping all of the bags. But he quickly sensed that the officers barking out orders were not interested in his ideas of how to make the army more efficient. Perhaps this was just the first of many exercises in discipline. Zar reasoned that, with his Hasidic appearance, he stood out enough; he didn't need to draw more attention to himself by challenging his superiors.

They were then divided into units and introduced to their commanding officers. Zar, along with around sixty other new recruits, was directed to an open space outside a large tent with a "101st Infantry Unit" sign. Waiting at attention outside the tent, in a crisp officer's uniform, was the commander of the unit. He was a muscular man with tanned bronze skin, fine wrinkles around his eyes, and a stern face. On the right side of his thick neck was a tattoo of a blue-and-white soccer ball. The unit commander related his rules. They were few and simple, but all present understood that these rules were not to be broken under any circumstances. He promised that he would work them hard, but they would be rewarded for their hard work. There were several rewards, including free time on the base, extra snacks, and above all else, soccer. But in his unit, he explained, soccer was not simply a reward; it was also part of their training. They would play when he allowed it, how he allowed it, and where he allowed it. They would learn teamwork and camaraderie, which would be essential, he assured them, on both the soccer field and the battlefield.

Zar was mesmerized. This was a dream come true. He would have the best possible reward—soccer! Zar looked around the group. Many other soldiers were smiling broadly. They too had chosen this unit in order to play soccer. Then Zar noticed a face in the crowd that he recognized: the kibbutznik with the golden-blond hair, the wonder child from the Youth League championship match. Egel's eyes widened with joy when he spotted Zar. As soon as they were "at ease," Zar and Egel embraced like old friends reuniting after a long absence. "Now we can be teammates and win the army championship," Egel exclaimed.

"I already told you," Zar corrected him. "We're not stopping with the army championship or even the Israel national championship. You and I are going to win the World Cup!"

CHAPTER 24

Zar had been exposed to secular people (he'd played informal games of soccer with the *traif* boys, and he'd competed with—and even befriended—his teammates in the youth league), but he had never before actually lived among them. In the lone soldiers' apartment, he had minimal contact with the other men, but on the army base he was completely immersed in a world of secular people. Initially, he felt apprehensive of   even intimidated by   his secular surroundings. He was concerned that his religiosity would be compromised, and fearful that he would be ridiculed or shunned by the other soldiers in his unit. Surprisingly, none of his apprehensions materialized. His peers generally respected him for his faith, discipline, and commitment. Egel echoed the sentiments of the group when he said, "I don't even know if I believe in God, but if there *is* one, I sure hope that he's on our side. So keep on praying, buddy. We're depending on you!"

For the first few months, they went through basic training. Although time was scarce, they still had some opportunity to play soccer. Zar, Egel, and a handful of other soccer fanatics managed to squeeze in a match most days, but most of the recruits didn't have the stamina to play. Zar and Egel really enjoyed being teammates, and the more they played together, the more each learned the other's style and pace. After playing only a few games together, they became such a formidable pair that the others complained, demanding that the two stars be split up onto separate teams. But even as opponents, each was able to scrutinize the other's techniques and strengths; when they did play together, they would be even more effective.

A drill sergeant took charge of the unit for basic training. He introduced himself simply as *Mefakked*, "Commander." The recruits were not privy to his first name; they were to refer to him simply as Commander. He was a head shorter than most of the recruits, so he was more commonly known as Napoleon. He seldom smiled and never spoke in any tone softer than shouting—and he only got louder from there. His first drill involved running around the perimeter of the base again and again and again. Napoleon was trying to wear them down physically and emotionally, to break them in and establish his dominance over them. The guard dogs at the entrance to the base would bark wildly as the new recruits passed by. Most of the recruits paid no attention to the dogs, but Egel had a near-pathological fear of dogs, or as he called them, "wolves." The dogs seemed to sense his fear and barked louder and more savagely when Egel was in close proximity. Some of the guys jokingly referred to Egel as "the boy who cried wolf."

After three days of running around the base and trying to avoid getting nipped by the angry guard dogs, Napoleon led the recruits on longer runs through the surrounding desert and into an old artillery practice firing range. He neglected to mention that the unexploded ordinances were empty and basically harmless, so the recruits thought Napoleon was crazy, reckless, or both. By the end of the first week of training, two soldiers had sustained leg or ankle injuries. One soldier had a mental breakdown and required hospitalization.

Most nights, they would return to the base to sleep, but occasionally, they would sleep in the desert on paper-thin mats; as the temperature dropped precipitously, they were completely exposed to the elements. The following mornings were the hardest for Zar and the few other religious soldiers, who had to relinquish precious minutes of sleep in order to hastily say their morning prayers.

Zar, who was inclined to melancholy, started feeling the stress of training and was worried that he too would break. Egel, who had already earned a reputation in the unit for being easygoing and charismatic, fed Zar with a steady stream of encouraging words. One particularly grueling drill was running for about six miles at high noon in the desert heat, carrying one of the recruits on a stretcher. Napoleon always chose one of the heavier soldiers to lie on the stretcher. When Zar was one of those carrying the stretcher and he felt like his arms would fall off or that he'd collapse from heat stroke, Egel would sneak up behind him, grab onto the stretcher, and whisper to Zar, "Take a drink of water and come back in ten or fifteen minutes when you're feeling stronger." Zar would be forever grateful to Egel for his kindness.

During one of their runs, Egel sustained a laceration on his hand from carrying the stretcher, which had a bolt protruding from it. He was sent back to base to have the wound sutured, and he ended up spending the night in the infirmary tent. Zar wondered why Egel had to stay in the infirmary to convalesce after what appeared to be a relatively minor injury. Later the next day, Egel went back to the infirmary to have his bandages changed. When Zar spied a young female paramedic leaving the tent and greeting Egel warmly, Egel's motives became clearer.

Midway through the third week of training, they were issued out-of-date M16 rifles. An attractive female officer came to the base to teach them the basics of assembling, disassembling, cleaning, and proper handling of their firearms. It didn't take long for Egel to find out her name and, with some persistence, her phone number.

CHAPTER 25

One day, Zar was delayed by his morning prayers and missed the bus that took the soldiers to a firing range for target practice. Fortunately, Zar bumped into the unit commander, who radioed to Napoleon, then summoned a truck to take Zar out to the range. Zar had seen the truck driver around the base, but he'd never interacted with him. The driver was plump, and his sagging uniform suggested that he'd previously been much heavier but had lost some weight since joining the army. Zar hopped into the truck. The driver extended his hand, which had been cradling the stick shift, and greeted him in Yiddish: "*Vus tut zich, Reb Yid?*" ("What's up, buddy?") Zar looked at him, wide-eyed, but responded in kind.

The conversation continued in Yiddish. The driver's name was Yoli, a nickname for Yoel. Back in Brooklyn, he'd been Yoily, but Israelis had difficulty pronouncing the "oi." He'd grown up as a Hasid, he said, and he'd had a "difficult" childhood. (He didn't elaborate, and Zar didn't probe any further.) Upon reaching the age of eighteen a few years earlier, he immigrated to Israel and joined the army as a lone soldier. For Yoli, this was both an act of rebellion and a means of liberation. Physically unfit, without a secular education or Hebrew language skills, he was deemed "not combat-worthy," and he gladly became a non-combatant *jobnik*. In his case, this meant driving a truck, cleaning, doing basic plumbing, and a multitude of other random job assignments on and off the base.

Zar, in turn, related a very truncated version of his own personal history. Like Yoli, he'd grown up in an insular Yiddish-speaking community and had enlisted in the IDF as a lone soldier, but Zar had no skeletons in his closet, and he was enlisted in a combat unit. Yoli and Zar formed an instant bond. They were landsmen of sorts. Literally and figuratively, Zar was the only one on the base who could speak his language. In time, Zar learned that with Yoli he could discuss pretty much anything that was on his mind. Yoli, on the other hand, always seemed to keep his cards closer to the chest, as if there was something too personal or too painful for him to disclose.

Basic training was arduous, and with the additional hours of soccer practice, Zar pushed himself to his limit. He was at his peak of fitness, and he could run faster and with more endurance than ever before. His body was trim and muscular, and his skin was tanned bronze. He had always been good-looking, but now he was downright handsome.

The culmination of basic training was a twenty-two-mile overnight hike through the Judean foothills in full gear, ending with a ceremony in Jerusalem at Ammunition Hill, the site of an important battle during the Six-Day War. The hike was grueling. Zar developed blisters on his feet from his ill-fitting boots, and as the unit approached Jerusalem, he was numb with pain. Sleep deprivation had also taken its toll on Zar. Enduring the final few miles took all of his adrenaline, plus a few energy drinks, incessant shouting from Napoleon, and ample words of encouragement from Egel. When they reached Ammunition Hill, most of the troops collapsed into a few minutes of much-needed sleep. Zar wanted to say his morning prayers, but he simply didn't have the physical or mental energy to do it.

Parents and other close family members of the soldiers arrived, and the ceremony took on a positively festive air. Zar was the only one with no family present; his lone soldier adoptive family had other commitments that day. During the ceremony, the soldiers received their berets, and Napoleon "broke the distance," revealing his real name and his true demeanor. As it turned out, Napoleon was very personable, with a sharp sense of humor. He had even composed a poem with crude rhymes and hilarious jabs at all the members of his unit. Then the soldiers reunited with their families and posed for pictures. Zar met Egel's parents, then discreetly left Ammunition Hill and took a bus back to the lone soldiers' apartment by himself. The whole unit was given a much-deserved weekend off to spend time with family—or in Zar's case, to nurse his aching, blistered feet back to health.

For Zar, the ceremony had been anything but festive, and the weekend off was lonely and dismal. Before going to bed Saturday night, he cried for the first time since he was a child. Zar then did what he often did when he was feeling down: he spoke with God. But he was physically and emotionally depleted, lacking the vigor and fortitude for prolonged supplication. So before collapsing in his bed, he composed a succinct entreaty to his creator: "Dear God, I am lonely and sad. And more than anything else, I feel hopeless. Dear God, please give me hope."

CHAPTER 26

The next day, Zar woke up late and went to a synagogue near the central bus station for morning prayers. He caught the 470 bus to Be'er Sheva, then another bus to his base, arriving just in time for lunch. As he walked to the dining hall, he noticed a small group of soldiers congregating near the administrative offices. When Zar had finished eating and was on his way back to his tent, he saw the same group of soldiers; they seemed to be just loitering. Perhaps they were from another base and were waiting for a ride to pick them up, Zar thought to himself. Three of them were men and the fourth was a woman. Instinctively, he turned his eyes to the ground. It is sinful to gaze at women, he had always been taught; just looking at them would surely conjure up forbidden thoughts. But something inside him urged him to take another glimpse at the female soldier. Zar nervously brushed his shortened sidelocks behind his ears. He couldn't help but notice, even from a distance, that she was strikingly beautiful. Again he turned his head away. Even looking at a woman's finger or clothing is prohibited, the Talmud teaches, lest it lead to impure thoughts or actions. But again, he couldn't resist the temptation; he discreetly scrutinized the visitor. Suddenly, she looked up and caught his eye. Zar averted his eyes, but not before observing that she'd smiled at him. Now he was doubly inhibited from looking at her again. Not only would it be sinful, he thought, but also awkward, now that she had noticed him and even smiled at him.

But her smile seemed sweet and genuine. How could he ignore her and her sweet smile? He looked toward her again, but now she was looking away. With her attention now elsewhere, Zar was able to examine her more closely. She was above average in height, with a slim but athletic build. Her dark brown hair was thick and wavy, and tied back into a ponytail. Her face was pretty, with dimples and kind brown eyes. She looked at Zar again and smiled, and this time Zar smiled back. Only then did Zar notice something about her that he'd missed before: the tag on her left shoulder displayed a green-and-white circle with a Star of David in the center. The soccer battalion! Zar was now overcome with curiosity. Who was she? Where did she come from? And what was the significance of that shoulder tag?

Zar had never had a conversation with a woman outside his own family. He had taken orders from female officers and responded as per protocol, but he had never actually had a *conversation* with one of them. He didn't even know where to begin, how to break the ice. One thing he did know, however: he had to speak with her. He had to meet this mysterious woman with the dimples, pretty smile, kind eyes, and the shoulder tag with a soccer ball and a Star of David. Hesitant but determined, Zar approached her. "Hi!" he said awkwardly, as he fiddled with his sidelocks, partly concealed behind his ears.

"Hi!" she responded, extending her hand to shake his. Zar froze. Jewish religious law forbids men to touch women except for close family members, Zar had been taught. So he began to rationalize: it was forbidden for men to touch women, but perhaps that was only if the touching was done in an affectionate way. Also, thought Zar, it would be rude to rebuff her; it might even offend her. And he remembered hearing that some businessmen shake hands with women in the course of business dealings. Furthermore, there was an imperative to treat all of God's creations with respect—perhaps in this case, he was forbidden *not* to shake her hand. After these lightning-quick calculations, Zar took her hand and shook it. Instantly, he felt flooded with a mixture of warmth and guilt.

"Hi!" she said again, "My name is Tikvah." Zar again froze, unsure how to respond.

"You're supposed to say, 'Hi, Tikvah. So nice to meet you. My name is...' and then say your name."

"Oh, I'm sorry. Umm... Hi, Tikvah. So nice to meet you. My name is...Zar."

"Zar? That's a *strange* name," she said, making the obvious pun.

"Zar is my nickname. It's short for Elazar. Is Tikvah a nickname?"

"A nickname?" Tikvah giggled. "No, Tikvah's a name. You know, like *Hatikvah*...Israel's national anthem?"

Although he had never sung *Hatikvah* as a child—it was unheard of in his ultra-Orthodox community—he knew it well. It was sung at all of the matches in the youth soccer league. "Of course I know," said Zar, and proceeded to sing the second verse of *Hatikvah*, "*Od lo avdah tikvatenu, hatikvah bat shnot alpayim...*" Tikvah joined in, and they finished with exaggerated soulfulness: "*lihyot am chofshi be'artzenu, eretz Tzion vi-Yerushalayim.*" They burst out in laughter as the small crowd that had gathered to watch this spectacle applauded. Zar again felt guilty. The Talmud teaches that it is forbidden to hear a woman's voice singing, Zar recalled—though of course he hadn't anticipated that she would sing along, and he wouldn't want to offend her, and it might even be *forbidden* to offend her because there is an imperative to treat all of God's creations with respect...

Zar then clarified his seemingly foolish question: "What I meant was, well, I can tell from your accent that you're probably not a native Israeli. I thought maybe you're American or Canadian or something like that. So I guess I was asking if you had another name, in English or whatever."

"You're very astute," Tikvah answered. She spoke quickly, almost hurriedly "I *am* American, from California. My English name is Hope—that's English for *tikvah*. I mean, I was named Tikvah *and* Hope when I was a baby, but no one ever called me Tikvah, except for my grandmother; everyone else always called me Hope. Then I made *aliyah* a little over a year ago, and my official name here in Israel is

Tikvah, so that's what everyone here calls me."

"You've only been here for a year? How do you speak Hebrew so well?"

"I don't speak *that* well. After all, you picked up my American accent in, like, two seconds."

"Okay. But aside from the accent, you speak pretty fluently."

"Thank you. That was a compliment, I think. As a kid I went to a Jewish summer camp. It wasn't really so religious—I guess I would call it 'nondenominational'—but it was very Zionistic. All the announcements were in Hebrew and there were classes in Hebrew and a lot of the staff were Israelis. So I was already pretty comfortable with basic Hebrew, even before I made *aliyah*. And then I enlisted in the army. I've pretty much been immersed in Hebrew since then. I don't really have anywhere else to go even on weekends when I'm free. I'm a lone soldier."

"So am I!" Zar replied enthusiastically. "I'm a lone soldier too."

But before Tikvah had a chance to respond, a truck pulled up, and the three male soldiers hopped in. "Come on, Tikvah. Enough flirting. We've got to go. We're late!"

Tikvah climbed into the truck and waved. "Bye, Zar. It was nice meeting you. Maybe I'll see you again soon."

Zar wanted to say, "I enjoyed meeting you too. When will I see you again? Can I have your phone number?" but he couldn't get the words out of his mouth, and as quickly as it had arrived, the truck pulled away, speeding off the base and out of sight.

Later that night, as Zar was getting ready for bed, he heard Egel strumming his guitar and singing. Zar didn't recognize the song, but it was the Beatles' "I've Just Seen a Face," which describes becoming infatuated with a woman after seeing her beautiful face.

CHAPTER 27

Zar had difficulty falling asleep; he simply couldn't get Tikvah out of his mind. She was beautiful and witty and kind—he could tell from her eyes and her smile that she was kind. But Zar was also tormented as he rested on his cot. She's secular, he thought. She doesn't observe the laws governing male-female interactions: she shook my hand and she sang with me. Does she observe any of the laws? She probably doesn't keep kosher or observe *Shabbos*. She may not even believe in God! But Zar couldn't stop thinking about her, and he couldn't stop regretting that he hadn't had the chance—or, more accurately, the courage—to say goodbye and get her phone number. I'll track her down, he decided. How many Tikvahs could there be in the unit with a soccer ball shoulder tag? And she's a lone soldier, just like me. Surely there's only one. Tomorrow morning, I'll start searching for her. As he drifted off to sleep, he envisaged Tikvah, her pretty face with the dimples and sweet smile and kind brown eyes…

The next morning, Zar awoke early. He hastily got dressed and rushed to the synagogue tent to say the morning prayers, inserting an impromptu prayer of his own: Dear God, he prayed, I've always tried to be faithful to you. Perhaps I don't study as much Torah as I should, but Torah study has never been my strength. Dear God, you've given me strengths and talents, and I will strive to sanctify your name by using them. God, yesterday, you sent me an angel—Tikvah, an angel of hope. Did you send her to help me in my life's mission? Or, heaven forbid, did you send her to tempt me, to lure me away from you, away from performing my life's mission? God, please send me a sign.

At breakfast in the dining hall, Zar asked Egel and some of the other guys at the table if they'd noticed a bunch of soldiers, three men and a woman, visiting the base the day before. They hadn't. "Wait a second," joked Oren, a dark-skinned soldier who spoke Hebrew with a thick Yemenite accent. "We had a female visitor on the base yesterday and Egel didn't notice her? I'm getting worried." "Quick, check his pulse!" advised someone else. Oren put two fingers on Egel's wrist and started counting out loud, "One, two, three…"

"Hey, look at that!" laughed Egel, "Oren can count. It's not true what they say about him." Egel wrestled his wrist free and gave Oren a light punch in the arm.

"Some soldiers were visiting from another base yesterday," Zar persisted, "and I was wondering where they came from, what unit they're in. Their shoulder tags had a ball, like a green-and-white soccer ball with a Star of David in the middle. Does anyone know what unit that is?" No one did.

"Why do you need to know?" asked Egel.

"Just curious, that's all."

"I think you liked one of them," Egel guessed. "Was it the girl—or maybe one of the guys?" Egel asked, raising his eyebrows, at which point two of the others embraced each other in mock passion.

Another soldier joined them at their table. "Hey, Zar," he said, "I had the honor of enjoying your duet yesterday. Nice rendition of *Hatikvah*. And who was your singing partner? She's cute."

"Oh! Now I get it," announced Egel. "Zar has a crush on the girl. Why didn't you get her phone number? Geez, if it was me, I'd have her number and we'd already have dinner plans for tomorrow night."

"If it was you, Egel, she'd probably be curled up in your cot right now," joked Oren, and everyone at the table except Zar laughed uproariously. "Hey, hey, hey," Egel admonished them. "Don't talk about Zar's girlfriend like that. He's liable to get mad…and sing you to death!"

"Well, guilty as charged," admitted Zar, fiddling with his sidelocks behind his ears. "I met a nice girl yesterday and, stupidly, I didn't get her

phone number, so I want to track her down. I got her name: Tikvah."
Zar was rudely interrupted by two of the guys, who began a duet of their
own, singing "Zahav," an Israeli pop song about a beautiful woman.

"Okay, enough," said Zar. "Cut it out—seriously! I just know her
name, her first name, and I know that she's from America...California,
actually." The duet again broke out in song, strumming imaginary
guitars as they sang "California Girls," the old Beach Boys classic. Zar
stared at them in annoyance and they promptly stopped. "She was
wearing a shoulder tag with a ball, like a soccer ball, with a green-and-
white Star of David in the middle, but no one seems to know what it
means."

"I know what it means," the late-arriving soldier chimed in. "It's
army intelligence. Those soldiers are from a military intelligence unit;
they came to our base yesterday for some reason. If you want to track
down Tikvah, you'll have to get to the military intelligence offices near
Be'er Sheva somehow. That's where she's based."

"Good luck with that." Oren said. "You need high-level security
clearance to get anywhere near that place."

"But this is top priority: a soldier missing in action," Egel insisted.
"Zar lost his girlfriend and we have to find her!" And again, everyone
at the table except Zar laughed.

CHAPTER 28

After breakfast, Zar lingered in the dining hall after everyone left. He was planning his next move, attempting to contrive a strategy that would somehow get him assigned to visit the military intelligence offices, but he couldn't think of any plausible pretext. After he'd squandered the better part of an hour, Yoli entered the dining hall, sucking an ice-pop he held in one hand while pushing a mop with the other.

"Hey, Rabbi!" Yoli shouted in Yiddish. "You look like you're lost in thought. Are you trying to decipher some insoluble Talmudic passage?"

Zar explained the whole predicament to Yoli. "So that's my problem," he concluded. "I don't know how to get into the military intelligence building. Apparently, you need security clearance to get anywhere near it."

"You sure do," said Yoli. "And it's not just a building; it's a whole complex of buildings surrounded by a barbed wire fence, with some high-tech infrared cameras and motion detectors. It's like a fortress. Once, I had to deliver a package there from our commanding officer. I drove my truck up to the front gate, but they wouldn't let me in. They sent one of their guys in a jeep to get the package from me. I don't think you could come up with any excuse to get in there." Yoli paused, pondering Zar's dilemma. "But here's a novel idea: Why don't you try telling them the truth?"

"Are you kidding, Yoli? I can just imagine the scene: 'Hi, my name's Zar. I have a crush on one of the female soldiers in your impenetrable fortress. I don't even really know her name. Could you please let me in, without any kind of security clearance, so I can be reunited with her?'"

"Of course that won't get you anywhere, but maybe speak to our commanding officer. He loves you. You're his soccer superstar. Anyway, you'll never know unless you try."

"I guess I have nothing to lose...except my pride and reputation."

"Rabbi, let me share with you some words of wisdom: Life begins where your comfort zone ends."

"I like that. It's pretty deep. Where did you hear it?"

"I read it somewhere."

"Where?"

"Inside a candy wrapper. Bubblegum, I think."

"Well, here I go," sighed Zar, "risking my pride and reputation, and all because of something Yoli read on the inside of a bubblegum wrapper."

CHAPTER 29

Zar went to the base's administrative building to look for the commanding officer. Inside, he found Egel flirting with the secretary. "Hi, Egel. And hi, umm…"

"Rotem," the secretary replied.

"Hi, Rotem. Is the unit commander here? I have a question for him."

"Go knock on his door," Rotem instructed Zar dismissively, gazing longingly at Egel.

Zar knocked gingerly on the door. "Come in," barked the commanding officer. "Oh, it's you, Zar. Come on in. Have a seat," he said, in a tone that was cordial but not quite affable. His face was stern, and he had fine wrinkles around his eyes. Zar glanced at the tattoo of a blue-and-white soccer ball on the right side of his thick neck. His office was no bigger than a closet, and his small desk was cluttered with papers. There were two plastic chairs that barely fit between the desk and the wall, one of them already occupied by a box of files. Skittishly, Zar sat down on the other chair.

"What's up?" asked the officer, and Zar briefly explained his predicament. The officer's response startled him: "Listen, lover boy. This is the army. We're here to protect our country—and in your case, to protect our country *and* excel at soccer. We're not here to fall in love, marry a princess, and live happily ever after. I recommend that you stop fantasizing about this intelligence soldier and start doing something *really* intelligent…like practicing your penalty kicks!" The officer started rummaging through some papers on his desk, indicating to Zar that he had more important things to do and that this unscheduled and unnecessary meeting was over. Zar thanked the officer for his time and, head lowered, left the room. Egel and Rotem were still flirting as Zar exited the building.

CHAPTER 30

Z ar was dispirited. As he walked away, he looked up at the sky and whispered, "God, is this the sign you sent me? A dead end?" Just then, a truck pulled up to the administrative building. It looked like the truck in which Tikvah had arrived the day before. In fact, thought Zar, it *was* the same truck. Zar's heart skipped a beat as a few soldiers hopped out. Was Tikvah among them? The soldiers had alighted on the other side of the idling truck, which was obstructing his view.

When it pulled away, Zar spotted Tikvah. Zar couldn't help but notice her dimples and kind eyes, and the distinctive shoulder tag with the green-and-white circle and the Star of David. She looked up, and their eyes met. She exchanged a few words with the other soldiers and walked briskly to Zar, a broad grin on her face. "Zar! Hi again!" She greeted him with open arms, intending to give him a hug. Zar recoiled slightly; he could rationalize shaking a woman's hand or even hearing her sing, but hugging Tikvah was way beyond his comfort zone, Yoli's advice notwithstanding. Secretly, of course, he wanted nothing more than to embrace her.

"Oh! Sorry if I made you uncomfortable, Zar...if I overstepped some sort of boundary."

"No, it's fine," Zar answered, although he felt anything *but* comfortable. He felt awkward talking to a woman, and he was uncomfortable and even somewhat embarrassed to be putting his religious observance on public display like this. Gathering all of his fortitude, he continued, "It's nothing personal. Really. But I *am* religious. I guess you can figure that out from my *kippah* and beard and sidelocks. And there are rules that we follow, that I follow. And touching women is against the rules."

"How do you touch your wife, then? Well, not *you*, but how does a religious man touch his wife and, you know, make babies? Orthodox women have a lot of babies."

"Obviously, married couples can touch each other and...make babies. That's not against the rules. Actually, it's a commandment for married couples to, um, be intimate with each other. The prohibition is against *unmarried* men and women touching each other."

"But you shook my hand yesterday, and I'm a woman. And we're not married. Was *that* against the rules?"

"It probably was, actually...more than probably. But you kind of caught me with my guard down, and I guess I failed the test."

"Now that I think about it, you did sort of hesitate before we shook hands. Well, I'm sorry if you sinned because of me." And, looking up at the sky, Tikvah called out, "Hey, God! It's me, Tikvah. Please excuse Zar for breaking your rules yesterday. It's my fault." She tapped on her chest in a gesture suggesting that she accepted the blame and any consequences.

"Thanks for putting in a good word," said Zar. "Do you talk to God often? You seem to be on a first-name basis."

"Actually, I do. All the time. Not a first-name basis kind of thing, but I do talk to God a lot. My grandmother taught me that." With that statement, there was a noticeable change in her tone, followed by an awkward silence.

Zar broke the silence: "You know, I really enjoyed meeting you yesterday. I wanted to get your number so we could keep in touch."

"Touch?" asked Tikvah, in mock surprise. "I thought touching was forbidden."

"No, it's just an expression. I meant—"

"I know what you meant," Tikvah interrupted him. "I was just trying to be witty."

Zar laughed out loud. "Oh, that's funny! Now, where was I?"

"You were flirting with me, trying to get my phone number so you could call me and ask me out on a date." Zar was taken aback by her brazenness until he saw her smirk.

"Oh, you're trying to be witty again. Well, I don't think you need to try anymore. You're very good at it already."

"Thank you." She scribbled her phone number on a piece of paper, folded it, and carefully dropped it into Zar's hand, making a show of the exaggerated effort she took to avoid touching him.

"Thanks. But next time, please put the paper at the end of a long pole so we can be sure that there's no unintended contact."

Tikvah smiled. "You can be witty too. I like that."

"It must be a match made in heaven," Zar said, unsure if he was crossing the line now, but he continued: "So, you're in an intelligence unit. I can tell from your shoulder tag. I'll tell you a story someday about a tag I once had, one just like yours. But first, what kind of top-secret work are you doing here two days in a row?"

"Honestly, I have no clue. My superior officer drags me along with him to his meetings. I don't even take notes—another officer does that. Most of the time, I'm not even allowed in the room when they have their meetings."

"Why do they bring you along, then?"

"No good reason, really. I don't know, to fetch a cup of coffee. To make phone calls. Mostly just to stand there and smile. I honestly think that's it. My superior thinks it makes him look more important if he has a woman accompanying him, smiling and looking pretty."

"Well, you're doing a great job."

"Doing what?"

"Smiling and looking pretty."

Tikvah blushed. "Thank you. You know, I wasn't even supposed to come today. They were going to leave without me. But I wanted to come back to your base."

"To see me?"

"Yes, Zar. To see you." Now it was Zar's turn to blush. "I enjoyed speaking with you yesterday and I regretted that we didn't exchange numbers. I wanted to keep in touch too. That's just an expression, you know." Zar smiled, and Tikvah continued, "Also, I wanted to share something with you." Again, the tone in her voice changed. She was more serious, maybe even a little sad. "Remember how I said that my grandmother taught me to talk to God? Well, I was very close with my grandmother, my Bubby. That's what I called her, 'Bubby.' She survived Auschwitz, miraculously, as a little girl. After the war, she was an orphan. She was sent to America to live with an aunt. I was her only granddaughter, and we were very, very close. She taught me so much. I really feel that anything I accomplish in life, any good that I do, is all thanks to her. She didn't just teach me to talk to God. She taught me to say the *Shema* prayer. For as long as I can remember, every night before bed, I would cover my eyes with my right hand and say those six words: *Shema Yisrael, Adoshem elokeinu, Adoshem echad.* It's a verse in the Bible somewhere. But you already know that, I guess. When I was little, I didn't even understand what I was saying, but I said it anyway. When I was a little older, Bubby taught me what it means. 'Listen, Israel: God is our Lord. God is one.' And she told me that as they walked into the gas chambers, some Jews would say those six words so they'd be the last words out of their mouths before they died, words of complete devotion to God. Bubby said that's what Jewish martyrs have done for a long, long time."

"That's also why we say the *Shema* prayer at night, before we go to sleep," Zar observed.

"What do you mean?"

"When you go to sleep for the night, God takes your soul temporarily, then returns it to you in the morning. So when we go to sleep at night, it's almost like dying...sort of."

"That's really interesting. That makes a lot of sense."

"You were telling me why you decided to come back to the base today."

"Right, okay. When I decided to make *aliyah*, to move to Israel and join the army, I was so afraid to tell Bubby. I thought she would be so mad at me for leaving her. But do you know what she did when I told her? She cried. Tears of joy. She was proud of me. And she made a blessing: 'Bless you, God, for you have kept me alive and brought me to this moment in time.' She didn't have to explain herself; I understood. She was saying that she had survived Auschwitz and built a life for herself in America all for one reason: so that one day, many years later, she would have a granddaughter who would move to Israel...to go back home. When my Bubby made that blessing, she was saying that she could move on. With my *aliyah*, her life's mission was finally complete. She was crying like a baby when she said goodbye to me at the airport in Los Angeles. We were both crying like babies. That was the last time I saw Bubby. We spoke on the phone a few times after that, but she died only a few weeks later. She really meant it when she said that God had kept her alive just to see the day that I would move home, to Israel. And yesterday was the first anniversary of her death. There's a name for that in Yiddish."

"Her *yahrzeit*."

"Right. *Yahrzeit*. For some reason, I have a mental block against that word. Anyway, yesterday was her...*yahrzeit*. And I was so sad thinking about her. I miss Bubby so much. She was so proud of me for enlisting in the army, but she made me swear that I wouldn't go into a combat unit. She wanted me to defend Israel, but she was also worried about my safety—that's how I ended up in this intelligence unit. Actually, there were other issues; I probably wouldn't have been eligible for a combat unit anyway. But I don't do *anything* in this damn unit. I'm not protecting anyone. I'm not reading intelligence briefings or anything like that. I just get coffee. And smile and look pretty. I was so down yesterday. So I did what Bubby would have wanted me to do: I spoke to God. Really! Right before I got in that truck, I looked up at the sky and said, 'God, please send me a sign. Something to connect me with Bubby and make her proud.' That's what I said. And then I noticed you."

"I guess it's hard *not* to notice me with my *kippah* and beard and sidelocks. I stick out like a sore thumb."

"No, I noticed you because you're gorgeous! You're all muscle, and you have such a sweet smile."

Zar froze again. He was unaccustomed to speaking with women generally, but completely unprepared for such unabashed flirting. "No one ever called me gorgeous before," he finally managed to mutter, fiddling with his sidelocks. "Besides, there are lots of gorgeous guys in the army. You must have guys hitting on you all the time."

"You're right. There are lots of hot guys in the army, and they *do* hit on me all the time. But none of them ever interested me. They're too shallow. They're only interested in one thing. I'm looking for something deeper, more meaningful in a relationship."

"And you weren't turned off by my *kippah* and all that?"

"No. That's part of what attracted me to you, actually."

"Huh? What do you mean?"

"Like I was saying before, yesterday was my Bubby's..."

"*Yahrzeit.*"

"You see what I mean about having a mental block? It was her *yahrzeit*, and I was really sad thinking about her, getting all depressed and everything. Okay, I know this is going to sound super-weird, but I'd asked God to show me some sort of sign, and then I noticed you and I thought to myself, 'Is he the sign that God sent me?' And then you told me your name—Zar—and I was blown away. My Bubby's real name was Odella, but no one called her that. Everyone called her Ella. So when you said your name was Zar, I couldn't believe it. Put together your name, Zar, and Bubby's name, Ella, and what do you get?"

"Zarella?"

Tikvah laughed. "*Zarella?* That's funny. No! Ella plus Zar makes Elazar, your full name. Don't you see it?"

"I guess so...but what's the significance?"

"I don't know. Maybe it's just a coincidence, but—" Just then, the driver honked impatiently. "Zar, I have to go now. You'll call me, right?"

"Tikvah, of course I'll call you..." Before he had a chance to finish his sentence, the truck pulled away.

CHAPTER 31

Zar watched the truck until it was completely out of sight, then remained there, staring into the distance, wondering if everything that had transpired that morning had just been a dream, a fairytale. But it hadn't; he really *had* just met the most wonderful young woman in the world. But when it came to Jewish ritual, he reminded himself, she was only marginally observant—at best. Zar was torn, confused, and restless.

Zar related his thoughts to Egel after dinner that night: "Egel, I have a problem. Can I talk it over with you?"

"Sure. But I have only two areas of expertise—soccer and women—so I hope your problem is related to one of those."

"I guess today's my lucky day. It's about women. Well, one woman in particular: Tikvah, the one we spoke about the other day in the dining hall."

"So you tracked her down at the military intelligence complex in Be'er Sheva? Now *that's* what I call persistent!"

"Actually, she came back to the base today. I couldn't believe it! And it was specifically to see *me*."

"Wow! Women are flocking to you, Zar. I'm starting to rub off on you."

Zar laughed, nervously brushing his sidelocks behind his ears. "But that's where my problem begins."

"I think I'm missing something," said Egel.

"Well, she seems to be a really nice, good person, definitely the kind of woman I'd want to meet. And she was attracted to me specifically because I'm religious. And physically, I'm totally attracted to her. She's beautiful! The problem is that *she* isn't religious, at least not Orthodox. And I couldn't seriously date a girl who doesn't observe Jewish religious law."

"Okay, so she doesn't observe Jewish religious law. But if she was attracted to you *because* you're Orthodox, she probably respects religion, more or less. Maybe with time she would, I don't know, become more religious? Zar, my expertise is women, not philosophy; I don't know how much more I can help you."

"I just need to talk it over, to think this through clearly before I get involved in something I shouldn't be involved in."

"Okay, I'll try my best. Let's start from the basics. Does she believe in God?"

"Yes. She does believe in God. She even speaks to God."

"So we're off to a good start. And she's nice. You said so yourself. Is she Jewish?"

"Of course she's Jewish. I mean, she made *aliyah*. She enlisted in the army."

"That doesn't prove anything. There are Christians and Druze and Bedouin Muslims and all sorts of people in the army."

"But she made *aliyah*. Don't you have to be Jewish to make *aliyah*?"

"Yes and no. I think you only need one Jewish grandparent to make *aliyah*. Take Vlad in our unit, for example. His father is Jewish, but his mother isn't. And I dated a girl in high school...her father was a Jewish Israeli, but her mom was a gentile from Brazil who never converted, apparently—at least not how the rabbis here in Israel wanted. It caused a whole controversy on the kibbutz because her mother wasn't recognized by the government as Jewish."

"According to Jewish religious law, your Brazilian girlfriend wasn't Jewish either, if her mother wasn't Jewish."

"I see. Well, do you know anything about Tikvah's parents?"

"Egel, I hardly know her. But she did mention that her grandmother was Jewish."

"Well, there you have it. She has Jewish grandparents, so she's Jewish."

"Maybe not. I've heard there's a lot of intermarriage in America. Maybe only *one* of Tikvah's parents is Jewish. And if her father is Jewish but her mother isn't, then according to Jewish religious law, Tikvah isn't Jewish either."

"What's the big deal? She's Jewish enough in my book."

"But she's *my* girlfriend—I think she is, anyway—not yours. Your book is irrelevant here!"

"Alright. Fine. Let's assume that her parents *are* intermarried. It's still a fifty-fifty shot that her mother is the Jew in that relationship."

"But let's say she's not. Let's say her father is Jewish and her mother is a gentile. Then what?"

"So she'll convert. It's as simple as that."

"But there's something I didn't mention yet: I'm a *kohen*. And a *kohen* can't marry a convert."

"Oh," Egel conceded. "I see the problem. So do what I do. Don't marry her. Live with her in sin! It's much simpler that way."

"Thanks for being so understanding. With friends like you, who needs enemies?"

"Sorry, Zar. Looks like you'll just have to ask her."

"That will be a pretty awkward conversation."

"Ask her which grandmother she was talking about—was it her mother's mother or her father's?"

"I don't know. I'm afraid to ask like that; it's too direct. I want to find out indirectly."

"Then ask her what her last name is. If it's McKenzie or something, then her father's a gentile and her mother is Jewish, so you're good to go."

"And if her last name is Goldstein?"

"Well, then...give *me* her phone number!"

CHAPTER 32

Zar pulled the folded paper out of his pocket. He examined it close-ly. The letters and numbers were shapely and feminine. He saved Tikvah's number in his phone contacts, then called her.

"Hello?" said the voice on the other end of the phone.

"Tikvah? Hi! It's me, Zar."

"Hi, Zar! What took so long? I've been waiting all day for you to call me."

"I know. And I've been waiting all day for some free time and privacy so I could call you. Tikvah, I really enjoyed talking with you yesterday. I'd love to learn more about you—"

"And I want to hear your story too," Tikvah said, cutting him off. "You haven't told me anything about your childhood."

But Zar wanted to steer the conversation back to her life story. "Sure. Of course. I'd love to share my story with you. But first, can I ask you your name, Tikvah? Your last name?"

"Sure. Pristino. Hope Pristino. Well, now I'm Tikvah Pristino. I mean, I've always been Tikvah Pristino, but no one called me that before I moved here."

"Pristino? That's an interesting name. Where's it from?"

"It's Italian." Tikvah paused before she continued. "Zar, my parents are intermarried. I should have told you already. I certainly would've told you before our relationship got more serious. But there's no time like the present."

"Thank God!" Zar exhaled.

"Thank God? What does that mean?" Tikvah asked, puzzled by Zar's strange response. When Zar explained the concerns he'd had—and the relief he now felt—regarding Tikvah's Jewishness, Tikvah seemed to be offended, but Zar was still surprised when she abruptly ended the phone call.

Afterwards, Zar reflected on the awkward conversation and the sour note it ended on, and he wondered if he'd just cut short this budding relationship. He felt conflicted. On the one hand, he was attracted to her, and she was clearly attracted to him—she'd said so herself. And he'd enjoyed talking with her. But on the other hand, she wasn't religious, at least not Orthodox. Zar felt guilty for entering into a relationship (of sorts) with a secular girl, and part of him was relieved that he'd inadvertently rebuffed her. He was unsure whether to call her back and apologize or to move on and be thankful that the relationship ended before he got too involved.

Zar's dilemma was resolved moments later when Tikvah called him back. He didn't answer her call the first time or the second. But when she called him a third time in as many minutes, he succumbed to pressure and accepted the call. They both apologized, then Tikvah told her story. Her mother had fallen in love with her father, an Italian-American Roman Catholic. Tikvah described him as a wonderful man, and said she couldn't have asked for a better father. But her Bubby hadn't thought so; she was furious. So her parents eloped. Bubby more or less disowned Tikvah's mother, and she'd say hurtful things like, "I survived Auschwitz so you could marry a *goy*?" and, "What Hitler couldn't do, you're doing!" The family ended up moving to Los Angeles, leaving Bubby behind. When Tikvah's grandfather died, her mother and grandmother reconciled their differences. Later on, Bubby moved in with Tikvah's family.

The hour was getting late, and Zar sensed that Tikvah would go on talking indefinitely if he didn't attempt to end the conversation. "Tikvah, I want to hear more—really, I don't want to hang up the phone—but our curfew is any minute now, and I still have to say my evening prayers and get ready for bed before lights out. When will I see you again? Can you come back to the base?"

"Not tomorrow, no. My officer is taking me to Tel Aviv for some stupid meeting. You know, I just smile and try to look pretty. But maybe the day after. I'll find out and be in touch."

"Just an expression," they both said together, laughing.

"Zar, before you hang up, can you do me a small favor?"

"Sure."

"Can you say the *Shema* prayer with me?"

"Tikvah, I'm so moved that you asked me. Of course! Let's say it together."

CHAPTER 33

Zar and Tikvah spoke often by phone over the next few days, but only briefly and superficially. Finally, early the next week, Tikvah came back to the base. They walked together as they talked. Tikvah stopped briefly to gaze at her reflection in the window of a parked truck.

"You mentioned that you were in college before you moved here," said Zar. "Did you graduate? What did you study?"

"No, I didn't graduate. I was a psychology major. I was only there for one year, so I only took a few introductory courses. Besides, I was there on an athletic scholarship, so I spent a lot of time on the field and out of the classroom."

"Athletic scholarship? What kind?"

"Soccer," Tikvah answered. Zar was speechless.

"Did I say something wrong?" Tikvah asked. "I was an honor student in high school. I could've gotten an academic scholarship, but the athletic scholarship basically paid for my full tuition."

"No, of course. I'm sure you're really smart. I'm just shocked that you play soccer."

"Oh, you don't think a woman can play soccer? Well, I'm pretty good."

"No, it's not that. I mean, you got a scholarship, so you must be very good. It's just that I really like soccer too. I *love* it. It's been, like, an obsession of mine since I was a little kid." Zar filled Tikvah in on some of his life story: his rebellious childhood, playing soccer with the *traif* boys, secretly joining the youth soccer league, winning the championship, and being awarded MVP. He also told her about his soccer-loving unit commander, and how a number of guys in the unit, including Zar and his good friend Egel, played a lot of soccer on the base. His soccer skills, he said, had improved a lot, and the unit commander thought that he and Egel had a decent shot at going professional someday.

"Well, can I see you play?" Tikvah asked.

"I guess so. I mean, I can see if any of the guys want to play a quick pick-up game or something."

"Maybe *I* can be your opponent," suggested Tikvah. "One-on-one. You won't have to touch me—just the ball. I'm pretty good too, you know. I may give you a run for your money."

"I kind of doubt that, but hey, why not? Let's go! Come with me. I have to get a ball from our tent and change into shorts."

"Hey, that's an unfair advantage. You can't wear shorts if I'm in uniform!"

"Okay, that's true. I won't change. We'll both be in uniform, with our boots on. I won't play my best game, but neither will you."

A few minutes later, Zar and Tikvah were on the field. "Why don't you start on offense? Ladies first." Tikvah started dribbling from the top of the field. As Zar approached, she moved back a few paces. Zar lunged forward and deflected the ball between her legs, then skillfully went behind her and, with great force, kicked the ball nearly twenty meters, straight into the goal.

"Impressive!"

"You start again," said Zar. "Give it another try." Tikvah started out slowly this time, then increased the pace. Zar studied each of her moves. He could hear her breathing heavily as she approached the goal. Zar again went on the offensive, stealing the ball and directing it between her legs and into his goal.

"Wow. I think I've met my match!" Tikvah exclaimed. "Now you start."

Zar began at the top of the field, slowly, teasing Tikvah by dribbling back and forth. She was trying to keep up with him, moving back and forth, up and down the field. He was tiring her out, but she was enjoying it. Finally, Zar charged forward, right toward Tikvah. Instinctively, Tikvah moved back to accommodate him. Skillfully and with all of his might, he kicked the ball into his goal, leaving Tikvah flat on her back, panting. "You won!" Tikvah shouted, as she lay there, smiling broadly.

Zar lay down on the grass beside her. "And I couldn't have asked for a better trophy."

"Then I suppose we're both winners!" Tikvah declared.

CHAPTER 34

Later that day, after Tikvah had left the base, Zar saw another religious soldier in the dining hall. They were in different units, and Zar knew his face, but not his name. The other soldier was fair-skinned, with sideburns, a mustache, and a scraggly goatee, none of which connected, as if he were trying—and failing—to grow a full beard. Their eyes met. Zar half-smiled. The other soldier did not return the half-smile; his eyes narrowed, he grimaced disapprovingly and looked away, then left the dining hall. Zar was puzzled by the scraggly-bearded soldier's unfriendliness. But he pushed the awkward encounter to the back of his consciousness, grabbed some food, and ate dinner with some of the other soldiers from his unit.

Later that night, Zar was walking aimlessly on the base, recollecting the day's events. He thought about the impromptu soccer match with Tikvah. He smiled, remembering her intensity and her playfulness. Then he recalled the scraggly-bearded soldier. Was he just an unfriendly guy, or was there a meaning behind his cold demeanor? Had he seen the one-on-one soccer match? Was the soldier's behavior meant as a silent but scathing show of disapproval? Zar again pushed these uncomfortable thoughts aside, but they lingered in his subconscious.

After he said his evening prayers and retired to bed, Zar lay awake, twirling his sidelocks, thinking again about the scraggly-bearded soldier. He vaguely remembered having seen him earlier in the day as well, shortly before the impromptu soccer match with Tikvah. He had certainly witnessed Zar and Tikvah interacting, although Zar wasn't sure if the soldier had seen them play soccer. The more Zar thought about it, though, the more certain he became that the scraggly-bearded soldier's unfriendliness *was* a condemnation of sorts. He was telling Zar, ever so subtly, that he had gone too far. What had started off as an innocuous friendship with a girl—admittedly, a girl whose commitment to Jewish ritual was relatively lacking—had evolved into something much more precarious. Indeed, Zar could see now that his budding relationship with Tikvah was jeopardizing his own devotion to Jewish religious law and ritual. Was it realistic, he asked himself, to think that this relationship could flourish? Religion would certainly be a source of conflict for them. She'd never be able to live up to his standards, and he'd never be able to satisfy her needs. And then there was Tikvah's persistence and intensity: the way she called him multiple times a day, the way she hung up the phone so abruptly, and her cryptic reference to "issues" that made her ineligible for a combat unit. For all these reasons, Zar concluded, he had to end this relationship before he got trapped in a predicament he could not easily escape.

Zar decided that he would call Tikvah the following morning to break up with her. He wasn't brave enough to reveal his true concerns. Instead, he would explain that between his army duties and his soccer practice, he didn't have the time for a serious relationship. In the morning, though, he couldn't muster up even that much courage, so he simply didn't call her at all. Tikvah called him shortly after breakfast, but Zar rejected the call. Tikvah tried again a few minutes later, and again shortly thereafter. Then she started sending text messages:

"Good morning Zar!"

"Hi, are you there?"

"What's up...HELLO???"

"WHERE ARE YOU??????"

After avoiding her all morning, Zar finally answered the phone. He reassured her that he was okay and fibbed that he'd been busy all morning. He still had every intention of breaking up with her (gently, of course), but he didn't have the opportunity—or the backbone—to interrupt Tikvah. And he was genuinely enjoying their conversation. Her voice was at times frenzied and at times soothing. She was witty and intelligent and charming. Zar thought of her dimples and pretty smile and kind eyes, and he soon forgot his intention. By the end of the conversation, they had decided to go on a "real" date, to spend an afternoon and evening together off the base. After he hung up, Zar twirled his sidelocks—or what was left of them—and wondered where this relationship was headed, and if, at this point, there was any turning back.

CHAPTER 35

Later that week, Zar requested permission to leave the base for an outing with Tikvah. The unit commander wasn't thrilled about it, but as a lone soldier, Zar was entitled to certain perks, and an occasional free day off the base was one of them. Technically, these "personal errands" days were for taking care of mundane chores like going to the bank or shopping for groceries, but Zar calculated that it was well worth using up one of his scarce days off to spend an afternoon and evening with Tikvah.

Tikvah had suggested that they go to a restaurant on the beach in Ashkelon, so Zar asked Yoli to drive him to Be'er Sheva, where he and Tikvah planned to meet at the central bus station. When they reached the station, Tikvah was waiting for them, wearing a simple light-blue blouse and a straight black skirt that reached just below her knees. She didn't want to make Zar uncomfortable with her choice of clothing for the evening, but she was unfamiliar with the norms of women's dress in Orthodox Jewish circles. She asked one of the Orthodox soldiers at the complex, who explained some very basic guidelines: nothing too short or revealing. Zar thought she looked lovely. After some brief introductions, Yoli got back into the truck. "Just let me know when you're on your way back to Be'er Sheva and I'll pick you up right here where I dropped you off." Yoli drove away, and Zar and Tikvah boarded a 364 Egged bus to Ashkelon.

Ashkelon is a modern city built in the vicinity of ancient Ashkelon, one of the five cities of the ancient Philistines, along with Ashdod, Gat, Gaza, and Ekron. The 364 bus runs along Highway 34, skirting the Palestinian-ruled Gaza Strip by just a few miles. Tikvah found a window seat in the middle of the bus.

Zar briefly hesitated before sitting down. "You know, in my old neighborhood, men never sat next to women on buses...not even a husband and wife."

"Then I guess I'm glad we're not going out to eat in your old neighborhood. Have a seat!" Tikvah instructed him, gesturing toward the empty seat next to hers. Zar complied. On the bus, Zar and Tikvah mostly made small talk and looked out the window. Billowing smoke was visible from somewhere deep in the Gaza Strip.

They arrived at Ashkelon about an hour later. "Do you want meat or dairy?" asked Zar.

"Doesn't matter. I'm vegetarian, so I'll just order a salad anyway." They walked along the boardwalk until they found a dairy restaurant with a kosher certification that Zar accepted.

"Is there really a difference between the different kosher certifications?" Tikvah asked, as they were seated at a table for two with an ocean view.

"Sure. For meat, it's a bigger deal because there are different standards for kosher slaughter. But even for dairy or vegetarian, there's the issue of bugs."

"Bugs?"

"Yeah. Bugs aren't kosher, and certain vegetables—lettuce and broccoli, for example—can have a lot of bugs. So they have to be soaked and then checked.

"That's a little disappointing."

"Huh?"

"Well, all these years I've been a vegetarian—since I was in middle school. I was kind of grossed out by the whole idea of animal slaughter. But I also thought that I was sort of keeping kosher. And now I find out I'm supposed to find all those bugs and slaughter them, with tiny little knives on their tiny little necks."

Zar laughed. "That wouldn't help. A bug isn't kosher, dead or alive. But that's still pretty cool that you tried to keep kosher. I think you still get some credit for that." Zar cupped his hands around his mouth and directed his eyes heavenwards, as if talking to God: "*Isn't that right?*"

"You're so sweet, Zar. Thanks for the vote of confidence."

"Anytime. So, tell me: How did a girl growing up in a secular home in California even know about keeping kosher?"

"Well, like I was saying last week, my grandmother lived with us my whole life. Bubby was basically Orthodox. My grandfather—I never met him—would never work on *Shabbat*. Bubby said he got fired from a lot of jobs for that. Nowadays there are laws protecting people from getting fired over religion; I bet it still happens, but it was probably much more common back then. And Bubby kept *Shabbat*. Maybe not a hundred percent, but she lit candles on Friday nights and we usually had a Friday night dinner. My mom and dad would watch television and Bubby and I would sit and talk for hours, watching the candles burn.

Thanks to Bubby, our family became affiliated with a synagogue...not your kind of synagogue. It was Reform, very Reform. Bubby wasn't very comfortable there, either; she thought it looked more like a church than a synagogue. And thanks to Bubby, we kept a kosher home—not to your standards, I'm sure, but still nominally kosher. After Bubby died, I think my mom gave up the whole kosher thing. She always thought it was too much of a hassle, but she did it out of respect for Bubby."

"Wow. It's one thing to keep kosher at home out of respect for your grandmother, but you said you even tried to keep kosher outside your home. It must've been tough to be surrounded by other kids at school or at birthday parties or hanging out at other kids' houses and still try to keep kosher."

"I can't say that I was a hundred percent successful—not even close. But, growing up, I never really felt like I belonged. I always felt different."

"Because you're Jewish? Weren't there other Jewish kids in your school?"

"Sure. There were lots of other Jewish kids. But they were all basically embarrassed to be Jewish. If they even acknowledged their Jewishness, it was just some random fact, like their birthday or favorite flavor of ice cream. Their Jewishness didn't identify them. Or maybe I should say they didn't *want* their Jewishness to identify them. I remember when I was in seventh grade, one of the other Jewish girls in my class left school about a week before Christmas break. She didn't tell anyone, but it was pretty obvious when she came back that she'd had plastic surgery—you know, a nose job. Honestly, I didn't think her nose was so big in the first place, but obviously *she* did! The next year, a few other girls got nose jobs too. And in high school, a bunch of girls dyed their hair blonde. Bubby said they looked like Nazis. I couldn't even think about dyeing my hair—Bubby would have killed me. But anyway, I wouldn't have wanted to dye my hair."

"I'm glad you didn't. I think you're beautiful just the way you are."

"Thank you, Zar. But as a kid, I didn't feel that way. I didn't feel beautiful. I always felt different, like most of my peers were one type and I was different. I think I was always searching for something more meaningful."

"More meaningful than what?"

"More meaningful than the suburban life we were living. Even in grade school, I thought the things that interested everyone else— movie stars, music, et cetera—were so superficial. Except sports. I always loved sports: the teamwork, the discipline, the physical fitness. It felt more meaningful—not in a religious kind of way, but still not a waste of time. In high school, the other kids would always go to the beach to hang out. I would go too sometimes, but I always found it unfulfilling. Toward the end of my senior year in high school, there was a pre-graduation party at the beach. It was supposed to be the highlight of the year. We were planning it for weeks. After the party, I came home and cried all night. I just felt so empty. My mom asked me why I was crying. I couldn't even explain it to her. She thought I was depressed or something, but it was more than just depression; I just felt so empty. But Bubby understood. She knew I was searching—you know, for something more meaningful."

Just then, the waitress came to get their orders. "We're not ready yet," Zar told her. They hadn't even opened up their menus yet.

"I've told you a lot about me. Now it's your turn," Tikvah said.

"Okay. I grew up in a very Orthodox neighborhood in Jerusalem—you can't really *get* more Orthodox. It's called Mea She'arim."

"Oh! I was there once. For winter break in college, I went on a free trip to Israel. I can tell you more about it someday; it really changed my life. In fact, that's how I ended up making *aliyah*. Anyway, our guide took us to that neighborhood. We all had to cover our legs and shoulders and stuff. It was kind of funny. Most of the girls on the tour were wearing tank tops and short shorts. We got some angry stares from some of the residents there. At the time, I thought the whole thing was hilarious."

"Yup, that's my neighborhood. You're lucky you got away with just angry stares. I once saw a woman get spat at for dressing immodestly. And kids would throw stones at cars that drove through the neighborhood on *Shabbos*."

"Wow! That's pretty crazy. It reminds me of something my dad likes to say."

"What's that?"

"Ignorance is lethal."

"What do you mean?"

"If someone is ignorant, if he doesn't have access to information for whatever reason—in this case, lack of a decent education—then he can make decisions that endanger himself or other people. And the same principle could apply, on a much bigger scale, to an entire community."

"Hmm. I see what you're saying, and there's a lot of truth to that. But I don't want to condemn the whole community because of a few crazy people. For the most part, the people there are very nice and neighborly. I've seen a bunch of Hasidim clear a path on a main street on *Shabbos* so a car could get out safely. And there was a group of people who would run over to cars on *Shabbos* and give out pastries and stuff and say 'Gut

Shabbos!' They thought it was better to bring people closer to religion with love rather than drive them further away by throwing stones. And because there are a lot of tourists in my neighborhood, people mostly kind of tone it down. In other parts of the country where there aren't a lot of tourists, like Beit Shemesh, it's much worse. That's what people tell me, at least. But I had one run-in with religious fanatics that had a big impact on my life—and, in a roundabout way, you fit into this part of my story."

"Whoa! Well, now you've really piqued my interest. Go on."

Just then, the waitress came back. "Can I take your orders?"

"We're still not ready," Zar said.

"Well, make up your minds already! Did you even open your menus? There are people waiting for tables, and you two are just sitting here taking up space!"

"Tikvah, how hungry are you?" asked Zar.

"I'm not really hungry at all. I just want to talk."

"Okay, you can have your table. We're leaving!" Zar declared. And the two of them got up and left the restaurant.

CHAPTER 36

Z ar and Tikvah walked to the boardwalk and sat on an empty bench facing the water. The beach was serene and beautiful. To the north, they could see the hotels and high-rise luxury buildings of Ashkelon. To the south, just barely visible in the distance, were a watchtower and a border fence, and beyond that, the drab apartment buildings of Gaza City. To the west, the turbulent waters of the Mediterranean stretched out to the horizon, as far as the eye could see. Somewhere deep in those waters, thought Zar, Navy submarines were constantly patrolling to keep Israel safe.

"If a missile was launched at us from Gaza, how much time would we have to run for cover?" Tikvah asked.

"I don't know, maybe thirty seconds?"

"That's not much time. Are there bomb shelters here, by the beach?"

"I don't know. Maybe?"

"Well, that's not very helpful. Maybe we could run into the water. I imagine shrapnel can't travel very far through water."

"Yeah, but that would be mixed swimming. In my world, men and women don't swim together."

"You're kidding, right?"

"Of course! I mean, it's true that men and women don't swim together, but running away from a missile would definitely be an exception."

"I sure hope so."

"Hey, I have a better idea," said Zar. "I could put my soccer skills to good use and kick the missile right back where it came from. *That* would teach them a lesson!"

"You were going to tell me about something that happened when you were a kid and about how Hope Pristino from L.A. somehow ties into the story." She sat there wide-eyed with anticipation.

Zar told her the story of how he saved a religious soldier from a lynch mob and how the soldier gave him his shoulder tag as a token of his appreciation. "Here comes the funny part. I had no clue what that tag meant; I thought it was a soccer ball. I thought maybe that soldier was in some sort of soccer battalion in the army!" Zar and Tikvah laughed. "That shoulder tag was my prized possession. I really loved it. I kept it hidden in my bedroom. I'm sure my parents would've thrown it away if they'd found it. And I'd look at it from time to time and dream about playing soccer in the army, in the 'Soccer Battalion.' Years later, when I enlisted in the army and broke the news to my father, he went ballistic. I mean, he *really* lost it. I didn't feel safe there; I ran out of the apartment and ran away. I actually went back and snuck into the apartment the next morning to get some stuff, but I haven't gone back home since. I didn't think about it when I ran away, but I left pretty much all of my possessions in my room—including the shoulder tag. I basically forgot all about it until the day you came to my base for the first time. So you may think that God sent me as a sign to you…"

"He did!"

"I agree, I really do! But when I saw that tag on your shoulder, I had a flashback to that day, that Friday in Mea She'arim with the soldier. My point is, God also sent *you* as a sign to *me*."

Tikvah said nothing as she reflected upon Zar's words.

"You know," Zar continued, "When I think about it, your whole life you've been 'moving up,' searching for more meaning, and I've been sort of 'moving down,' away from all the meaningful stuff."

"Just because you don't dress like other people in your community, I don't think that makes your life any less meaningful. You're contributing to society through your army service, and maybe you can do a lot of good when you play soccer professionally."

"How?"

"Building bridges between the religious community and the secular community?"

The light from the late afternoon sun refracted through the mist coming off the ocean waves. Zar spotted a rainbow, visible just above the horizon, and pointed it out to Tikvah.

"Oh! I love rainbows. They remind me of my grandmother. This might sound a little weird, but I'll tell you anyway. There's an old movie—you may not know it, but everyone in America does, and people all over the world do—*The Wizard of Oz*. It was Bubby's favorite movie, and it's my favorite movie too. We would watch it together sometimes. It scared me a lot when I was a kid, but I grew to really love it. It's about a girl named Dorothy. I guess her name isn't that important, but anyway, Dorothy somehow ends up very far from her home in Kansas, and in the end, after this long adventure, she finally gets to go back home. And in the movie she sings a song called 'Somewhere Over the Rainbow.' I know it by heart. It's really lovely."

Tikvah sang the first verse in the sweetest voice Zar had ever heard. He fleetingly considered informing Tikvah that it was forbidden for him to hear her sing, but she had again caught him off-guard, and now he couldn't possibly have stopped her. "That song in the movie is about Dorothy's desire to go home, to Kansas. But my Bubby told me that the song was written by a Jewish composer, and it's about the desire of every Jew throughout our long exile to return home, to return to Israel. I don't know if that's what the song is *really* about, but that's how my Bubby understood it. Actually, I looked it up later online, and it turns out that's something of an urban legend—that the song is really about Zionism, I mean. I even tried confronting Bubby, but she insisted that the song *is* about Zionism and that she knew it from the moment she saw the movie, many years ago. She was very stubborn, you know."

"That explains why she was so proud when you told her that you were moving here."

"I know. It makes me proud too, but also sad because it makes me think of my Bubby."

The rainbow dissipated. They continued to gaze into each other's eyes for a while, then took off their shoes and walked along the beach as the sun began to set. They walked along the beach for what seemed like an eternity, until Zar's cellphone started ringing. It was Yoli. "Did you guys fall into the water and drown? I want to go to sleep eventually tonight. What's taking so long?"

"Sorry, Yoli. We just lost track of time. The next bus leaves in about twenty minutes and takes about an hour to get to Be'er Sheva. And I want to go with Tikvah back to her base—you know, 'the fortress.' I'll meet you in front of the fortress in about an hour and a half."

Zar and Tikvah both fell asleep on the bus ride back to Be'er Sheva. Zar dreamed that he was in paradise. He couldn't describe its appearance, but he could sense that it was warm, soft, and fragrant. As the bus pulled to a stop and roused the two young soldiers, Zar realized that Tikvah had fallen asleep with her head resting on his shoulder, and he had been resting his head on hers.

Zar and Tikvah walked silently back to the intelligence complex. Zar was the first to break the silence. "Tikvah," he said, "I had a dream on the bus. I dreamed that I was in paradise. It was warm and soft, and it smelled, I don't know, sweet—the way I imagine paradise should smell."

"You weren't dreaming, Zar. You *were* in paradise tonight. We both were. Goodnight, Zar."

"Goodnight, Tikvah."

On the ride back to the base, Zar asked, "Yoli, do you ever speak to God?"

"I'm not sure I believe in God. I sort of lost my faith years ago."

"Well, I believe in God. I speak to him a lot, you know. And tonight... tonight I felt God speaking to me!"

CHAPTER 37

Yom Ha'atzma'ut, Israel's Independence Day, was less than a week away. All of the lone soldiers had been invited to a barbecue in a large park in Jerusalem. Zar and Tikvah arranged to meet on a street corner just west of the park and walk to the barbecue together. Zar was dressed casually, in slacks and a T-shirt, but Tikvah was wearing her olive-green uniform. "What's with the uniform?" asked Zar. "I thought the invitation said to dress casually."

"It's a long story," said Tikvah. "I almost didn't make it. For the past year, I've done almost nothing in the army, and just this week they decide to give me some real work. I practically had to beg to get off today. And my superior made me go to Tel Aviv with him."

"I thought *Yom Ha'atzma'ut* was a national holiday. The banks are closed, and most businesses are too."

"That's what I thought, but my superior read me the riot act. 'The army never goes on vacation, blah, blah, blah…' I guess he's right. I mean, we can never let down our guard. But I'm a pretty small cog in this big machine."

"I think you're a small, pretty cog," Zar said, winking at her.

Tikvah laughed. "Thank you. Anyway, long story short, I had to wear my uniform, I forgot to bring a change of clothes, and there wasn't enough time to go to Be'er Sheva and back—I wanted to be on time to meet you."

"Well, I'm glad you got here on time. And I think you look gorgeous in your uniform. Heck, you could wear anything and still look gorgeous."

"You're too sweet, Zar. And keep 'em coming…the compliments, that is."

The barbecue was in Sacher (pronounced like "soccer") Park, and while there were always people playing soccer there, the park was named not for the game, but for the wealthy Sacher family, who had donated a lot of money years ago to build the park.

Sacher Park is a popular destination on any holiday, but it gets particularly congested on *Yom Ha'atzma'ut*. Thousands of people, mostly large families, flock to the park for picnics and barbecues. This year, the park was even busier than usual, with a few dozen soldiers there for the lone soldiers' party. There was a festive atmosphere in the park; music was blasting, the smell of grilled meat wafted through the air, and impromptu games of soccer, Frisbee, and volleyball were sprouting up in every empty patch of grass. Tikvah spotted a familiar face: Yoli was behind the barbecue, tending the grill. He spotted them too, and shouted in Yiddish, "Rabbi and Rebbitzin! How are you?"

"I'll translate," said Zar. "What he meant was, 'What a handsome couple!'"

Tikvah laughed. "I'm no expert in Yiddish," she retorted, "but I think what he actually said was, 'My, how beautiful Tikvah looks in her uniform—like a true green princess!'" They all laughed. "Zar, I have a question for you," Tikvah said. "I should've asked you weeks ago. Yoli and I both moved here from America, so we're lone soldiers. But you're a native Israeli, Zar. What makes you a lone soldier?"

"Well, if we decide that I don't really qualify as a lone soldier, do I still get a hot dog?"

"I'll smuggle one out to you," Yoli joked. "But shhh! Don't tell anyone. Oh, and they're kosher—very kosher! Even you, Rabbi Zar, would trust the certification."

"Well," explained Zar, "a boy from an ultra-Orthodox family who enlists in the army—or a girl, I suppose—they'll often be disowned by their parents. And even if they aren't *literally* disowned, they still don't get the kind of support that most Israeli kids get from their families. In some ways, kids like that, like me, are more alone than lone soldiers from other countries who still have loving families, just far away."

"And I get the worst of both worlds," observed Yoli. "I was disowned by my family *and* they're thousands of miles away."

"Then you deserve a second hot dog," Zar declared.

"I've already had three!" declared Yoli, patting his protuberant belly.

A group of lone soldiers, including one of Zar's roommates from the Jerusalem apartment, were playing soccer nearby.

"Hey, Zar!" his roommate shouted. "You want to join our game?"

"No, I'll pass, thank you. I'm hanging out with my girlfriend. Maybe another time."

"C'mon, Zar," said Tikvah. "Join them. You have my permission."

"It's fine," said Zar. "Really. Why don't *you* join them? *You're* the one with the athletic scholarship."

"I would, but I think it's kind of a men's club on the field. I'm happy to watch and cheer you on from the sidelines. Besides, I'm wearing my uniform. You remember what happened the last time I tried playing soccer in my uniform."

"Remember? How could I forget? I dream about that day!"

With Tikvah's encouragement, Zar accepted his roommate's offer and joined the game. It was a friendly game; the players were clowning around, not taking it too seriously. To impress Tikvah, but also to put the clowns in their place, Zar decided that he was going to play hard— very hard. He was going to give it his all.

The ball started out on the other team's side. They were dribbling lazily and passing wide, slow passes. Easy to steal. Zar sprinted to the opposite side of the field, stole the ball effortlessly, dribbled past two defenders, and with a powerful kick from his right foot, knocked the ball past the goalkeeper and into the lower left side of the goal. When play resumed, Zar repeated the trick, but this time he struck the ball left-footed and into the upper right corner of the goal. Play after play, Zar took command, exploiting each and every hole in the defense, scoring goals from all over the field, short goals and long goals, using both feet and his head. His teammates all but stopped playing; some of them even switched teams mid-game. Zar was double-teamed, then triple-teamed, but there was no stopping him. He grew more confident with each passing minute. Tikvah cheered boisterously. A small crowd gathered to watch the spectacle. By the end of the game, there were dozens of people watching Zar score again and again and again.

After the game, Zar was bombarded by congratulations from the crowd. Some of them, mostly children, asked him for his autograph. He had never signed his autograph before. He didn't even know what language to sign in. He improvised, making a big letter Z with a small stroke on top so that his signature also resembled the Hebrew letter *zayin*. After the crowds dispersed, Tikvah and Yoli approached him. Tikvah whispered something in Yoli's ear and Yoli ran to Zar, kissing him on each cheek, then embraced him tightly, lifting him into the air like the champion that he was. "Those are from Tikvah," Yoli explained. Then, taking Zar's right hand warmly in both of his hands and shaking it, he said, "And that's from me. And now I've been told to scram. Tikvah wants you all to herself!"

The park had mostly emptied out. All of the families and younger people had left; only Zar and Tikvah and a few other couples remained. "Zar, you were amazing today, really amazing! I've been playing soccer almost my whole life; I started when I was five years old, in a peewee league, and I played through high school and into college. I've played with and against some very talented players. Some of my coaches in high school and college played professionally at one time or another. I've been watching soccer matches in person or on television for as long as I can remember. And I've *never* seen anyone as good as you. Okay, maybe Ronaldo or Messi in their primes. But you're in their league. I was so proud watching you today."

"Thank you, Tikvah. Thank you so much. Hearing those words from you means more to me than I can describe. More than hearing them from our unit commander, or my youth league coaches, or anyone else. Really. Thank you."

"And I have a surprise for you!"

"A surprise?"

"Yes, a surprise—a gift for you. Not something completely new. It's more of a replacement for something you once had and then lost." She removed her shoulder tag, with the green-and-white circle and the Star of David, and gave it to Zar. "Here! Take this. Put it in your sock, either one. It'll be your lucky charm."

Zar was awestruck. He had no words to say in return. He just stared at the tag, and caressed it, and smelled it, and embraced it, and kissed it.

CHAPTER 38

Back on the base, Yoli had been showing everyone some videos that he had on his phone of Zar's incredible soccer performance at Sacher Park on *Yom Ha'atzma'ut*. At dinner, Egel teased Zar that he'd only played so well because he'd been among amateurs. "If I'd been on the other side of the field that day, you wouldn't have scored a single goal."

"You're just jealous of my talent, that's all," said Zar.

"I think he's jealous of your new girlfriend," Oren quipped.

"Yeah!" Egel added. "If she were *my* girlfriend..."

"Hey, cut it out!" Zar shouted. "It's one thing to treat women the way you do, but leave Tikvah out of it!"

Oren, seeing where this was going, quickly got up and left the table, muttering under his breath, "I'll leave you two alone to fight this battle."

"Oh, so you don't approve of my social habits?" asked Egel. "I didn't think I needed your approval."

"It's not *my* approval you need."

"Whose, then?"

"God's."

"And let's just say that I don't believe in God?"

"You don't believe in God? Are you sure of that?"

"Well," Egel continued, "we had a class in comparative religion when I was a senior in high school. I wasn't a very good student, but this class I actually liked."

"Why? Was it interesting?"

"Not really, but the girl who taught it was *very* interesting, if you know what I mean," Egel winked. "The old philosophy teacher had retired," he explained, "and the Ministry of Education sent us this

Russian girl who was doing national service in lieu of army service. Her name was Marina...or Malena. One of those names. Or maybe it was Natasha or Natalie. It's been a while."

"Wait a second," Zar interjected. "You mean to say that you had some sort of relationship with this Russian teacher of yours and you don't even remember her name?"

"Well, I was pretty busy. I had a lot of girlfriends."

"That's exactly my point! Even if you're not afraid of God's punishment for adultery..."

"Adultery is only with married women; I don't go near married women."

"But let's say you met one and she was pretty and willing?"

"I guess it depends on *how* pretty and *how* willing," joked Egel. "I'm just kidding," he reassured him. "Even *I* have standards."

"Well, can't you at least show a little more respect for your girlfriends? And aren't you worried about getting one of them pregnant, or getting a sexually transmitted disease? I mean, what about AIDS?"

"Heterosexual men don't get AIDS."

"Are you sure about that?"

"Pretty sure. That's what I've heard, at least."

"I don't think that's true."

"Whatever. Anyway, what's the punishment for adultery?"

"Death," answered Zar. "The punishment for adultery is death."

PART THREE

CHAPTER 39

Hajji continued visiting the checkpoint sporadically for several years. At first, he would visit the soldiers every day, but with time, his visits became less frequent. As he grew older, he became more committed to practicing and playing soccer. He would often have to travel to play matches in other cities, and he had little time to hang out with the soldiers at the checkpoint.

Every few months, a new group of soldiers would arrive to man the checkpoint. Some were friendly to him, while others were less receptive. But he still enjoyed going up to the minaret of the mosque for the evening call to prayer. It wasn't so much the call to prayer that interested him; he loved the view. He could gaze forever at the green and bronze and auburn hills, and the stones, and the red wildflowers, and the lush Jordan River Valley. He could observe the sapphire blue of the Sea of Galilee to the north, and beyond that the towering heights of the Galilee and the Golan.

He would scrutinize the checkpoint and the villages on the other side of the border. Once in a while, there would be protests at the checkpoint. Palestinian youths with scarves covering their faces—some of them likely his cousins—would use slingshots to hurl stones at the soldiers. Sometimes, actual riots would erupt, and the youths would burn tires and throw Molotov cocktails. Then reinforcements would be called in, and dozens of soldiers with heavy armor would arrive. On those days, the acrid smell of tear gas wafted through the village.

CHAPTER 40

One afternoon, after a long day playing soccer, Hajji went up to the minaret. From his perch, he spied the checkpoint. There was a new group of soldiers in olive-green uniforms, and one of them was a woman. He couldn't make out her features from such a distance, but he could tell that she was a woman, and he imagined that she was beautiful.

For the first time in many months, he felt drawn back. As he walked past the entrance to the village and down the road toward the checkpoint, he had a better view of the female soldier. She was, in fact, strikingly beautiful, with bronze skin and thick, wavy auburn hair. And her eyes were a deep blue, like two sapphires. Slowly, he approached the young soldier.

"Hi! My name is Hajji," he said to her. "I work here," he said awkwardly, not sure what to say next and a bit flustered by her beauty.

"You work here?" she asked. "What do you mean?"

"I...load and unload trucks...at the checkpoint. Palestinian trucks... at the checkpoint."

"Why? Do you get paid for it?" she asked, with a gentle smile.

She spoke with a certain confidence. He felt awkward, but she seemed completely cool and at ease. She was different from the girls in his village, who were more quiet and reserved. She seemed a bit older and more mature. She was strong and in control. He was mesmerized and couldn't even remember what she had just asked him.

"I'm sorry. What did you say? You asked me something."

"I asked you why you load and unload trucks. Do you get paid?"

Meanwhile, two of the other soldiers walked over to see what was going on. "This guy says he loads and unloads trucks at the checkpoint.

Do you know anything about this?" she asked the other soldiers.

"Let me check with our commanding officer," suggested a Druze soldier who seemed to be more senior. A few moments later he asked, "Is your name Hajji, from Al'ard Alhamra?"

"Yes."

"He did mention that, that his name is Hajji," the female soldier added.

"Okay. The lieutenant said he's safe," the Druze soldier said, and he and the other soldier walked back to the guard post.

"So, where were we? Right. So you work here...loading trucks? And the army pays you for it?"

"Well, I don't get paid—except for a can of Coca-Cola, sometimes."

The female soldier laughed out loud. "Wait, so you work here for free? Is everything okay up there?" she asked, tapping softly on his head.

Hajji recoiled. He hadn't expected her to touch him—not yet, anyway.

"Oh, I'm sorry. I didn't mean to startle you," she said.

"No, no. It's fine. I just didn't see it coming. It's fine. So what's *your* name?"

"Adin," she answered, offering her hand to shake. Hajji again recoiled and clumsily extended his hand to shake hers.

"Adin means gentle. Delicate. You don't seem delicate. In my culture, names have a lot of significance. Yours doesn't seem to fit."

"Well, you don't know anything about me. I'm an Israeli. Native Israelis are known as *sabras*, like the cactus fruit. Rough on the outside, but soft and sweet inside."

"Well, I'm an Israeli too, an Israeli Arab. Does that make me a *sabra* too?"

"That's a good question. I've never thought about that. I always kind of associated *sabra* with Jewish Israelis. But I suppose Arabs can also be rough on the outside and soft and sweet on the inside," she said, again smiling playfully.

"Now, back to my original question: Why do you come here if you don't get paid? To flirt with female soldiers? Don't you have anything better to do with your time? I mean, a handsome young man like yourself could certainly find a nice young Muslim woman."

Hajji was speechless. He simply didn't know how to respond. Why *did* he come to the checkpoint that day? He just stared into her sapphire eyes, then looked down.

"So, you say names are important," Adin remarked. "What does Hajji mean?"

He paused for a moment, collecting his thoughts. "It means 'pilgrim.' My full name is Hajji Al-Salem, which means 'pilgrim of peace.'"

Then he heard the late-afternoon call for prayer, signaling that their brief meeting was over.

"Have a good night, Adin," he said, as the muezzin's voice drifted through the hills: "*Allahu akbar.* God is great."

Hajji had difficulty falling asleep that night. His mind was flooded with thoughts. Why had he gone back to the checkpoint after so many months? He was attracted to a woman, to a Jewish woman. A soldier! Was it sinful to feel this way? Was he betraying his people by forging a relationship with a Jew? Certainly Allah had orchestrated the whole thing; it couldn't have happened otherwise. He concluded that it was his destiny to have met Adin.

And he couldn't get her image out of his head. Her curves, her bronze skin and thick, wavy auburn hair, her deep-blue sapphire eyes... and her name. What could it mean? Delicate? How was she delicate? She was a soldier. An Israeli. Tough. Strong. Was she also gentle and fragile? As he drifted off to sleep, he wondered if he would ever find out.

He was awoken by the early morning call for prayer: "*Allahu akbar.* God is great." He went to morning prayers and added in a prayer of his own: "Allah, please protect Adin, the delicate one."

CHAPTER 41

Hajji had an important match to play early that afternoon. He'd heard that scouts would probably be there to watch him play. His coach had scheduled practice for late morning; he didn't have much time. After morning prayers, Hajji hurried to the checkpoint. When he got there, Adin was in front of a truck, talking to the driver. Hajji approached and, as he had done countless times before, lifted up his shirt and his pant legs to show that he wasn't hiding anything. After years of playing soccer, Hajji's torso and legs were lean and muscular. He helped to unload and reload the truck, and the truck passed through the checkpoint, followed by a few cars. After the last car pulled through the checkpoint, there was an awkward silence. Hajji was the first to speak.

"I very much enjoyed meeting you yesterday. I thought about you last night—a lot."

"I thought about you too," Adin responded. "You came early today."

"I have a match to play, so I don't have much time."

"A match?" Adin asked.

"Soccer. I play soccer. It's a youth league."

"What position do you play?"

"Goalkeeper. I don't mean to brag, but I'm pretty good. Everyone says I'll play professionally, maybe next year."

"Wow! I'm impressed. My brothers play a lot of soccer. They're pretty good, I guess, but not professional or anything."

"Well, I just wanted to stop by and say hello and good morning. So...hello and good morning."

Adin laughed. "Well, hello and good morning to you too. And good luck in the game!"

"Thank you," he answered. He waved, then raced back up the road to his village.

Hajji thought about Adin a lot afterwards, about her bronze skin and thick, wavy auburn hair and deep-blue sapphire eyes. He enjoyed her wit and her playful smile, he respected her maturity and her strength, and he wondered about the significance of her name.

CHAPTER 42

O ver the next few weeks, Hajji and Adin learned a lot more about
each other. Hajji's family had lived in his village for generations;
much of his extended family lived across the green line and suffered under the occupation. He told Adin that his mother had died in childbirth
and that he was raised by his widowed father. Hajji's father had never
said so explicitly, but Hajji suspected that his father resented him for
unwittingly causing his mother's death. His teachers had told him that
he would never have any success in life, so he had basically dropped out
of school. His father thought he was a failure. He thought soccer was
a waste of time and never went to any of the matches to see him play.
Hajji was unequivocally the best goalkeeper in the youth league. Fans
he didn't even know would come and cheer, but his own father never
showed up at any of the games. His father particularly resented Hajji's
frequent visits to the checkpoint, and he resented Hajji even more for
disobeying him. He assumed that his father was unaware that he had
a relationship of sorts with a female soldier, but wondered—feared,
actually—how his father would react if he *did* find out.

Adin revealed that she was raised in Dimona, a poor town in the
Negev Desert, best known for the nuclear reactor that stands on the
outskirts of the town. Three of her four grandparents had emigrated
from Morocco to Israel in the 1950s. Her paternal grandmother
was a Polish Jew who had survived Auschwitz as a child and then
came to Israel after the war. Several years later, she volunteered in a
poor development town inhabited by recent immigrants from North
Africa. It was there that her paternal grandparents met and fell in
love.

"So that explains your blue eyes!" Hajji exclaimed, after hearing Adin's family history.

"I suppose; I'm one-quarter Ashkenazi." Adin replied. "My grandmother was a very beautiful person, inside and out."

"Is that a picture of her on your phone?" Hajji asked, pointing to the screensaver on Adin's cellphone.

"No," Adin answered, laughing. "That's Marilyn Monroe. She was also a beautiful woman, but she wasn't my grandmother."

"Who was she?"

"A famous American actress. My grandmother was very fond of her. She loved beautiful things. So do I. That's why I have her picture on my phone—Marilyn Monroe's picture, that is."

"There are a lot of beautiful things in this world. Why her? Why do you have a picture of—what's her name again?"

"Marilyn Monroe."

"Right. Why do you have a picture of her?"

"Because, to me, she represents Israel."

"Huh? Was she Jewish?"

Adin laughed again. "No. I mean yes, she did convert to Judaism. But that's only part of why my grandmother admired her. Marilyn Monroe was beautiful—some people think that she was the most beautiful woman in the world in her day—but she wasn't perfect. She had a blemish on her face, like a mole or pimple. Some people call it a birthmark, and some people call it a beauty mark. Isn't that funny? People call a pimple a beauty mark. What's beautiful about a pimple? Well, I think her birthmark made her more human, more real. She wasn't some kind of fictional or imaginary beauty, like a princess in a fairytale. She was human, and *imperfect*, but she was beautiful. I mean, if you looked at a picture of her, of Marilyn Monroe, and just zoomed in on the birthmark, at very high magnification, what would you see?"

"I don't know, a pimple," Hajji said.

"You would see something ugly, grotesque. You would see bumps, deep crevices…But that's just one perspective, one very skewed perspective. If you zoom out and get the big picture, and see that ugly birthmark from a different perspective, what do you see? Something beautiful, something very, very beautiful." Adin had tears in her eyes as she said this. "And that's how I see my country."

"*Our* country," Hajji interjected. "It's my country too, you know."

"You're right. I'm sorry. Our country," Adin said, wiping her eyes.

"People in the world, even in this country, I mean even *Jews* in this country, and people of all backgrounds all over the world, are so critical of Israel. They point out every flaw. And believe me, there are flaws, plenty of them. But they're zooming in on a birthmark and missing the big picture. I know the flaws in my country—*our* country, I mean. You think I want to be in the army at my age? Anywhere else in the world, a girl my age, eighteen, would be in university, studying science and poetry and art. And here I am at this godforsaken checkpoint."

Adin was openly weeping now. "Do you think I want to stop these cars and search them? It's humiliating for them. It's humiliating for me, for God's sake! But I do it to protect my country. *Our* country. Is there a perfect country anywhere in the world? Look at Europe or really anywhere in the world, anywhere! Nothing is perfect. We all have flaws. And so does Israel. But that doesn't change the fact that Israel is beautiful. I think so, anyway. The love affair of a people and their homeland, preserved in exile for two thousand years…and this people, the Jewish people, survived, against all odds, despite persecution and pogroms and inquisitions and the Holocaust. And then to return to that homeland, despite all the odds. And to fight for themselves—with God's help, I believe—and win wars and build a country with an economy and an army, and to revive this language which was hardly spoken for all these years. I think it's the greatest, most romantic story ever written. It's messy. I know it is. How do you, an Arab, a Muslim, fit in? And the Palestinians? I don't have all of the answers. I don't even have all of the questions."

"But my people are suffering," Hajji objected. "Their villages were destroyed and their homeland was stolen! And they suffer terribly under the occupation. My cousins often don't have electricity or water. They can't move freely through the land. They're constantly waiting at checkpoints, where they're harassed. Soldiers raid the villages and the refugee camps and search houses in the middle of the night. And the houses of the *shuhada* (martyrs) are destroyed. Why does the whole family or the whole village have to suffer because of the acts of one man?"

"I'm not denying that they suffer. But I don't benefit from their suffering. Israel doesn't benefit from their suffering."

"So who *does* benefit?"

"Your leaders benefit."

"What are you talking about?"

"Your leaders exploit the suffering of the people to use it as a political weapon."

"Well, maybe because they're outgunned, they need any weapon they can get their hands on."

"Why? How about putting down all of the weapons? What about peace? Do you know that I pray for peace every day? Can you believe that? I'm a soldier, and I'm trained to kill if necessary. But what I dream of more than anything else is peace. And it's not just me. All of my friends and fellow soldiers...all of us dream of peace. Here, look at this," she said, extending her wrist to reveal a sapphire-blue silicone wristband with the words *shalom* and *salaam* imprinted in Hebrew and Arabic. "Do you see this wristband? Why do I wear it? And so many of my friends wear similar wristbands. Why? Because, more than anything else in the world, we dream of peace."

Adin's voice cracked and she couldn't go on speaking. Hajji watched her, perplexed. He didn't know the history; he had dropped out of school. But he knew that her narrative was vastly different from the one that he had heard his whole life.

He just saw a beautiful woman, an extremely beautiful woman who was also intelligent, articulate, passionate, gentle, delicate...and vulnerable. Now he understood her name. Adin: gentle and delicate and vulnerable. He heard the late-afternoon call for prayer; it was time to go home. "Have a good night, Adin," he said, as the muezzin's voice drifted through the hills: "*Allahu akbar*. God is great."

CHAPTER 43

Hajji couldn't go to the checkpoint to visit Adin the next day. He had an important match, a playoff game in Tel Aviv. The team bus was leaving early in the morning. He went to morning prayers and again inserted his own personal prayer, asking Allah to watch over and protect Adin.

Hajji's performance was excellent, but it wasn't perfect. No one is perfect. He was somewhat distracted. He couldn't stop thinking about Adin. She had really impressed him the previous night. He didn't agree with all of her politics—he didn't like to think too much about politics—but he was overwhelmed with her. She was a paradox: so strong, so passionate, but so vulnerable...the way she cried when she spoke about things that were important to her, about Israel.

Despite his distractions, Hajji's team narrowly won the match. On the bus back to Kiryat Shmona, Hajji's teammates asked what was wrong. They could tell that he hadn't played his best: he'd allowed two goals that he would ordinarily have blocked. He revealed only that he'd been up late the night before. He was tired. The teammates guessed, correctly, that Hajji had been up with his girlfriend (he *had* been up late at night thinking about Adin), so he had to endure jeers and crude jokes from his teammates for the rest of the ride home.

When he finally got back to Al'ard Alhamra, he headed straight for the checkpoint. As he walked down the road, he saw a single red wildflower at the side of the road. He picked the flower, intending to give it to Adin. When he approached the checkpoint, he saw several armored trucks and a small cadre of border police in riot gear. There were dozens of stones littering the ground around the guard booth.

Military police stopped him before he could reach the checkpoint. "What do you want?" an officer barked at him, gun drawn, anticipating the worst.

"My friend. I came to see my friend," he pleaded.

"There was a riot today. This is a closed military zone," the officer responded.

"But I need to see my friend. She's a soldier. There she is!" he said excitedly, pointing toward Adin, who by then had spotted him too, and was walking toward him.

"He's okay. He's safe. It's okay." she shouted. "He can come in."

"No he can't," the officer replied. "We have strict orders. No exceptions. Not even for lover boy over there," gesturing toward Hajji, who was still arguing with them.

"Okay, okay. He won't come in. Can I go out? To talk with him? Just for a minute or so?" Adin pleaded.

"I'll give you one minute," the officer said.

"We won the game, but barely. We almost lost," Hajji told her. "I gave up two goals. I should have blocked them, but they got by me. I was distracted because of last night. I can't stop thinking about you. Here! For you." Hajji extended his arm and handed the wildflower to Adin.

Adin smiled broadly when she accepted the unexpected gift. "Do you know what kind of flower this is?" she asked excitedly. "It's a *kalanit*, Israel's national flower. It's also my favorite flower. Thank you!"

She put the flower in her hair, just above her left ear. She looked stunning in the late afternoon sun with the single red wildflower in her wavy auburn hair.

"Now I have to give you something in return," Adin said, unsure of what to do next. She removed from her wrist the blue silicone wristband with the words *shalom* and *salaam* imprinted in Hebrew and Arabic. "For you," she said. "Wear it when you play. It'll be like a good luck charm. Nothing will get past you now," she joked, with a twinkle in her sapphire eyes.

CHAPTER 44

The acrid smell of teargas wafted through the village and woke Hajji early the next morning. The riots have gotten more violent, he thought to himself. I should go and check on Adin. First he went to morning prayers and again added in his own personal prayer: "Allah, the most awesome, the most powerful, please watch over Adin, the delicate one, and protect her."

He went up to the minaret to assess the situation. From his perch he had a bird's-eye view of the riot. Burning tires churned out black clouds like smokestacks. Dozens of Palestinian youths were hurling stones from slingshots. Some of them are probably my cousins, he thought again, though he couldn't recognize them from so far away. Besides, they were wearing scarves to cover their faces, and the tear gas made it hard to see clearly even from up close.

Heavily armored reinforcements in riot gear were at the front, close to the action. Adin was easy to spot with her thick auburn hair. She was in the back, in relative safety. Hajji realized that all of the other soldiers were wearing helmets. "Put on your helmet!" he screamed, as if she could hear him from so far away.

He raced down the steps of the minaret and out of the mosque. He ran through the village and down the road, screaming, "Adin! Put on your helmet! Adin! Put on your helmet!" But she couldn't hear him. There were sirens and yelling, and Adin could hardly hear herself, let alone someone else screaming from down the road.

Again, the military police wouldn't let him near the checkpoint. "It's a closed military zone!" a policeman yelled.

"Tell her to put her helmet on!" insisted Hajji. "Please! Tell her to put her helmet on!" But nobody would listen to him. A riot was blazing, and no one wanted to listen to this Arab kid ranting and raving.

He could see Adin, toward the back. She looked beautiful, as always. She was talking on the phone, presumably getting orders from her superiors. "Adin! Put your helmet on!" he screamed again. But she didn't hear him. And she didn't see the stone as it sailed over the men up front and collided with her head at high velocity. Hajji instinctively dove, as any great goalkeeper would, in a futile attempt to block the stone, but to no avail. The stone smashed her left temple, the temporal bone, the most delicate bone in the skull, just above her left ear. She collapsed to the ground. Blood spilled forth onto her beautiful auburn hair and stained the earth a crimson red.

Hajji let out a mortal scream as he watched, helplessly, from afar. Paramedics quickly put Adin on a stretcher and started an intravenous line, then whisked her away in an ambulance. The shrill siren of the ambulance drifted off in the distance. Hajji lay on the ground crying bitterly as he heard the piercing sound of the muezzin's call to prayer: "*Allahu akbar*. God is great. *Allahu akbar*. God is great."

CHAPTER 45

Hajji desperately sought to find out what had happened to Adin. Where did they take her? Which hospital? Was she even alive? He had no access to information, and he was sad and angry and frustrated and confused. He knew that the nearest hospital with an emergency room was in Tiberias, and that, he assumed, was where they must have taken her. So he borrowed a car from a friend and drove to Baruch Padeh Medical Center in Tiberias. When he pulled into the parking lot, he already knew he was in the right place. There were several military vehicles parked there, and ten or fifteen soldiers were standing near the emergency room entrance. As he approached, several soldiers converged toward him, blocking the entrance. He recognized one of the soldiers—the Druze who was stationed at the checkpoint with Adin.

"Hi. I'm Hajji. You know, Adin's friend," Hajji said, playing with the blue silicone wristband.

The Druze soldier extended his hand and rested it on Hajji's shoulder. "I'm sorry. I'm so sorry," he said in Arabic, as he lightly squeezed Hajji's shoulder in an attempt to offer him some comfort. He didn't need to say anything else. Hajji could see in the soldier's eyes that his greatest fear had come true. "No! No!" Hajji cried out, then rested his head on the Druze's shoulder and wept. As he stood there crying, a car pulled up, and from it emerged a man and a woman. They both looked like Sephardic Jews; they walked hand in hand, with heads lowered. A few of the soldiers silently escorted the couple into the hospital. The man had sapphire-blue eyes.

Regaining his composure, Hajji asked the soldier when and where the funeral would be. "I don't know anything specific," he answered.

"Her parents just arrived. If they decide to donate her organs, then the funeral might be delayed a day or so. Otherwise, it will be sometime tomorrow."

Hajji drove home in a daze. He was partially in shock and partially in denial. He didn't speak a word at dinner, and he didn't attend evening prayers that night. The following morning, he again skipped prayers. He was angry at God and angry at himself. Besides, he was in a rush. He hurried over to the checkpoint, imagining that Adin would still be there, that yesterday's events had been a horrible dream. The situation at the checkpoint was much calmer today: no rioting or tear gas or burning tires. But stones were everywhere, and the ground was still stained red where Adin had been hit, where Adin had died.

Adin wasn't there, but the Druze soldier was, and the two men embraced briefly.

"Any updates about the funeral?" Hajji asked, in Arabic.

"It will be tomorrow, around noon, maybe a bit later, at the military cemetery in Jerusalem."

CHAPTER 46

Getting to Jerusalem wasn't going to be easy. Hajji wouldn't be able to borrow a car for such a long trip—at least three hours each way, plus however much time he spent in Jerusalem. With public transportation, it would take a lot longer. So the next day, he awoke before sunrise and hitchhiked to Tiberias. From there he caught the first bus of the day to Jerusalem. He had been in Jerusalem only twice before in his life. The first time was as a young boy, when he accompanied his father to pray at the Al-Aqsa Mosque in the Old City. The second time was earlier that year, for a soccer match. Thanks to a solid performance by Hajji, his team had won the match against the Jerusalem youth soccer team 1–0.

Mount Herzl is a tranquil sanctum in the center of Jerusalem, only a few stops on the light rail from the central bus station. It houses both the main military cemetery and the Yad Vashem Holocaust museum. When Hajji arrived at the cemetery, there were two young female soldiers stationed at the front gate. They asked him a few questions and grew suspicious. What was a young Arab man, a Muslim, doing at a military funeral? He wasn't a soldier and he wasn't part of the family, so they refused to let him in.

"We were close friends, Adin and I," he pleaded with them. "She was a very special person. I'm here to pay my last respects to her. I'm not armed. I'm not here to harm anyone. Please let me in!" A few other soldiers came to assist the two guards. The situation started to become contentious; Hajji was afraid he would be arrested. Then he remembered that the lieutenant of the unit that manned the checkpoint knew about him. "Please ask the lieutenant, Adin's lieutenant. Tell him that Hajji is here, the... unofficial truck loader. I load and unload trucks at the checkpoint where Adin worked. Where Adin died."

"Okay, hold on. Let me check," one of the more senior soldiers said. A few minutes later, a middle-aged officer with multiple colorful stripes on his uniform approached the small crowd that had formed by the gate.

"Hajji?" he asked, extending his hand in a friendly gesture.

"Yes. That's me."

"It's nice to finally meet you," the officer said. "I've heard a lot of good things about you."

"He's clear," the lieutenant called out, waving Hajji past the gate and into the cemetery. "I'm sorry for your loss. For our loss. She was a beautiful person. And a good soldier. We'll all miss her terribly." Hajji didn't know how to respond; he just looked at the lieutenant with tears welling up in his eyes.

The two of them walked silently past row after row of graves. Most of those buried there were around Hajji's age or a few years older. In the distance was a large group of soldiers. As they approached the group, Hajji saw at the front, closest to the grave, the couple he'd seen in the hospital parking lot a few days earlier, her parents. Surrounding them were several muscular men who appeared to be in their twenties or thirties—her brothers, he presumed. All of them were crying.

He watched Adin's coffin as it was carried to the grave, draped in an Israeli flag. The flag was then removed and folded, and the simple pinewood coffin was lowered into the grave, returning her to the earth. One by one, men mostly, but a few women as well, took a shovel to cover her coffin with dirt and stones. The lieutenant said a few words and saluted. Then, on command, a few soldiers in crisp uniforms let off a volley of ceremonial gun shots into the air. Finally, a rabbi recited the Prayer for the Soul of the Departed:

> *Oh God, full of compassion, who dwells on high, grant true rest upon the wings of the Divine Presence...to the soul of Adin, the daughter of Chaim, who has gone to her eternal world...*

May her place of rest be in the Garden of Eden…
May she rest in her resting-place in peace, and let us say amen.

Hajji covered his ears when he heard the shrill cry of the muezzin's call for prayer from a mosque on a nearby hilltop: "*Allahu akbar.* God is great. *Allahu akbar.* God is great."

CHAPTER 47

Hajji's denial quickly progressed into anger. He was angry at God for betraying him, for not answering his prayers. He was angry at his cousins for killing Adin. Invisible cousins. Faces covered with scarves. He was angry at the military police for not letting him get closer to Adin, for not letting him warn her to wear her helmet. He was angry at Adin—why hadn't she worn her helmet? And he was angry at himself for failing to protect her, for failing to block the stone that took her life. What kind of goalkeeper was he if he couldn't block the most important shot of all?

He even contemplated suicide, imagining that he would climb the olive-green and bronze and auburn hills of the Galilee or the towering heights of the Golan and leap to his death in the water below. His body would be carried into the sapphire-blue waters of the Sea of Galilee, and he would remain there for eternity, forever enveloped by her beauty.

Then he saw the wristband, the sapphire-blue wristband that Adin had taken off and given to him, the good luck charm emblazoned with the most beautiful words of all, in Hebrew and in Arabic: *shalom, salaam*. As he played with the wristband, he vowed never to remove it from his wrist. He vowed to use all his energies to block every attempt at goal, never letting one slip by him as he had a few days earlier at the checkpoint. And he vowed to spread Adin's message of peace, *shalom, salaam*. Perhaps, with the money and fame he'd earn as a professional soccer player, he could start a soccer club in Adin's memory, a soccer clinic for Israeli children from all backgrounds, Jew and Arab, Muslim and Christian and Druze. He would teach not only soccer, but coexistence and inclusion and peace.

One week later, Hajji's team lost in the semifinals to a team from Haifa. Hajji allowed only one goal, a shot that couldn't possibly have been blocked by any goalkeeper, with or without a good luck charm. The goal was scored by a blond-haired and blue-eyed kibbutznik who had such impressive sportsmanship that he actually hugged Hajji and apologized to him after the game. Notably, Hajji's father was not in attendance. Over the next few weeks, Hajji received many attractive offers to play for professional clubs. He rejected a lucrative offer from an Egyptian club and ultimately signed a contract to play for Hapoel Haifa, an Israeli club.

PART FOUR

CHAPTER 48

"We've been together for weeks and we've never spent *Shabbat* together!" Tikvah declared one day during a phone conversation.

"I have a free *Shabbos* off of the base this weekend. Are you free? Maybe we can celebrate *Shabbos* together in Jerusalem."

"I'm almost always off for *Shabbat*," Tikvah replied, "and yes, I'd *love* to join you this weekend."

"Awesome!" said Zar. "I'm really looking forward to it. I can ask Yoli to drive me to Be'er Sheva on Friday, and we can take the bus together to Jerusalem."

It didn't take much to convince Yoli to drive Zar to Be'er Sheva. The roads were pretty empty at that hour, and it took less than thirty minutes to get there. Tikvah was already waiting outside the base when they arrived. Yoli honked, hollering, "Rebbetzin! Come on! The Rabbi is waiting for you."

Tikvah, carrying an olive-green knapsack, hopped into the truck. Zar had the same army-issued knapsack, and he joked that it would be pretty funny—and embarrassing—if they accidentally switched knapsacks. "If you see me walking around the base in tights," he told Yoli, "you'll know why!"

Zar and Tikvah caught the 470 bus just as it was about to pull out of the station. The bus was only half-full, and they easily found two empty seats toward the back. Zar thought again of his old neighborhood, where men never sat next to women on buses. It was considered too close, too intimate, and the risk of inadvertent contact too high. Such contact, he'd been taught, would surely provoke the *yetzer hara*, the

151

evil inclination, and stir up forbidden thoughts. After falling asleep on the bus from Ashkelon a few weeks ago with Tikvah's head resting on his shoulder, he could attest to the wisdom of such precautions. Nonetheless, he sat next to Tikvah, telling himself he'd be extra-vigilant and avoid any inadvertent—and forbidden—contact.

They chitchatted for several minutes and watched the scenery. The bus traveled directly north. The Bedouin Israeli city of Rahat sprawled out to the west, and the South Hebron hills of the lower West Bank were discernible only a few miles to the east. The conversation flowed unabated for the duration of the trip. Tikvah was charmed by Zar's humor and keen intelligence, and Zar was equally impressed by Tikvah's sharp wit and insightful commentary. After an hour and a half or so, the bus arrived at the central bus station in Jerusalem. They disembarked and walked the few blocks from the central bus station to the Machane Yehuda market.

The outdoor market was bustling when Zar and Tikvah arrived. Immediately, they were flooded with the pungent scent of spices and fresh fish, a kaleidoscope of colorful fruits and vegetables, the sweet taste of *halvah* and other confections that vendors offered as free samples, the sounds of shopkeepers advertising their wares and entertainers performing in the street, and the constant brushing of shoulders as they elbowed their way through the crowd.

The headlines of the newspapers on sale reported a bombing in a marketplace in Indonesia. "Do you think that could happen here, in Machane Yehuda?" asked Tikvah.

"I was wondering the same thing," admitted Zar. "I assume there's security here, even if we can't see it. There must be hidden cameras everywhere—like in that gourd over there!"

"Good point. I knew that gourd looked funny, just kind of staring at me."

"And there are probably undercover agents all over this place, like that guy playing the guitar."

"And that beggar, he's got '*Shabak* operative' written all over him!" Tikvah joked, using the Hebrew acronym for the Shin Bet, the Israeli intelligence force.

"Well, you should know. After all, you do work for military intelligence."

"Of course. I'm *so* important—indispensable to military intelligence, basically. Maybe I'm an undercover agent myself; maybe I've been observing you since we've met and I know all about your nefarious schemes!"

"I don't know what nefarious schemes you mean, but if they involve spending *Shabbos* with a beautiful young woman, then I'm guilty as charged," Zar said, raising his hands as though he were under arrest.

They were having so much fun that they nearly forgot to buy food for *Shabbat*.

"Wow! It's getting late," observed Tikvah. "We'd better stop frolicking and start buying stuff or we'll have to eat Bamba for dinner tonight," she said, referring to the ubiquitous peanut butter-flavored Israeli snack food.

"I happen to love Bamba—but not for Friday night dinner."

Tikvah, who was a vegetarian, offered to make some salads Zar showed her how to look for the kosher certification on a bag of lettuce that indicated it was free of insects. Tikvah selected a variety of vegetables and fruit, negotiating a better price for each.

"She's pretty and smart *and* she can haggle like a real Israeli!" said Zar, impressed.

"I have many hidden talents."

They also bought several challah rolls, grilled chicken cutlets, soup, some side dishes, drinks, and desserts. When they left the marketplace, the crowds were thinning out and some of the vendors were already starting to close their gates.

Zar and Tikvah rushed to catch the number 7 bus as it stopped by the Davidka monument on Hanevi'im Street. There were no empty seats, and they had to jostle for space as the bus coasted down King George Street, then wound its way past Liberty Bell Park and onto Hebron Road. Tikvah was staying at a friend's apartment in the Baka neighborhood, so she got off at Bethlehem Road. Zar remained on the bus for a few more stops and disembarked near his apartment in the Arnona neighborhood, only a few blocks from the U.S. embassy.

CHAPTER 49

A few hours later, after showering and changing into Sabbath clothing, Tikvah walked to Zar's apartment. She lit Sabbath candles there, then the two of them walked to a nearby synagogue for the evening services. Like most Israeli synagogues, this one was Orthodox, with men and women seated in separate sections. Tikvah was unfamiliar with the prayers, but thanks to a young woman who sat next to her, she was able to follow along. The man leading the services had a sweet voice, and the congregation sang along heartily. After the services were over, Zar and Tikvah mingled for a few minutes with the other congregants, who were mostly young and single, and declined numerous offers to join others for their Sabbath meals. They left the synagogue and walked several blocks back to Zar's apartment.

"Are we all alone here?" Tikvah asked as they entered the apartment.

"Yes and no. No one else is here right now, but my roommates are constantly coming and going."

"I guess our exclusive dinner for two might not be all that exclusive," Tikvah commented, peeking at the mirror and smoothing out her hair.

Zar recited the *Kiddush* blessing over wine, formally inaugurating the Sabbath. They washed their hands, recited the blessing over bread, and began the meal.

"You seem to be pretty familiar with the Friday night dinner ritual," Zar noted.

"Well, Bubby and I had Friday night dinner together almost every week, so I was already somewhat familiar with it. But then in college, I got involved with Jewish life on campus and had a lot of Friday night dinners. It's actually a funny story how that all started."

"I'm all ears!"

"At the beginning of the school year, there was this big event where all of the clubs set up tables to advertise and attract new members. I stopped by the table for Hillel, which is this large Jewish organization on campus. I met a lot of other Jewish students there, including this really cute guy named Dan. He was wearing a *kippah*, which was pretty uncommon on campus. We exchanged email addresses, and a day or so later, he invited me to join him for Friday night dinner. I thought it was a little weird that he lived in an apartment off campus rather than in one of the dorms, but I assumed he was an older student or maybe a grad student. I was a little hesitant to accept the invitation—I mean, he could've been a serial rapist or axe murderer or something crazy like that—but he seemed sweet and genuine, so I accepted. That Friday night, I got dressed up for a date, for what I thought would be a romantic night out. Anyway, I walked to his apartment, knocked on the door, and when the door opened, I almost fainted!"

"Why? What happened?"

"A woman answered the door. She was really pretty—radiant, actually—and she had the sweetest smile in the world. And she was like *nine months pregnant*! And there was a little boy running around in diapers and a baby in a high chair with baby food all over his face and bib. Then Dan came out of the kitchen in a suit and tie. He welcomed me warmly and offered me a seat. I learned that *Rabbi* Dan worked for a Jewish outreach organization; I had thought he was just some nice Jewish guy who happened to be Orthodox! I was sort of shocked and a bit embarrassed that I wasn't wearing something more modest, but he and his wife were totally cool and made me feel completely at home."

"I guess it wasn't the romantic evening you were expecting."

"That's the crazy part. It *was* romantic. It was the most romantic, beautiful *Shabbat* dinner I had ever experienced! We spoke about everything, from sports and movies and music to politics and religion. They were very accepting, and not at all judgmental. We sang songs, some of which I knew from my Bubby. The environment was really peaceful—except for the occasional baby crying. I left their home that night on a total high! I went back a lot for other *Shabbat* dinners and got involved with Hillel and Chabad."

"That's a great story. Is that why you decided to move to Israel?"

"Indirectly. Rabbi Dan and the other campus Jewish groups definitely sparked my interest, but ironically, it was some of the *anti-*Israel activities that convinced me to explore Zionism."

"How so?"

"There was this girl Becca—that's short for Rebecca. I knew her pretty well because we went to the same temple back home. Well, neither of us *went* very often, but both our families were members. Our bat mitzvahs were supposed to be the same week, so our families had all these discussions to reach a compromise. Basically, she got the original date and I had to move mine to a later week. In hindsight, it wasn't such a big deal, but at the time I sort of resented it. Becca's grandmother was the president of the local chapter of Hadassah, which is this big Zionist women's organization, and Bubby was sort of friendly with her. Now that I think about it, we had pretty similar upbringings. Both of us are the daughters of a Jewish mother and a Christian father, and both our grandmothers were Holocaust survivors who were strong-willed and ardent Zionists.

Anyway, Becca somehow got involved in one of the anti-Zionist campus groups. I saw her once at some small anti-Israel demonstration—they were having a prayer vigil for a Palestinian terrorist who was assassinated by Israel. They were actually saying *Kaddish* for him as if he was some sort of hero! I didn't pay much attention to it at the time; there was always a lot happening on campus, and I guess my brain didn't really process what was going on. A few weeks later, some Israeli politician came to speak on campus. I can't remember who it was, but his speech was about some sort of Arab-Israeli social initiative. Anyway, during the speech, Becca and some of her friends got up and started yelling, 'You're a Nazi! Zionism is apartheid!' and other stuff like that. Security guards had to drag Becca and her cohorts out of the lecture hall. I remember looking at Becca, staring right at her, and our eyes met. She had this crazy look, like she was on drugs or something. I saw her a few days later, and I debated with myself whether I should say something to her or not. Finally, I decided to confront her. I asked her how she could go against her people, against her grandmother. She answered that 'my people' were racists and that her grandmother was also a racist. I was shocked! I tried arguing with her, but I really couldn't."

"Why not?"

"First of all, she was well prepared with all of these talking points. I didn't even know the history; for me, Zionism was more of an emotional thing. Also, she still had that bugged-out look in her eyes. I don't think she was on drugs, but I think she was kind of brainwashed—although she accused *me* of being brainwashed for supporting Israel despite its 'crimes.'"

"She kind of has a point there."

"What are you saying? You agree with Becca? Do *you* think I'm brainwashed?"

"Not really brainwashed. It's just—and please don't take this the wrong way—it's just that your grandmother was so pro-Israel and you were so close with her that I don't know if you could really think about it without being kind of...biased, I guess. You know what I mean?"

"I think what you're trying to say is that because of my strong emotional attachment to my grandmother, I can't think about Zionism objectively, that somehow, opposing Israel would constitute, indirectly, a betrayal of my grandmother. You know, Zar, that's a little insulting..."

"I'm sorry."

"But there may be some truth to what you're saying. That doesn't make me wrong, though. I mean, just because I'm emotionally attached to something, that doesn't make it wrong."

"That's true. It doesn't make it right either. I'm just saying that you can't really think about it—what was the word you used?—objectively."

"And do you think Becca was being completely objective?"

"What do you mean?"

"Don't you think she was being influenced by peer pressure?"

"Maybe a little."

"Maybe a *lot*! You may not have felt the pressure growing up in Israel, especially in an ultra-Orthodox neighborhood, but *I* certainly felt it. Jews in the diaspora have this constant need to be accepted by the gentile society around us; my Bubby would say things like, 'What will the *goyim* think?' Becca may not even realize it, but she's ashamed to be Jewish. And she's ashamed of an Israel that represents exactly the opposite of what Jews in the diaspora need most: to be accepted. Deep down, she's terrified of being labeled a traitor, of having dual loyalty. So maybe Becca didn't have such a close relationship with her grandmother—and having met her grandmother a few times, I don't blame her—but she's still pushed and pulled in lots of different directions. If she thinks I'm brainwashed, so be it. But she's brainwashed too, just in a different way! Have you ever heard of cognitive dissonance?"

"Nope."

"I learned about it in a psychology class last year. Basically, there's an inner conflict when we see things that contradict our belief systems. It's called cognitive dissonance, and it's really uncomfortable. And we have to either just walk around with this inner turmoil, or we change our beliefs. That's pretty hard to do, so people usually find some sort of rationalization. In the case of Zionism, or anti-Zionism for that matter, we have strong beliefs, and we'll try to reinterpret current events or history to somehow fit into our belief systems. So Becca might view a Palestinian terrorist as a 'freedom fighter,' no matter how horrible his actions may have been. Or a Zionist might dismiss Palestinian suffering or civilian casualties as 'collateral damage' rather than hold Israel accountable."

"Okay, I see your point. It reminds me of a parable I heard as a kid. You know what a parable is?"

"Sure, like Aesop's fables?"

"Huh?"

"You know, like the story of the fox and the grapes, or the boy who cried wolf."

"I'm not familiar, but those sure *sound* like parables. Anyway, there was a famous storyteller, the Dubno Maggid—I don't even know where or when he lived."

"Well, presumably he lived in a city called Dubno," Tikvah suggested.

"You're right. Anyway, somewhere in Europe. And he lived maybe a hundred years ago, maybe even earlier; I'm not too sure. I heard some of his parables when I was a kid and I never forgot this one because it really sums up human nature. It goes something like this: There was a king—or a prince—"

"I've heard parables like this. They always seem to involve a king or a prince."

"So true! Anyway, this prince was traveling through the countryside looking for young men to join his army. He reached some village and he saw lots of arrows stuck into trees, and every single arrow was right in the middle of a target, right in the bull's-eye. The prince got very excited. 'Whoever shot these arrows must be the world's greatest archer!' the prince said. 'We have to find this archer and get him to join my army!' So the prince went into the village and asked around and eventually found the archer who'd shot the arrows. So the prince said to the archer, 'Are you the one who shot these arrows?' The archer said yes. 'Well,' said the prince, 'you must be the world's greatest archer. I want you to join my army! So, what's your secret? How do you always get the arrow right in the middle of the target, right in the bull's-eye?' 'It's easy,' the archer responded. 'First I shoot an arrow, then I paint the target around it!'

I love that parable because it really sums up human nature. We all have opinions, and we're so committed to them that we're not willing to let go of them, even if there are strong arguments against them. We just draw targets around the arrows we've already shot—or around arrows that other people have already shot *for* us—so the facts fit our opinions and not the other way around."

"But Becca is also painting targets around arrows. They're just different arrows and different targets. I think we all do that. We have to, in order to deal with cognitive dissonance. Imagine if someone wrote a book about us," Tikvah continued, "about two Israeli lone soldiers. And one of the soldiers is this amazing soccer player and he ends up playing for the Israeli national soccer team and wins the World Cup."

"Sounds like a great book!"

"Right! *You* think so. And maybe anyone who loves Israel would think so, even if the book really wasn't that great from a literary perspective. But anti-Zionists would criticize the book. They'd label it as trash, even if, from a literary perspective, it was a masterpiece. People have a very hard time being objective—*because of cognitive dissonance.*"

"So, if I understand what you just said, the Dubno Maggid's parable isn't about cognitive dissonance; it's about how people *react* to cognitive dissonance. Painting targets around arrows is the way we deal with cognitive dissonance."

"Yes, I think that's right. You're a fast learner. I'm impressed!"

"It's all those years of Talmudic learning that sharpened my brain," Zar said, smirking.

"I thought you were kicked out of like ten schools and just played soccer during high school."

"It was more like six schools, thank you very much. Now, what were we talking about before?"

"I was telling you about Rabbi Dan and how I got interested in Israel when I was in college."

"That's right. So what happened?"

"Well, after my confrontation with Becca, I decided that I needed to learn more about Israel. I spoke to Rabbi Dan about it, and he hooked me up with an organization called Birthright that offers free tours of Israel to young Jewish people. I applied for the trip and I was accepted."

"That's awesome! How was the trip?"

"Amazing! Eye-opening! Life-changing! Literally—it changed my life. Of course, I still didn't have all the answers. Actually, I had more questions after the trip than I had before. But that was when I decided to move here...not only to move here, but to join the army."

"Did you tell Rabbi Dan that you wanted to make *aliyah* and join the army?"

"Of course I told him. And he was very supportive of my plans to make *aliyah*. Surprisingly, he wasn't so keen on me joining the army. He wanted me to enroll in a seminary here to learn more about Judaism. He thought the army would actually *endanger* my growing commitment to Judaism. What do you think?"

"I'm glad you joined the army...because that's how we met."

"Me too!"

They continued talking for hours as the *Shabbat* candles flickered nearby. Zar enjoyed the food they had bought at the shuk, but Tikvah only picked and nibbled. Zar's roommates came and went, but for the most part, they were alone. Finally, when they realized how late it was, they decided to finish the meal and skip dessert. They left Zar's apartment and continued talking all the way to Tikvah's friend's apartment. They stood outside and talked for several more minutes before Tikvah invited Zar in for a drink.

"No, thank you. I don't want to disturb your hosts," Zar said.

"Actually, no one's home but me. The whole family went to a bar mitzvah or something in Modi'in, so it's just me here." Tikvah wasn't sure what to expect. Part of her really wanted to spend the night with Zar, and part of her understood that, as much as she desired it, it might jeopardize their relationship. But Tikvah went ahead, saying softly, almost in a whisper, "You're welcome to come inside."

Zar was struggling too. There was nothing in the world that he wanted more than Tikvah. He knew that spending the night with her was unequivocally forbidden by Jewish religious law, but the temptation was nearly insurmountable. Zar recalled the biblical verse from the end of the *Shema* prayer: "And you shall not stray after your hearts and after your eyes, after which you are inclined to indulge." Summoning all of his fortitude, Zar declined Tikvah's invitation.

"Thank you, Tikvah, for your offer. You know—I'm sure you know—how much I want to join you tonight...all night. But I can't. You know that too. There are certain lines I can't cross, that *we* can't cross. Tikvah, I love you. I love you too much to endanger our relationship. Our first time together should be on our wedding night, in purity and holiness."

"Was that a marriage proposal?" Tikvah asked with a mixture of longing and reservations, secretly fearing the numerous changes and sacrifices she'd have to make to accommodate Zar's religiosity.

"It was a proposal to make a proposal, at the right time and at the right place. God willing, we'll be together, as one, someday—but not yet. I love you, Tikvah. Good night."

"Good night, Zar. I love you too."

After Zar left, Tikvah closed the door and stood leaning against it, absorbed in her thoughts, for several minutes. Finally, she undressed and got into bed and, as she did every night, she spoke to God. She thanked God for giving her Zar. Then she recited a blessing: "Bless you, God, for you have kept me alive, and sustained me, and brought me to this moment in time."

And then she said the *Shema* prayer.

CHAPTER 50

Z ar overslept the next morning and had to rush to get to synagogue on time. The rabbi was an energetic young man with a wispy beard and a powerful voice. He gave a sermon about Moses, who had desired more than anything else to enter the promised land, but was denied entrance to the Land of Israel by God for what seemed like a minor infraction. We all have very human desires to "enter the promised land" before we are granted permission, the rabbi said. All of us are faced with tests throughout our lives. We have desires and are forbidden from fulfilling them except as prescribed by God, in the proper place and at the proper time. Zar was mesmerized by the sermon, which seemed tailor-made for him, given his inner struggle the night before.

Tikvah showed up at the synagogue just as services were ending. She was wearing a simple white top and a floral blue skirt. They greeted each other warmly and walked to Zar's apartment. As he had done the night before, Zar made the *Kiddush* blessing, consecrating the Sabbath. They silently washed their hands, then Zar made the blessing over the *challah* loaves.

Tikvah opened the conversation with a question: "Zar, I was wondering, when you were in the youth league, did you have to play soccer on *Shabbat*?"

"When I first joined the team, I was really worried about that, about having to choose between keeping *Shabbos* and my dream of playing soccer; I had some sleepless nights. For my first *Shabbos* team practice, I actually walked from Mea She'arim to Talpiot. It took me almost two hours. When I got there, the coach saw me drenched in sweat and asked what happened. I explained everything to him, and he took care of me:

164

for the rest of the season, all of our *Shabbos* away games were either moved to another day or until well after sundown on Saturday nights. I still walked to practice on Saturdays, and we did have a few home games on *Shabbos*, but we never had to travel on *Shabbos* for a game."

"I love how committed you are to *Shabbat* observance—and you still won MVP in the championship game. You were a real Sandy Koufax!"

"Who?"

"Sandy Koufax! Maybe the greatest pitcher ever to play professional baseball—I think so, at least, because he played for the Los Angeles Dodgers. I'm a huge fan of all the L.A. sports teams."

"Okay, but what does that have to do with me?"

"Oh yeah. He was Jewish, and around fifty years ago—actually, it was the sixties, so more than fifty years ago—the first game of the World Series fell out on Yom Kippur. Koufax was supposed to be the starting pitcher, but he decided not to play on Yom Kippur. His team lost the game, but they came back and ended up winning the World Series, and Sandy Koufax, who had refused to play on Yom Kippur, was named MVP. And you—you refused to play on *Shabbat*, your team won the championship, and you were named MVP! So that's what I meant when I compared you to Sandy Koufax."

"That's nice of you, but I don't think I'm *that* good. I mean, I don't think I'm the greatest soccer player in the world."

"Well, I do!"

"You sound like a Jewish mother."

Tikvah laughed. "Does your mother think you're the greatest soccer player in the world?"

"My mother didn't approve of my playing soccer. Actually, she was sort of neutral: she wanted me to be happy; she just wished that I'd find something else, something more Jewish, I guess. My father, on the other hand, was *really* against soccer. He was ashamed of me."

Tikvah paused before asking her next question. She was hesitant to probe too much into Zar's childhood, but he had opened up to her, so she seized the opportunity to explore this sensitive topic. "Do you miss your parents?" she asked.

Zar took a few moments to gather his thoughts. "Yes and no."

"What do you mean?"

Zar paused again before answering. "I never had a close relationship with my father. He was very strict. I can't say I miss him. My mother is a different story. She was—*is*—a loving mother. She cried whenever I came home too late from playing soccer, and she cried the night I ran away from home. I think about that night a lot.

You know, when I was really young, maybe first or second grade, I was reviewing Bible homework with my mother—at that age, she would do my homework with me; my father didn't take over until around fifth grade, when I started learning Talmud—and we got to the verse in Genesis where God creates Eve and brings her to Adam to be his mate. It says something like, 'A man will leave his father and mother and go to his wife and become like one flesh.' As kids, we were taught that 'one flesh' meant the children that came from a man and a woman. When we learned that verse together, I looked up and saw my mother wiping tears from her eyes. I asked her why she was crying, but she wouldn't answer. I didn't understand it at the time, but I never forgot about it. Now, when I think about the way she cried whenever she thought I was going off the right path, and especially the night I announced I was joining the army and ran away, I finally understand why she cried over that verse in Genesis when I was a little boy. She loved me so much that, even then, when I was maybe seven years old, she couldn't bear to think that one day I would leave her. So yes, I do miss my mother...a lot."

Zar cleared his throat, holding back his own tears, and continued. "Tikvah, I want to share something with you. The night before we first met, I was really down. I guess you could call it depression. I get that way every now and then—not suicidal or anything like that, just sad. I don't know if it's depression or just the normal mood swings that everyone has. Maybe you know; you're the psychologist."

"I'm not a psychologist, just a college student who took a few classes. But I think you're right—everyone has mood swings. It's normal. Believe me; I've had tons of them. That's how we deal with stress and all the difficulties in life."

"But the night before I met you, I was at a real low point. I felt lonely and hopeless. That really sums up how I felt: hopeless. For the first time since I was a child, I cried. I think it was a combination of burnout from basic training plus loneliness and missing home and worrying about the future. So I did what I always do in situations like that. The same thing you would do in a situation like that."

"You prayed? You spoke to God?"

"Exactly! That's what I did. I spoke to God. And do you know what I asked for? I asked God to give me hope. And the very next morning, you showed up on my base: *Tikvah*, hope. God answered my prayer and gave me exactly what I asked for...you!"

CHAPTER 51

Z ar and Tikvah were so absorbed with each other that they barely ate their food and hardly noticed the occasional interruptions when Zar's roommates barged into the apartment. Finally, Zar suggested that they finish the meal and go for a walk.

"Where should we go?" Tikvah asked.

"Why don't we walk to the Western Wall? Along the way, we can stop at a really beautiful place with an amazing view."

"Sounds great!"

Zar recited *Birkat ha-Mazon*, the grace after meals, and the two of them left the apartment. They walked the few short blocks to Hebron Road, which follows the ancient road connecting Jerusalem in the north with Bethlehem and Hebron to the south. Zar and Tikvah walked north on Hebron Road, and after a few minutes, they reached a beautiful park officially known as the Haas Promenade, but more commonly just called the *Tayelet*, "the promenade." The *Tayelet* is on a hill at the nexus of three neighborhoods: to the west, Jewish Talpiot; to the east, the Arab neighborhood of Jabel Mukaber and the mixed Arab-Jewish Abu Tor. Its strategic location on a hill connecting East and West Jerusalem meant that it was the site of fierce battles during the War of Independence in 1948–1949 and the Six-Day War in 1967. Later, the hilltop was made into a park, to serve as an oasis of peace in a land too often marred by conflict.

The *Tayelet* offers unparalleled panoramic views of ancient Jerusalem and its environs, including the Mount of Olives. On any given day, Jewish, Muslim, and Christian brides pose for photographs there in their wedding gowns. When Zar and Tikvah arrived, they found dozens of people enjoying the mild weather and the beautiful view. Many were Jews dressed, like themselves, in Sabbath clothing. A small group of Asian tourists were taking photographs, and a tour group of Christian pilgrims were listening to a lecture from a young priest. A few armed border policemen in olive-green uniforms were laughing and smoking cigarettes. Zar and Tikvah were relishing each other's company, the amazing view, and a gentle, cool breeze.

Their serenity was shattered by the sound of screeching car tires, followed by a thud, then people shrieking. Moments later, Zar and Tikvah were knocked to the ground; they felt the wind knocked out of them. At first, they thought they'd been struck by a car that had lost control and veered into the crowd, but they quickly realized they'd been knocked down by a pedestrian who had herself been struck by a car intentionally driven into the crowd. Fortunately, concrete barriers prevented the car from penetrating any further. Zar and Tikvah were on the ground, still processing the unfolding events, when a young man jumped from the now-disabled car, wielding a butcher knife, which he raised above his head. He screamed "*Allahu akbar!*" and lunged directly at Tikvah. Zar was only a meter away, but he was unable to react quickly enough to protect her. Tikvah screamed.

CHAPTER 52

As Zar watched helplessly, the sound of gunfire rang through the air. Tikvah instinctively put her arms up to protect her head, rolling toward Zar and out of the knife-wielding terrorist's reach. As the terrorist attempted to lift himself off the ground and attack Tikvah again, more shots struck him. Tikvah was still screaming, her head buried in Zar's chest.

As quickly as the attack had started, it was over. Six people had been struck, one fatally, by the terrorist's car. Thanks to an alert civilian bystander who fired the first shots, and a border policeman who fired the second volley, no one was stabbed.

Within minutes, several police cars arrived on the scene, as well as ambulances and "ambucycles" to assist the injured and remove the dead, including both the victim and the terrorist who had killed him. Zar and Tikvah reported their accounts of the attack, but declined to be taken to a hospital for medical treatment. Miraculously, neither of them were harmed. Zar sustained a relatively minor abrasion on his arm, and his shirt was torn; other than some blood stains on her skirt, Tikvah was completely unscathed—physically, at least. Emotionally, she was a wreck. For the better part of an hour, she sat on the ground next to Zar, hugging him and sobbing.

Zar too was struggling: there was, of course, the shock of having just been the victim of a terror attack and nearly witnessing the savage murder of his love. But he was also grappling with the proper response to Tikvah's embrace. He felt at once the burning desire to hug Tikvah and comfort her, and the imperative to follow tradition and avoid intimate contact with a woman. But Zar's internal struggle was quickly resolved: Tikvah was holding on to him so tightly that it would've been nearly impossible to undo her grip. Anyway, he could certainly touch a sick woman who needed medical care, couldn't he? Tikvah was emotionally bruised, so she probably qualified as a sick person. In fact, he reasoned, he'd be *obligated* to touch a sick woman in need of care, so really, he was *obligated* to hug Tikvah. They got up and sat together on a park bench, speechless, for another hour.

Finally, Tikvah's sobs subsided, and she released her grip.

"Is this what it takes for you to hug me?" she asked with some ill-placed sarcasm.

"Tikvah, did you stage this whole thing just so I'd show you some affection?" Zar joked.

"I'm sorry."

"Sorry for what?"

"Sorry if I made you uncomfortable by hugging you."

"It's okay. You needed it. I think we both needed it. Maybe that's what Yoli meant when he said that 'life begins where your comfort zone ends.'"

"And I'm sorry for making light of this situation with my crude humor."

"I think that's normal. Of course, you'd know better than me, with all those psychology classes you took last year. You know what's ironic?" Zar asked.

"How about the way you won't ever touch me, then we almost get killed and we hug for like two hours?"

"I suppose there's some irony there. But I was thinking about how we're both soldiers; theoretically, we're constantly putting ourselves in harm's way. But in the army, our lives have never really been in danger. And here we are, in civilian clothing, enjoying a beautiful day, and *that's* when we nearly lose our lives."

"I'm just grateful that we're alive and intact. Should we still go to the Western Wall, or should we call it a day and walk back to your apartment?"

"Let's visit the Wall. I think we need to go there now more than ever. There's a blessing for surviving a dangerous situation. I'll say the afternoon prayers there and say that blessing for both of us."

CHAPTER 53

They continued walking north on Hebron Road, crossed the busy thoroughfare via a pedestrian footbridge, and proceeded up a steep, winding path to the Armenian church that sits outside the Old City's ancient walls. They passed a monument to a young yeshiva student who was murdered on that spot twenty years earlier by a Palestinian terrorist. Just past the church on the right was Mount Zion, where the biblical King David is purported to be buried.

They entered the Jewish Quarter of the Old City through the Zion Gate, which was still pockmarked by bullets, remnants of the fierce battle to capture the Old City in June 1967, and a perpetual reminder that the threat of violence is always lingering.

The Jewish Quarter was a happening place at that hour. Mothers with baby strollers stood in small groups and schmoozed, keeping a watchful eye on their children playing nearby. Old men sat on benches playing chess and backgammon. Flocks of male yeshiva students passed small clusters of garrulous female seminary students, who would occasionally catch a stray glance from their male counterparts, only to erupt in giggles as they blushed and turned away. On a sign hanging outside a school were the words of the prophet Zechariah: "Old men and old women will again sit along the streets of Jerusalem... and the streets of the Old City will be filled with young boys and girls playing." Zar read the verse aloud to Tikvah. "My father would quote that verse as we walked to the Western Wall through the Jewish Quarter on *Shabbos*; it always puzzled me."

"Why?"

"Because it's referring to a messianic time, when the Jewish people would return to this land and to this city. But my father's very anti-Zionist; he believes that the modern State of Israel is the work of the devil, not a fulfillment of ancient prophecies. And yet, when he saw scenes like this—little children playing and old men sitting peacefully—he would quote that verse."

"He was condemning Zionism...and vindicating it at the same time. Cognitive dissonance?" Tikvah suggested.

"I suppose."

They lingered awhile, watching this biblical scene, then proceeded down innumerable steps to the Western Wall. Zar thought of the custom of tearing one's shirt upon seeing the Western Wall, a sign of mourning for the Holy Temple destroyed almost two thousand years ago. Of course, no public mourning was permitted on the Sabbath, and it would be a violation of the Sabbath to tear garments—but his shirt had already been torn, he realized, during the terror attack earlier that day.

"What should I do?" Tikvah asked Zar as they approached the Wall. "What prayers should I say?" Zar told her to just talk to God, with whatever words and in whatever language she was most comfortable.

"And then what?"

"You could recite psalms. That's what most people do. There are lots of copies of the book of Psalms here."

"Aren't there a lot of psalms? How do I know which ones to say?"

"You're right, there are a lot of psalms—150 of them. Most of them were written by King David. I guess the most popular ones are the Songs of the Ascents. If I'm not mistaken, there are only fifteen of those. Number 120 to 135, I think."

"I majored in psychology, not math, but I think 120 to 135 would make sixteen of them."

"You *are* sharp! Okay, so you'll have to look in the book. Maybe they start at 121 or end at 134, or maybe there are sixteen after all. I'm not totally sure. You could also ask someone for help."

"I think I'll be fine. When should we meet up again?"

"I'll need around fifteen or twenty minutes to say the afternoon prayers, so let's meet back here in twenty minutes."

CHAPTER 54

The plaza in front of the Western Wall was divided into two sections, one for men and one for women, as is the Orthodox practice. Tikvah gingerly entered the women's section, where she was greeted by a middle-aged woman. Her graying strawberry-blond hair peeked out from under her straw hat and she wore the badge of the organization that maintains decorum at the Wall. The woman's main job, it seemed, was to distribute scarves to women in sleeveless attire so that they could cover their shoulders. She also reminded tourists to refrain from violating the Sabbath by using their phones or cameras.

Tikvah asked why non-observant and even non-Jewish visitors had to comply with these restrictions. "Every shrine and holy place has its rules," the woman told her. "Up there," she said, pointing to the Temple Mount, "is controlled by the Muslim Waqf, even though Israel captured it in 1967. They have very strict rules about dress and what you can and can't do or say. A Jew can't even whisper a prayer up there without being thrown out, maybe even starting a riot. And there are rules you have to abide by in the churches too. Even museums and libraries have rules of decorum. We're not asking much, just to respect the holiness of this place and the holiness of the Sabbath." Tikvah was placated, if not completely satisfied. This woman was just doing her job; there was no point in arguing with her.

This wasn't Tikvah's first time at the Western Wall. She had visited it during her Birthright trip, and again shortly after she made *aliyah* and moved to Israel. But this visit to the Wall was more meaningful. Now she had Zar, and she was really starting to connect with her heritage— and she'd just survived a near-death experience. She felt an acute need to express her gratitude to God. Remembering Zar's advice, she looked on the bookshelves and found a copy of Psalms. She knew she was looking for the Songs of the Ascents, but she couldn't remember the chapter numbers. She looked in vain for a table of contents, then flipped through the book, but she still couldn't find them.

A woman standing nearby asked if she could help. She was ultra-Orthodox; Tikvah could tell from her head covering, which left not even one hair exposed. Her clothing was austere but dignified. She looked vaguely familiar. She had a cherubic face, a sweet smile, and a gentle manner. Tikvah explained her predicament, and the woman opened the volume, locating the desired passages in mere seconds: chapters 120 to 134. Tikvah thanked her, then looked at the crowd of women separating her from the Wall, not seeing any easy path to approach and touch it. She didn't need to say anything more; the woman understood what Tikvah needed. She was quite adept at navigating the crowds. She held Tikvah gently by the hand and guided her, with grace and determination, to a spot next to the Wall. "May all your prayers be answered," the woman said with a smile. Her face seemed to radiate wisdom. "May God bless you. And have a good *Shabbos!*" The woman let go of Tikvah's hand and walked away, disappearing into the crowd.

Tikvah caressed the aged stones. How many tears, she wondered, had been shed at this very spot? She began reciting the Psalms, softly at first, then louder and more fervently:

In my distress I called unto the Lord, and He answered me...
I am for peace, but even as I speak, they are for war...
The Lord shall guard your going and coming, now and forever...
...our feet are standing within your gates, Jerusalem...
Pray for the peace of Jerusalem...
They that trust in the Lord are like Mount Zion, which cannot be moved...
Peace be upon Israel!

When the Lord brought back the returnees to Zion, we were like dreamers...

The Lord will bless you out of Zion, and see the good of Jerusalem all the days of your life...

Peace be upon Israel!

Let them be ashamed and turned backwards, all they that hate Zion.

Out of the depths I have called to you, Lord...

For the Lord has chosen Zion; He has desired it for His habitation...

The Lord will bless you out of Zion...

Tikvah didn't have to compose her own prayer; King David knew exactly the right words to say.

CHAPTER 55

Meanwhile, Zar was on the men's side looking for the requisite quorum of ten men for reciting the afternoon prayers. He didn't have to search for long; groups were forming all around him. He joined one, a potpourri of Jewish men, Hasidic, Modern Orthodox, Sephardi, Ashkenazi, young and old. Even a pair of off-duty policemen had put on yarmulkes to participate in the short service. Zar made sure to say aloud the blessing for having been saved from danger: "Blessed are you, God, our Lord, King of the universe, who has granted goodness to those who are unworthy," and the other men all responded on cue, "He who has granted you goodness, He should grant you all of the goodness eternally."

As he was walking back to meet Tikvah, he heard a familiar voice saying the blessing over the Torah reading. The man was wearing a prayer shawl over his head, and Zar was a few paces behind him, so he didn't recognize the man at first. After the Torah reading, the man recited the second blessing. Zar, along with all the other men within earshot, answered, "Amen!" The man removed the prayer shawl from his head, draping it over his shoulders and back. Even from behind and at a distance, Zar knew his father.

Zar froze. He hadn't seen or even spoken with his father in months, not since the day he'd run away and enlisted in the army. Perhaps this was an opportunity to reunite and reconcile their differences? But Zar didn't have the courage or the will to take the next step. He was afraid that his father would reject him again. Or that, even though Zar was now an adult, his father would somehow intervene and prevent him from pursuing his dream of playing soccer. Or worse, perhaps he'd

179

interfere with his relationship with Tikvah. Even more than losing soccer, he feared losing Tikvah. Zar's father began reciting the silent prayer. It was too late—he couldn't disturb his father during the silent prayer. And it had been more than twenty minutes. He didn't want to keep Tikvah waiting. As his father swayed rhythmically in fervent prayer, Zar left the Wall.

When he met up with Tikvah, she noticed that he looked pale, even frightened. "Is everything okay? You look like you saw a ghost."

"Tikvah, I saw my father. My father is here, praying."

"Oh, my! Did you say anything to him?"

"No, I didn't know what to say. I was afraid."

"Afraid of what?"

"Afraid of confrontation. Afraid of rejection. Afraid that he'd interfere with my dream of playing soccer. But most of all, I was afraid that he'd somehow interfere with you."

"Most of all? Do you really mean that? On your list of priorities, the things you cherish most, I'm at the top of that list? Even more than soccer?"

"Yes, Tikvah. More than anything else in the world. Even more than soccer."

Tikvah was speechless. She wanted to tell Zar that she felt the same way. But she didn't need to say anything; he knew how she felt. He could see it in her eyes. After sitting there quietly for some time, Zar asked Tikvah, "How did it go for you, praying at the Wall on your own?" Tikvah described her experience: her confrontation with the scarf lady, then the kind woman who'd helped her find the right psalms and found her a spot next to the Wall, and that woman's kind words before she disappeared into the crowd.

"Zar, can I ask you a strange question?"

"Of course! Ask me anything."

"You said that, as a child, you sometimes walked to the Western Wall with your father on *Shabbat*?"

"Yes, he comes here maybe once a month. I would walk with him a few times a year, maybe more."

"Did your mother ever come with you?"

"Yes. Usually. Actually, she walked here all the time, more often than my father. She probably still does."

"Oh my God!" Tikvah said softly, covering her mouth in astonishment.

"What?"

"*Oh my God!*" she repeated louder, almost shouting. "Zar, that woman who helped me find the right place in the book, who held my hand and walked me to the wall and blessed me...it was your mother. I'm sure of it. She had your eyes and your smile. You're practically a clone of her. As soon as I saw her, I thought she looked familiar, like I knew her somehow. But where would I have met her, this ultra-Orthodox woman? But now it's clear. A hundred percent clear. A thousand percent clear! Zar, there were dozens of women at the Wall. I was obviously sort of lost, but no one else noticed. Or if they did notice, they didn't care to help. But she did. She didn't just help me; she *touched* me. Maybe you won't touch me, but she did. She held me by the hand and escorted me to the Wall. She was so kind, Zar. I saw it in her eyes. Now I understand you. I understand why you love her. I could see myself loving her too. I don't think you and I could live up to her standards—I mean her religious standards, her austerity. But she understands that. I *know* she does. I'm sure she accepts you for who you are. And she'd accept me for who I am."

"But what about my father? He's different. He doesn't understand me. He'll never accept me—or you, for that matter—unless we live according to his standards."

"I haven't met your father, so I can't say; maybe you're right. But your mother's very strong. You told me she cried when you read that verse in Genesis about men leaving their mothers and cleaving to their wives, and she cried when you ran away from home. But she didn't cry out of weakness. She cried out of love. If you wanted to reunite with your family, she'd make sure that your father complied."

"You may be right, Tikvah. You may be right. Someday, I'll have the courage to reach out to my parents. And you could help. But not yet. I'm not ready. And you're not ready—you're still on a journey. I'm on a journey. And I want to continue this journey with you. God willing, one day I'll reunite with them. *We'll* reunite with them."

CHAPTER 56

"Do you know what special day is next week?" Tikvah asked Zar on the phone one night.

"No. Give me a hint."

"Okay. Think *Hatikvah*."

"Like the national anthem?"

"Yes."

"I don't know. Is it the anniversary of the first time *Hatikvah* was sung publicly?"

"Close. It *is* the anniversary of a public singing of *Hatikvah*, but think about something more recent."

"Well, they sing it at sporting events. Is it the anniversary of an Israeli soccer victory?"

"Zar, think about *us*. Remember when you and I sang *Hatikvah* together?"

"Oh! Of course. It's the anniversary of the first time we met! I'm so dumb—or maybe I'm just careless. How could I not have known that?"

"If you have to choose between dumb and careless, choose dumb. Women can't really blame men for being stupid; it's just their nature. But you'll never hear the end of it if you're careless."

"Ouch. Well, either way, we have to celebrate!"

Tikvah didn't respond.

"Tikvah? Is everything okay?"

"Zar, we have to talk," Tikvah said, suddenly sounding melancholy.

"Tikvah, I'm sorry that I didn't realize that it was the anniversary of the first time we met. I'm just stupid. You just said you can't blame me for being stupid. I'm sorry, Tikvah. Please don't take it the wrong way. We've been together for a whole year—that's a reason to celebrate, right?"

"Celebrate, or maybe tear my hair out. I'm not sure."

"What do you mean? Did I say something or do something wrong? If I did, please tell me. I apologize sincerely—"

"It's not something you said or did. It's something you *haven't* said and *haven't* done. Zar, we've been dating for a year already."

"So what's wrong?"

"Zar, other than that first handshake of ours, and the time I fell asleep on your shoulder on the bus from Ashkelon, and the day we hugged after the terror attack at the *Tayelet,* and the occasional accidental bump, *you never touch me.* A woman needs to be touched. This woman does, at least! I need to feel affection, not just words, but physical contact, embracing..."

"But you know the rules about unmarried men and women touching. In the world I grew up in, a couple would never date for this long. They'd meet a few times, and if it seemed like a good match, they'd announce the engagement, then get married maybe a month or two later."

"And in the world I grew up in, no one gets married that quickly. If a guy and a girl are attracted to each other, they hook up. There isn't this constant tension. In our relationship, we have the worst of both worlds! We have all the restrictions of your world, but we seem to be in no rush to get married. It isn't normal. Sometimes I feel like I'm going to explode!"

"Tikvah, I feel the same way. I'm burning up inside. I dream about you every night and daydream about you every day. Sometimes I'm so distracted that people think I'm in outer space or something. But what can we do? I still have almost two years of army service left, but I can't imagine life without you. Can we hold off until my army service is over?"

"Why do we have to wait? Don't people in the army get married?"

"I don't know. I suppose so. But I live on the base. We would be separated most of the time. That doesn't sound like a normal married life."

"Well, our relationship now isn't exactly normal either! Listen, Zar, I can't go on this way. I can't…" There was a long lull in the conversation as Zar, not knowing what to say, listened to Tikvah weeping. Finally, she regained her composure and broke the silence. "Zar, I think we need to take a break from each other. We need time to think about this relationship."

"Tikvah, I think you're being a little too extreme—"

"I've thought about this a lot. I think this is the right thing for us to do now. Goodbye, Zar." And before Zar had a chance to respond, she had already hung up the phone.

Zar was in a state of shock and disbelief. He had been completely unprepared for Tikvah's outburst, but now he could see that he'd been complacent, that he'd taken their relationship for granted. Tikvah had given him signals of her frustrations over the past few months, but Zar had paid no attention. And he loved Tikvah. He loved her wit and her intelligence. He loved her dimples and her smile and her kind eyes. Without her, he felt alone and incomplete. Zar cried as he put his phone down, and he continued crying until he had cried himself to sleep.

For the next few days, Zar was listless. He declined numerous offers from Egel to play soccer and he hardly spoke at meals. Finally, Egel pressed Zar to reveal the cause of his melancholy. Egel listened, then reassured him that he would get over her eventually, that there would be other girls just as pretty and personable as Tikvah. But Zar was not consoled. He missed her terribly.

Later, he talked it over with Yoli, who suggested that Zar call Tikvah and attempt to patch up their relationship, and Zar resolved to do it. It took some time for him to muster up the courage, but after closing his eyes and taking some deep breaths, he managed to press the "call" button on his phone. He waited anxiously as it rang. When Tikvah didn't answer his call, he was discouraged—but also a little bit relieved. He waited a few minutes, then tried again. This time, Tikvah picked up.

"Hi," she said.

"Hi," said Zar, and then there was only the sound of Tikvah breathing, wordlessly. Zar felt uncomfortable enough making the call, and with this cold reception, Tikvah wasn't making it any easier for him.

"Tikvah, I called to apologize. I realize now that I've taken you for granted for the past year or so. I love you so much. I miss you so much. Tikvah, I can't go on without you. I didn't realize how much I loved you until you hung up on me the other day."

Tikvah finally broke her silence: "Zar. I love you too. Like crazy. If you hadn't called me I would have called you sooner or later. I guess we have no choice but to wait until you complete your army service. I just need some sort of commitment; if I knew for sure that we'd get married in two years, at least I'd have something specific to look forward to."

"You have my commitment, Tikvah. God willing, we'll get married as soon as I'm done with the army."

"Thank you. I just needed to hear you say that. I'm still going crazy inside, but at least there's a light at the end of the tunnel."

There was another lull in the conversation; Tikvah again broke the silence. "Zar, my army service is almost over. There's no special graduation ceremony or anything, but a few women in my unit and I have been together pretty much the whole time, and we're all finishing our service at the same time, so we're organizing something. Some of the women are friendly with some women at an intelligence base in Netanya who are also finishing their service, so they decided to pool resources and have a joint graduation ceremony. I wanted to let you know in advance because it would mean a lot to me if you came."

"Of course I'll be there. I wouldn't miss it for anything in the world!"

"And one more thing—guess who else will be at the ceremony."

"I give up. Who?"

"My parents."

CHAPTER 57

The next day at breakfast, Zar told Egel about his conversation with Tikvah.

"I don't understand you religious guys. You're either crazy or you have incredible self control. So are you going to get her a ring?"

"What do you mean?"

"An engagement ring. Are you going to buy her a diamond ring and formally propose to her?"

"Do you think that's what she expects?"

"Do I *think*? Of course she does! You basically proposed to her already, but she needs to see something tangible. She needs a ring. You have to get her a ring and propose to her properly."

"Are you sure?"

"Listen, I may know next to nothing about Jewish religious law, but if there's one thing I know about, it's women. Trust me on this one. You have to go out and buy her a ring. And then one day—or better yet, one night; nighttime is much more romantic—give her the ring and propose to her."

Zar remained in the dining hall after Egel and most of the other soldiers had left. He needed to speak with Yoli. Zar found him in the kitchen, munching on a pickle.

"Rabbi! What's new?" Yoli greeted Zar in Yiddish.

"Yoli! I'm so glad I found you. I need some help. It's about Tikvah."

"You're asking *me* to give *you* advice about your relationship?"

"Yoli, I'm not looking for advice. Well, maybe I am, sort of. I want to marry Tikvah."

"*Mazal tov!* When's the wedding?"

"The wedding won't be for another two years or so, but I want to propose to her. And Egel said I need to buy her a ring."

"I think Egel is right. He knows a lot more about relationships than I do."

"Right. So I need to get a ring, a diamond ring, and I presume they can be pretty expensive…"

"Don't ask me to lend you money. I'm broke."

"I didn't expect you to lend me money. I was wondering if you knew where I could buy a ring, if you had any connections or anything."

"Actually, I do. You know I have practically no contact with my family in Brooklyn, but my Uncle Zalman—my great-uncle on my mother's side, really—owns a jewelry shop in Bnei Brak. I'm in touch with him from time to time. He's the nicest man on earth—he's like a giant teddy bear! And you're a friend of mine, so I think he'd give you a good deal."

On a Friday morning a few weeks later, Zar and Yoli took the 446 bus from Be'er Sheva to Kiryat Gat, then caught the 550 bus to Bnei Brak. It was the first time Zar had been there since he'd been kicked out of *yeshiva ketana* several years earlier. As they walked from the bus stop, they passed the vacant lot where Zar had broken the school rules and played soccer.

Uncle Zalman's jewelry shop was no bigger than a single-car garage. In fact, his shop, along with all of the others in the narrow alleyway, *was* a garage that had been rented out for commercial use. Uncle Zalman was a jovial, corpulent man, with a bushy salt-and-pepper beard mostly concealing his ruddy face. His large body took up almost a quarter of the tiny shop, leaving little room for a few glass display cases, a safe, and a cash register. His customers had to stand outside. He greeted Yoli warmly, speaking in a familiar Hungarian dialect of Yiddish with a friendly singsong intonation. Uncle Zalman was eager to close up his shop after a long week, so they quickly got down to business. He asked what kind of price range Zar had in mind, then opened up a display case for him, but even the least expensive of the rings was beyond Zar's budget. Uncle Zalman saw the look of despair in Zar's eyes and was overwhelmed by empathy. He selected the least expensive ring, a thin white gold band simply set with a small diamond, and handed it to Zar for his inspection.

"Any friend of Yoily is a friend of mine. I'll tell you what—I'll sell it to you at cost, wholesale. I won't make even one shekel on the deal! Just do me a favor and don't tell anyone how much you paid. If I keep making transactions like this, I'll go out of business!"

Zar was overwhelmed by Uncle Zalman's kindness and generosity. "I don't know what to say. Thank you so much! You are a saint. May you live till a hundred and twenty years and perform many more good deeds."

"*Mazal tov*...and have a good *Shabbos!*" Uncle Zalman called out to them as the two young soldiers left his shop.

"Your uncle is a good man, Yoli. I can't thank you enough for bringing me to him," Zar said.

"I knew he'd give you a good deal, but that was really extraordinary. You know, I think he may have had ulterior motives. In his eyes, we're two lost souls. I think he felt bad for us, and maybe he thought that by treating us with such kindness, he could restore some of our faith in Judaism, and our faith in God."

"Well, did it restore your faith?"

"Maybe, Zar. Maybe just a little bit."

CHAPTER 58

Tikvah's unit and the unit from Netanya decided to hold their graduation ceremony in Yarkon Park, a large public park in central Tel Aviv. Zar had arranged to meet up with Tikvah at the park. She was already in Tel Aviv; she'd left the night before to meet her parents, who had flown in from the United States.

The ceremony started promptly at 4 pm, but Zar's bus was delayed in traffic, so he arrived a few minutes late. Zar was easy to spot—he was the only male soldier in attendance with a yarmulke and beard—and Tikvah's parents easily picked him out of the crowd. Zar recognized them at once too. Her mother had the same dimples and sweet smile and kind eyes, and her father had the same thick brown hair as Tikvah did, although his had thinned out considerably.

The ceremony itself was pretty boring. Several senior officers spoke, and one graduate from the Netanya base received special recognition as an outstanding soldier. After the ceremony was over, all the graduates cut up their ID badges as a sign of liberation from army service. There was a reception with light refreshments and musical accompaniment from a vocalist-guitarist. The crowd mingled and took lots of photos. Zar hung back for a few moments to allow Tikvah's parents to approach her first and embrace her. Tikvah greeted Zar warmly, but without embracing him, and introduced him to her parents. Zar shook hands with her father. Tikvah's mother, who had been notified in advance that Zar would prefer not to shake hands with a woman, greeted Zar somewhat cautiously, and the two of them awkwardly bowed slightly to one another, as if they were Japanese. Fortunately, the uncomfortable meeting was interrupted by several of Tikvah's friends from her unit.

They lingered at the reception for another half hour, then Tikvah's father suggested that they go out for dinner. Tikvah had anticipated this, and had already picked out an Italian dairy restaurant with an acceptable kosher certification. The restaurant was near the Jaffa port, only a few miles from the park, and Tikvah's parents drove them there in their rental car. The restaurant wasn't fancy, but it was clean and had a warm ambiance. Conversation was forced at first, largely due to the language barrier. Zar spoke only rudimentary English and Tikvah's parents didn't speak any Hebrew, so Tikvah translated when necessary and the conversation flowed more smoothly. Tikvah's father was perfectly affable. He was a genuinely friendly man who clearly adored his daughter; Zar understood why Tikvah was so fond of him. Her mother, on the other hand, looked at Zar with only measured friendliness. Her half-smile broadcasted her inner deliberation. She was happy that Tikvah had found a nice Jewish boy, but she secretly wished that he wasn't quite so Jewish. The food was served family-style, and they all shared the main dishes: lasagna, eggplant parmesan, and a tray of little pizzas on artisan bagels.

All the food was delicious, but Zar especially enjoyed the pizza bagels. "I love these!"

Tikvah's father laughed out loud. "I think I know why you like them so much."

"Why?" asked Zar, puzzled.

Tikvah smirked, quietly anticipating her father's response.

"When Hope was a little girl, do you know what I used to call her?"

"No, what?"

"Well, she's half Jewish and half Italian, so I used to call her my little pizza bagel!"

CHAPTER 59

After the meal, Tikvah's parents invited Zar and Tikvah to join them on a guided tour of the old Jaffa port. They declined, citing Zar's limited English. It was a lame excuse, but no one challenged it; Zar and Tikvah wanted to spend some time together without her parents, and Tikvah's parents, likewise, needed a respite to analyze their meeting with their daughter and her boyfriend.

Tikvah and Zar said goodnight to her parents, then walked a short distance to the shore. The Tel Aviv beach was surprisingly busy despite the late hour. A small group of young men and women were drinking beer and listening to music. A large family was having a barbecue; the children dug in the sand and built sand castles while the meat was grilling. Some teenagers were playing a friendly game of volleyball. Old men were seated at tables playing *shesh-besh*, a Middle Eastern variant of backgammon. And there were many other young couples walking along the boardwalk or sitting on blankets. Most of the couples were holding hands; some of them were being more intimate.

Zar and Tikvah sat down on the sand, facing the water. Gentle waves lapped up on the shore, and a cool ocean wind caressed them. They had much to discuss.

"I was really impressed with your father. He has such charisma!"

"Yeah, always the entertainer. You're not going to believe this, but for a few years when I was in middle school, he was the president of our temple."

"I can believe it. I would've voted for him too. But I'm not sure how to read your mother. It seemed like she was suspicious of me."

"I think you're right; she isn't sure what to make of you. In fact, I'm not sure she knows what to make of *herself*. I don't think she ever really got over her fractious relationship with Bubby." Tikvah paused to contemplate. "I think she's proud of me for connecting so much with Judaism and with Israel, but she's also scared that maybe I'm going too far with it. But at the end of the day, she just wants me to be happy...and she knows that when I'm with you, I'm on top of the world."

Hearing this, Zar seized the opportunity he'd been waiting for. He took the ring out of his pocket and looked at Tikvah silently. Tikvah saw the box and instinctively put both hands over her open mouth. Her soft brown eyes welled up with tears as she waited for Zar to say the words she'd conjured up in her dreams, in one form or another, a million times over the past year.

Zar had prepared a short speech; every word was measured. "Tikvah, one year ago, God sent me a gift from Los Angeles, the city of angels. He sent me my own angel, an angel of hope. Before I met you, Tikvah, I had no direction, no focus. I had soccer, but that was it. I felt lost and alone and hopeless. As the verse in Genesis says, 'Therefore man will leave his father and mother and cling to his wife and become like one flesh.' Tikvah, words can't possibly describe how much I love you. I'll paraphrase from the Sabbath morning prayers: if my mouth was filled with song like the sea, or my tongue filled with rejoicing like the deep waves...I couldn't possibly thank you enough. Tikvah, there's no limit to the words I need to express my love for you, so I have nothing further to say, except...will you marry me?"

Tikvah was crying tears of joy, tears of bliss. She, too, had no more words to say, save one. Holding back her tears for just long enough to catch her breath, she uttered the one word she'd been waiting to say for the past year: "Yes!"

CHAPTER 60

One Sunday, after a weekend on leave from the base, Zar went to a small synagogue near the central bus station for the morning prayers. This synagogue hosted an eclectic mix of Jews from across the religious spectrum, and it was always crowded—especially at the morning services, when people would stop there on their way to work or school. And on Sunday mornings, when soldiers would stop there to pray before traveling back to their bases, the synagogue was particularly crowded. For Zar, this synagogue was a refuge of sorts. The diversity of the people who congregated there meant that Zar didn't stand out. He even felt comfortable wearing his uniform there.

The synagogue, like many others in Jerusalem, also attracted a steady stream of charity collectors. Some were collecting for widows, orphans, or various charity organizations, but most were collecting for themselves. These beggars came mostly from the Hasidic and other ultra-Orthodox neighborhoods to the east and north, including Mea She'arim. They wore black caftans, sometimes with white pinstripes, and black hats of various shapes and sizes, indicating their respective sects. They would weave their way through the cramped synagogue during the prayer service, rhythmically rattling the loose change in their hands, like heartbeats pumping their lifeblood.

Most days, Zar didn't look up to see their faces. To him, they were faceless, with nearly identical black-garbed bodies. Zar was annoyed by them; they disrupted the service and distracted him during his prayers. In his estimation, they were, for the most part, able-bodied but lazy men who ought to be seeking gainful employment instead of exploiting the industriousness of others. And they reminded him of himself—or rather, of his former life.

194

Toward the end of the service, Zar glanced at one of the charity collectors, who turned to face him. Their eyes met, and Zar instantly recognized the beggar: it was Pinchas, the guy who had incited the mob that nearly lynched the soldier years ago. They were both older, and both had beards now, but Zar saw the fire in his eyes and knew that it was Pinchas. And he could tell from the expression on Pinchas's face that he recognized him too. A myriad of thoughts flooded Zar's mind. Would Pinchas start screaming *"Goy! Shaygetz!"* at him? Would he stir up a mob to lynch him? Certainly not; there were other soldiers in the room who would come to Zar's aid. And besides, he thought, this synagogue was a melting pot, a place where the unofficial policy was "live and let live." He also wondered why Pinchas was begging for loose change. He was a natural leader. Surely he could have been successful in business or in some profession. Was it his lack of secular education that held him back? Was he embarrassed to be a beggar?

Zar contemplated the situation further. Should he give charity to Pinchas despite the animosity that Zar still harbored against him? Would giving him charity be rewarding him for his apparent laziness, thereby cultivating a culture of dependency? But could Zar really blame Pinchas, who had no formal secular education, for his lack of industriousness? And Pinchas clearly needed the money, whatever the origins of his poverty. Zar reached into his pocket, retrieved a one-shekel coin, and put it in Pinchas's extended hand. "Be well," Zar whispered in Yiddish.

"Thank you. You should also be well," Pinchas replied, putting the coin in his pocket and moving on to the next row of pews to collect some more charity.

CHAPTER 61

Zar and Egel became very close during their army service. Although there were some very obvious differences between them—most notably, Zar was religious and Egel was not—there were also some striking similarities. They were both the great-grandchildren of Holocaust survivors who, coincidentally, had both been imprisoned at Dachau, although not concurrently (still, they had a macabre little joke that their great-grandfathers had probably played together on the Dachau soccer team). And more than anything else, of course, what Zar and Egel shared was a passion for soccer.

The soldiers were faithful to the unit commander and were rewarded, as promised, with soccer, soccer, and more soccer. Zar and Egel quickly established themselves as an unstoppable force. The more they played together, the more they learned each other's habits. Without even looking at each other, they would know where on the field the other was at any given time. They passed the ball back and forth fluidly, as if they were two legs on one body. When they played on opposing teams, other players would watch in wonderment as these two superstars battled each other. The unit commander loved Zar and Egel; he convinced his superior officer to keep these two young soldiers together in one unit, and to keep them out of harm's way. For two years, as other members of the 101st infantry were sent into combat or moved to other infantry units, Zar and Egel remained together in the 101st, and guard duty on the base was the only action they ever saw off the soccer field.

No one was surprised when the 101st infantry unit won the armed forces soccer championship, beating an Air Force team. Scouts from all of the Israeli teams and several European clubs showed up at these championship games, and Zar and Egel were offered attractive contracts, but one thing was made clear: they were a package deal. Midway through their final year of army service, they signed contracts to play for Beitar Jerusalem.

CHAPTER 62

Zar and Egel were on top of the world. They had less than six months of army service left, and they were all but guaranteed to be kept out of harm's way. When they weren't on guard duty, they had ample time to play soccer. Zar was engaged to marry Tikvah, who was now a psychology student at Hebrew University and lived in an apartment in Jerusalem not far from Zar's lone soldier apartment, and Egel had no shortage of girlfriends. Life was good. They anxiously awaited their day of discharge so they could start playing for Beitar Jerusalem.

One Sunday morning, returning to the base after a weekend off, they were summoned to the office of the unit commander, where a secretary greeted them and escorted them inside. Seated in the office was the unit commander, and next to him was a man in civilian clothing. Zar and Egel saluted at attention and were ordered to be at ease. The commanding officer introduced them to his guest, although he needed no introduction; Avi Saban was a local celebrity. He had been one of the best soccer players ever to play in Israel. He'd retired almost a decade ago, and had subsequently coached Maccabi Tel Aviv to three consecutive championships. The two young soldiers shook hands with Mr. Saban, who insisted that they call him by his first name. Egel told Avi that they'd met years ago at a youth soccer tournament, and added that the soccer jersey Avi had autographed was still proudly displayed in his bedroom at home on the kibbutz.

After a few more moments of small talk, Avi cleared his throat and revealed the purpose of his visit. "I've decided," he said, "to step down as the coach of Maccabi Tel Aviv."

"Wow! I'm guessing you got a lucrative offer from another soccer club," said Egel. "But why did you come here to make this announcement? And what does it have to do with Zar and me? I'm sure you know that we've already signed contracts to play for Beitar Jerusalem."

Avi didn't speak for a moment, and the others in the cramped office waited silently for his reply. "Yes, I did accept another offer, although it isn't more lucrative—it pays less, actually, than Maccabi. It's more of a career move, something I've always dreamed of."

"I don't get it," said Egel. "What team will you be coaching? What could be more prominent than Maccabi Tel Aviv?"

"Allow me to explain. Israel competes in the World Cup, you know—"

"Yes, of course. They even tied a game in the qualifying round in the last tournament," Egel said.

"True, true. But on the whole, Israel's performance has been—how should I say–less than stellar."

"Embarrassing, I'd say," the commanding officer chimed in.

"I'd have to agree with that," Avi said. "No Israeli team has ever won a game in the World Cup. Not a single game!" he said, banging his fist on the desk for emphasis. "Now, as you certainly know, we have a few terrific young players on Maccabi Tel Aviv."

"Of course! Weisman and Mizrachi are having an awesome year," Egel said.

"Yes, they are. Terrific! As good as the elite players in Europe and South America," Avi continued. "And you've heard of Hajji Al-Salem, I assume?"

"Who hasn't?" said Zar, who until now hadn't uttered a word. "He's the goalkeeper for Hapoel Haifa, and he's the best goalkeeper in the Premier League by far. He's got a save percentage of 82% this year. In fact, he has better statistics than any goalkeeper in any professional league in the world. I heard that an Egyptian club made him an offer, but he refused because it wasn't lucrative enough."

"You're right," Avi said. "Well, partially right, anyway. He *is* the best goalkeeper in the Premier League here in Israel, and he *is*, arguably, the best goalkeeper in the world. And he *was* offered a deal—a very good deal, in fact—by an Egyptian club. And he declined the offer...but not because it wasn't lucrative enough. I have some insider information about the whole matter, and I can't say much more about it, but suffice it to say that he had personal reasons for staying here in Israel and playing for Hapoel Haifa."

Avi paused for emphasis, then continued. "A few men from the Israel Football Association approached me recently. They showed me a video of the two of you playing in the championship match against the Air Force team. You two have talent. A lot of talent. I think the two of you, plus Weisman and Mizrachi and Al-Salem, and a handful of other great Israeli players around the league and in other leagues, would make a great team, a really great team, to represent Israel in the World Cup this year, in Germany. I was asked to coach the team; I've already accepted the offer, actually. And all the players we've spoken about today have agreed to join the team. I'm here today to recruit the two of you. We— the Israel Football Association and myself—want you two to join the Israel National Team. I've already spoken with Beitar Jerusalem, and they've given their approval. So, what are your thoughts?"

Egel and Zar looked at each other and, without saying a word, knew how to respond. Tears welled up in Zar's eyes as he said, "This is a dream come true. Literally, a dream come true. I've been dreaming about this, about playing for Israel in the World Cup, my whole life!"

"And what about you?" Avi asked Egel.

"Nothing in the world would give me more pride," he answered.

"Thank you, Egel, and thank you, Zar," Avi said.

"No, thank *you*!" the two young soldiers replied in unison, as if on cue. Avi laughed, and soon Egel, Zar, the unit commander, and the secretary—who had been eavesdropping all along—were laughing too. The commander rose and, out of respect, so did Zar and Egel. Avi stood up and shook hands with Egel and Zar. "I think we have a really great team," he exclaimed. "I'm very excited for you—for us!"

"But there's one problem," Zar said nervously. "We're still on active duty. We don't get discharged for another six months."

"I'm sure we can find a way to get around that," Avi reassured him. "Isn't that so, Officer?"

"There are many ways to serve our country," the commander agreed, a wide grin on his face. "Some shoot bullets at the enemy. Others shoot balls into goals." (In Hebrew, the same word means both "bullets" and "balls.")

"But in our absence, who will do guard duty on the base?" Zar quipped.

"Oh, I think we can find some other soldiers to fill your shoes here," said the commander, and everyone laughed again.

PART FIVE

CHAPTER 63

Zar and Egel were granted a sanctioned leave from active service. While playing soccer for the Israeli national team, they would still be enlisted soldiers—still serving their country, but in different uniforms. They packed their bags, said goodbye to their fellow soldiers, left the base, and boarded a bus to Haifa, where the Israeli national team practiced. They were greeted by Avi Saban, then met their new teammates. Zar and Egel immediately recognized every player on the team; each was a star in his own right. Mostly, they came from various teams in the Israeli league, plus several from the European leagues and one from South America. Zar and Egel were also already celebrities of sorts in Israel; a video of their victory over the Air Force team had gone viral on YouTube and was aired on all the major TV stations, earning them a cover story in a popular magazine.

All the other players were excellent. At first, it wasn't clear whether Zar and Egel would be starters or benchwarmers. After several practice sessions, though, it became evident that, as strikers, the two of them together made a dangerous pair, and they were assigned as starters.

Practice matches were arranged with several Israeli teams, many of them now playing without their best players, who now opposed them on the field. The national team easily won all these games, and practice matches were arranged with some European and South American teams.

Pressure from anti-Israel protesters forced the Argentine team to cancel its visit to Israel. A suggestion to fly in the Israeli team to play in Argentina was met with massive demonstrations. Hundreds of angry protesters converged on the Israeli embassy in Buenos Aires, waving

Palestinian flags and burning Israeli flags. Police were outnumbered and overwhelmed, and riot police were called in to create a barrier between the embassy and the angry mob. The situation spiraled out of control as more rioters joined the mob, and the riot grew progressively more violent. Molotov cocktails were hurled at the police and at the embassy. Police responded first with tear gas, water cannons, and rubber bullets, then with live fire. Armed rioters shot back at the police, wounding two officers; several also broke through the police line and threw firebombs through the smashed windows of the embassy. When the army arrived with armored vehicles, the situation was finally brought under control. The aftermath: eight riot police injured, two of them seriously, scores of rioters injured, one dead, and hundreds of protesters arrested. The southern half of the embassy was destroyed; the Israeli ambassador and his family and staff had to be evacuated. Needless to say, the friendly match between the two national teams was canceled.

After intense backroom negotiations, the match was rescheduled. It would be held at an undisclosed time and in an undisclosed location, but by the time the two teams played their match in Athens several weeks later, details of the planned match had leaked out. Dozens of protesters came to the match waving Palestinian flags, and on several occasions, they ran onto the field with banners and signs that read "Free Gaza" and "Zionism = Nazism." The organizers hadn't anticipated further protests, so they weren't adequately prepared for the disturbances. Police had to escort the Israeli team out of the stadium in the middle of the game, and the match ended after only thirty minutes of play, with the score tied 0–0.

The team learned two things from their practice games and from the fiasco with Argentina. First, the Israeli team was excellent; they could compete with any team in the world. Second, they had a lot of enemies, and could anticipate threats, violence, and even bloodshed. That would be the price to pay for representing the Jewish state.

CHAPTER 64

When the Israeli team arrived at Ben Gurion Airport for their flight to Germany, they were met with a warm reception: hundreds of adoring fans waving Israeli flags and signs attesting their love for the team. A much smaller group of Israeli fans greeted them at the airport in Berlin, and they were drowned out by a large, angry crowd that had also gathered there. An ample police presence ensured that, despite lots of yelling and cursing, there were no injuries, but in the confusion, some of the team's bags were trampled. The only major damage incurred was to Egel's guitar, which sustained a crack in its neck. "Welcome to Germany!" one of his teammates commented sarcastically.

The team bus, a Mercedes-Benz Travego, was to have been painted blue and white to match the national flag and the team colors, just as every other team bus was painted to proudly display the colors of the team it transported. After the chaos in Argentina and Greece, however, the Israeli team was advised to travel in a nondescript bus. And while other teams decorated their hotels with flags, and their hotels became meccas for their faithful, the Israeli team's hotel was kept secret, although the armed guards and heavy police presence for a block perimeter around the hotel soon revealed its location. The team's hotel then became a mecca for a different kind of faithful: those committed to denouncing and delegitimizing Israel, and intimidating anyone who felt otherwise.

There are three preliminary World Cup matches. A team doesn't have to win all three games to qualify for the tournament, but only the sixteen best teams proceed to the actual tournament. In that tournament, only the winners progress to the next round; the losers are eliminated.

Israel's first preliminary game was played in Hamburg against Croatia. The game was tense and low-scoring. Egel scored the only goal, leading Israel to victory. The Israeli newspapers the next day beamed with pride. *Yisrael Hayom*, one of the dailies, ran a headline that covered nearly the entire front page: *Egel Hazahav!*—"The Golden *Egel* (calf)," playfully recalling the idolatrous golden calf worshipped by the ancient Israelites in the Sinai Desert.

The game against Croatia was low-scoring, but it wasn't lacking in action. The action, however, was more off the field than on it: there were the now-usual protests outside the stadium, and fights broke out in the stands throughout the match. The Israeli and Croatian fans had been seated in separate sections, but the Croatian fans weren't the ones fighting with the Israelis; it was mostly Arab and North African fans who were involved in the fights, and who threw bottles at the Israeli fans and at the players on the field.

After that game, new regulations were put into place: No bottles— even nonalcoholic, even plastic—could be brought into the stadium; vendors would sell drinks only in cups, not bottles. Fans rooting for Israel had to notify security at least twenty-four hours before the game. Israeli fans were asked not to wear team colors or to bring flags or other patriotic paraphernalia. They would be separated from the rest of the spectators and surrounded by riot police at every game.

Almost a century after the Nazi party's rise to power, Jews in Germany were again being selected and segregated.

CHAPTER 65

A kinship of sorts had developed between Zar and Hajji. They had a lot in common: They were both religious, both keeping strict dietary laws; Zar kept kosher and Hajji ate only halal. Both prayed a lot; Zar prayed three times a day and Hajji five times. And both Zar and Hajji had, on some level, rejected their own communities and been rejected by them. Hajji had something of a love-hate relationship with his hometown. Many there resented him, even hated him, for his participation with—and de facto legitimization of—the Zionists. But many others respected him and were proud of him for his athletic prowess, his discipline, and his sophistication. Among the youth, there was no equivocation: he was imitated and idolized by hundreds of Israeli children—Jews and Arabs, Christians and Muslims. Even in the Palestinian territories, it was not uncommon to see a young boy wearing a soccer jersey with "Al-Salem" printed on the back.

Zar and Hajji also both avoided bars and discos. Zar avoided them because, as he'd been taught since childhood, they were *traif*. And even though his definition of *traif* had evolved considerably since he left Mea She'arim, bars and discos were still out of his comfort zone. Hajji, of course, avoided bars because, as a religious Muslim, he abstained from alcohol.

The night after the victory against Croatia, some of their teammates decided to celebrate at a bar down the block from their hotel. Neither Zar nor Hajji went with them. Six players, including Egel, went to the bar. It was an upscale establishment in an affluent neighborhood, so the players elected to go without security guards. They wanted to remain anonymous, and they thought a security detail would only draw attention. Within a few minutes, some Israeli tourists spotted them and approached, asking first for autographs, then for selfies. Word of their presence spread throughout the bar, and soon they were the center of attention, most of it good: more autographs, more selfies, some free drinks, and a general atmosphere of camaraderie.

At some point, three young German thugs, drunk, heavily tattooed, with shaven heads, entered the bar. They quickly gravitated to where the action was and learned the identity of these celebrities. "*Heil Hitler!*" one of them said, giving a Nazi salute. No one at the bar had any interest in an altercation, and the players ignored the taunt from the skinhead, as did everyone else. Meanwhile, one of the bartenders called the police as a precaution. "*Heil Hitler! Verdammte Juden!*" The skinhead yelled, again saluting and now goose-stepping toward Egel and his teammates. The other two skinheads drank their beers and laughed, but Egel, for one, didn't think it was funny. His brave great-grandfather had almost been killed in Dachau, but he'd been stubborn and stiff-necked, and he'd survived—he'd moved to Palestine under the British Mandate, and he'd helped build the country and defend it. Egel, himself a bit intoxicated, felt rage consuming him as he watched the skinhead. He stood up to confront him, and the skinhead responded by pulling out a knife and lunging at Egel. Egel deflected the skinhead's outstretched arm, but still got slashed across the back of his neck. Just then, several police officers rushed into the bar, tackling the knife-wielding assailant and restraining his two accomplices. The woman tending bar—Egel had been flirting with her just minutes ago—applied a makeshift bandage to Egel's neck, which was bleeding profusely. A few minutes later, an ambulance arrived. Egel was taken to the emergency room, where he got eight stitches and a tetanus shot.

CHAPTER 66

The next day, the Israel National Team played a game in Berlin against Germany, their host team and reigning World Cup champions. The Germans had been heavily favored even before Egel's injury. The match was a blowout; Germany won 6–0. Egel's injury kept him on the bench, and as for the rest of the team, the events of the previous night and the incessant taunts and curses of the spectators sank their morale. The score would have been even more lopsided had it not been for the extraordinary efforts of Hajji, who played valiantly despite the persistent onslaught of the star-studded German offense and the non-stop barbs directed at him from the stands.

Outside the Olympiastadion, another riot was underway. As they left the stadium after the game, the Israel National Team watched helplessly from a distance as stones were hurled at their bus. Through shattered glass, they spied violent protesters burning Israeli and American flags. The crowd was also burning an effigy of an Israeli soldier. Such revelry was now commonplace, and it no longer unsettled the players. Zar, however, noticed that the mock-soldier being tossed into the flames had a yarmulke, a beard, and sidelocks. The rioters were burning an effigy of Zar. For the first time since his arrival in Germany, Zar felt personally threatened. He watched with horror as his likeness was consumed by the blaze. Then he vomited.

The loss to Germany and the incidents before and after the game were a wakeup call to the Israeli team. They'd had such high hopes coming in, and now they were in serious jeopardy. For Israel to qualify, they'd have to win the next match, and several of the best teams would have to lose their next matches. Egel was instructed—doctor's orders—to sit out the next game as well, and without him, their chances of beating any good team were slim to none.

Two days later, they were scheduled to play in Stuttgart against Iran. Historically, in any international competition, from chess to table tennis, Iran would forfeit the match so as not to acknowledge Israel. In this case, however, Iran was almost guaranteed to win. With Egel sidelined by an injury, the Israel National Team was at a significant disadvantage. The Iranian coach and the team captain indicated to German media outlets that, to defeat the Zionists and possibly advance to the World Cup, they intended to play the game.

When these developments were reported in Iran, there was public outrage. Conservative hardliners in the government threatened jail time or worse if the Iranian team played the Israelis. Amid death threats to coaches and players, Iran forfeited the match, which was fortunate for Israel. Germany, France, and Brazil, three top teams, lost their next matches, so without even setting foot on the field, Israel advanced to the World Cup. They were the lowest-ranked team in the competition; statistically, it was unlikely that they'd win any matches, let alone the championship. But they'd made it to the World Cup—and that in and of itself was an accomplishment worth celebrating.

The night after their "victory" over the Iranians, the team held a small celebration in the hotel. Other than the players and coaches, no one was invited. A single bottle of champagne was served. Hajji declined the champagne and drank Coca-Cola instead. The mood was one of relief and cautious optimism.

During their small party, a security guard announced an unexpected and uninvited guest. He needed no introduction; everyone immediately recognized the Iranian team captain. He nonetheless introduced himself, explaining, in fluent English, the purpose of his surprise visit. "I want you to know that I didn't want to forfeit the game. Most of the team, players and coaches, wanted to play, and I'm confident that we would've won. Unfortunately, in my country, one can't always do as he likes. I was born after the revolution, so I know only the Iran of today, run by fanatics. But I was educated by my parents to respect all people. My parents remember life in Iran before the revolution, and they often tell me about their friends and business partners who were Jews. My father has a lot of warm feelings toward his Jewish friends, and he passed down those warm feelings to his children. So I came here tonight and risked my reputation, maybe even my life, to apologize for my team's cowardice and wish you the best of luck in the World Cup. Your chances are slim at best, but I'll be secretly rooting for you. *Shalom!*" He shook hands with the players and left.

CHAPTER 67

The players regularly checked their phones to follow the news from back home. Mostly, they kept up with sports news and popular culture; the players weren't much interested in politics, and there was an unwritten rule among them that discussion of politics was to be avoided. The players ran the gamut of political and religious affiliations, and they understood that talking politics would only cause friction within the group. But major political news is hard to avoid, so when the players checked their phones the next morning, they all learned about an incident that had occurred a few hours earlier at an Israeli army checkpoint in the southeastern Galilee.

A fifteen-year-old Palestinian boy came to the checkpoint on foot. As he approached the guard booth, he pulled out a knife and lunged at one of the soldiers, stabbing him in the upper torso. The boy ran away, pursued by a different soldier, who shot the boy in the back. The boy ran a few more steps, then collapsed. The stabbed soldier, who had sustained only moderate injuries, was quickly stabilized by an army medic and evacuated to a nearby hospital. The boy was left unattended for several minutes until, finally, an ambulance crew from the Palestinian Red Crescent arrived. The IDF battalion commander allowed the Palestinian medics to work on the boy, but not to evacuate him; as an assailant, he was technically in army custody. An Israeli ambulance crew arrived a minute later and brought the boy to an Israeli hospital, where he was declared dead upon arrival.

The incident had been filmed by an Israeli human rights organization, and a video of the incident—minus the stabbing—quickly circulated throughout the internet. The boy was clearly unarmed during the shooting; his knife, lodged in the first soldier's torso, was not visible from the camera angle. He was hailed as a martyr, and his funeral later that day was attended by thousands. The boy's name was Abdel Al-Salem.

Hajji did not recognize Abdel, but he suspected that the boy, who shared his last name, was a distant cousin of his. The checkpoint where the boy was killed Hajji knew very well; he'd been there countless times. In fact, he had worked there loading and unloading trucks. He had befriended the soldiers at that checkpoint, and he had even fallen in love with one of them.

Hajji was conflicted. Part of him shared the rage of the Palestinians. The boy was only fifteen years old, he was shot in the back, and technically, he had been unarmed when he was shot. He was left unattended, bleeding, while the soldier he had stabbed received immediate medical attention. On the other hand, the boy wasn't exactly innocent. He had just stabbed a soldier with the intent to kill him. Wasn't it the duty of the soldiers to fight back with lethal force against anyone who attacked their comrade, regardless of the age of the assailant? Hajji overheard some of the other players on the team call the soldier who "neutralized the terrorist" a hero. Hajji wasn't sure how to respond.

The incident reflected something much bigger than the killing of this particular Palestinian boy by this particular Israeli soldier. It was emblematic of the occupation itself, of power and subordination, and it highlighted the colossal challenge of existing as a nation that must defend itself by subjugating another people.

It became a cause célèbre, sparking protests throughout the West Bank and Gaza. "We are all Abdel" became a rallying cry, and within a few days, protests erupted in cities throughout Europe and the United States in solidarity with the Palestinians.

CHAPTER 68

Their first game in the tournament was played in Leipzig against Argentina. Argentina was favored to win, but after the half-match they'd played against them a few months earlier in Athens, the Israelis knew what they were up against. Also, one of the Israelis had played with an Argentine club, giving him a deep understanding of the Argentine national team's style and strategies, their strengths and weaknesses. Mentally, too, the Israelis were more prepared for the unfriendly reception they anticipated at the stadium.

The team bus departed from the hotel several hours before the match. Police had barricaded the sidewalks outside the hotel, and an angry crowd had assembled. As soon as the bus left the underground parking garage, it was bombarded by a barrage of stones and garbage, cracking the windshield and shattering several side windows. The team had to duck for cover as the bus, escorted by police, left the hotel for the long drive to the Zentralstadion in Leipzig, where another angry mob, and more stones and garbage, awaited them.

Inside, the crowd was deafening. The small cadre of fans rooting for Israel was drowned out by the thousands of spectators booing and cursing the Israeli players and fans. But the Israel National Team stayed focused, and—thanks to skillful offense and an unforgettable performance by Hajji—they won 2–1.

The Israeli victory on the field was overshadowed, however, by their fans' defeat in the stands. Hundreds of angry spectators overpowered the police assigned to protect the Israeli fans. Several enraged young men broke through the police barricades, seizing one of the Israeli fans and throwing him over the railing onto the seats below. Badly injured, he was evacuated by ambulance and rushed to a nearby hospital. The entire section of Israeli fans had to be escorted out of the stadium, shielded by scores of police in riot gear. By the time the game was over, with the Israel National Team victorious, there were no fans there to cheer for them.

When the Israeli players left the field for their locker room, they also required police protection; garbage was thrown at them—including glass bottles, which had been smuggled into the stadium—and onto the field. The Israeli players showered and changed. Then, accompanied by around a dozen police officers, they were finally able to leave the stadium. As they approached the parking lot, they heard the cacophony of shouting men, followed by the sound of breaking glass. Stones, then Molotov cocktails, were heaved at their bus. They watched helplessly as the bus was engulfed in flames. The players and their police escorts ran from the burning bus, then heard a massive boom as the gas tank exploded. None of them were injured, but the inferno and the accompanying blast made them feel frightened and vulnerable. Firefighters arrived quickly to douse the flames, but the fear and panic that had been ignited within the players continued burning for a long time. They had to wait another hour before the police provided one of their own buses (with bars on its windows) to ferry the players, surrounded by guards, back to Berlin and back to their hotel, where they'd be protected…and imprisoned.

CHAPTER 69

"I'm looking into flights from Tel Aviv to Berlin," Tikvah told Zar on the phone that night. "I finished my exams, and now I'm looking forward to cheering you on in person from the stands."

"Tikvah, I don't think you should come to Berlin. You can watch and cheer me on from your apartment in Jerusalem."

"Why? I want to be there in person, where all the action is."

"I'm scared," Zar confessed.

"Why? I mean, you don't *have* to win. Even if our team loses, you're all winners in my book."

"Tikvah, I'm not worried about losing. I'm fearful for my life. And I'd fear for *your* life if you were here in the stadium. I couldn't possibly have imagined how much they hate us."

"Who's 'they'?"

"Everyone! Okay, not everyone, but *so many* people. A lot of them are Arabs or Muslims, but a lot of them are white Europeans. There's a group from Iceland that hangs out at the stadium and heckles us as our bus pulls in. *Iceland!* Why would people from Iceland care about Israel so much? And these crazy fans from England and Ireland come to every game and curse us constantly. Are there even any Israelis in Ireland? And the Germans hate us too. You already know that Egel was stabbed in the neck by a skinhead in a bar. Some Germans bring Nazi flags and other Nazi stuff to the games. They give Nazi salutes and scream '*Heil Hitler!*' at us during the games."

"Aren't there laws against that in Germany?"

"I don't know, maybe. But if there are, they obviously aren't enforced. I think the police just aren't able to handle the mobs, so they pick their battles. They let people get away with holding antisemitic signs and Nazi stuff so they can focus on the violence. People say that the Holocaust could never happen again, but based on what I've seen the past few weeks, it definitely could! Angry mobs come to the hotel and throw rocks at our windows. The police had to close off a perimeter of a few blocks around the hotel to protect us, to keep them away so we can sleep at night. Avi bought a whole case of white noise machines—you know, the kind you put by a baby's crib—to block out all the noise outside. How are we supposed to play if we can't even sleep at night? Our bus gets pelted with stones and bottles wherever we go. All the windows were smashed, so we had to get a new bus—and then the new bus was firebombed right in front of us! Now they got us a military bus with reinforced glass and metal cages to protect the glass. It feels like we're in prison! Why do they hate us so much?"

"Holy cow, that's crazy—really scary! I don't know why they hate us so much. Are there mobs attacking other teams too?"

"I think that incident at the checkpoint where the kid was shot really shook things up. There are always spectators cheering and booing at soccer matches; that's normal. But no other team has to endure anything even remotely close to the abuse we've been subjected to."

"Is it political? I mean, are there signs and slogans against Israel and in support of the Palestinians?"

"Yeah, tons of them. They wave Palestinian flags and burn Israeli flags. And they burn effigies of Israeli soldiers. I even saw them burning one with a beard and sidelocks. They were burning an effigy of *me!*"

"Oh my God! Is that even legal?"

"I don't know. Riot police are constantly arresting people. And there have been people killed. Sometimes the rioters shoot at the police and the police shoot back. And did you hear about the Israeli guy who was thrown from the stands? He's lucky to be alive!"

"You know what I think?" Tikvah asked. "All this anti-Israel stuff is really antisemitism *masquerading* as anti-Zionism. Seriously! If you think about it, you'll see that I'm right. Soon these protests will become *overtly* antisemitic."

"They already *are* openly antisemitic—the Germans, at least. My mother would say that antisemitism is just part of the culture, even if they tried to change that after the Holocaust. The Muslims are mostly just anti-Israel. You may be right, and if you are, that's even scarier. I miss you so much, but I think if you came here to watch the games, I'd be so worried about your safety that I'd be distracted. Really. I'll play better if I know you're in Israel, watching and cheering me on in a safe place."

"Okay, I'll stay home and cheer like crazy! Just pretend that you can hear me. And as hard as it may be, you just have to ignore the crowd. You have to go out there and play the best soccer you can. Play with sportsmanship and grace, and maybe people will come to realize that Zionism isn't the boogeyman our enemies make it out to be."

CHAPTER 70

Over the next week, the protests grew even more violent. Riots broke out daily outside their hotel and outside the stadium, regardless of which teams were playing. By order of the police and their own security detail, the Israeli players were now barred from leaving the hotel except for games, and even then, only in an armored bus escorted by German troops in armored personnel carriers. Spectators had to go through metal detectors and body searches, and they were instructed to arrive at the stadium two hours before game time so everyone could be thoroughly searched by security. The Israeli fans were advised to conceal their nationality at all times; when they arrived at the games, they were escorted to a closed-off section of the stadium.

The game in Hamburg against Nigeria was tense. For the first eighty-five minutes, a Nigerian goal on a penalty kick was the only point scored by either team. With time running out and Israel in real jeopardy of being eliminated, Zar drove toward the goal and passed to Egel. With a skillful snap of his neck, Egel headed the ball past the Nigerian goalkeeper to tie the game. They went into overtime, which ended after thirty minutes of exhausting play with the score still tied 1–1. A shootout followed; Zar scored one goal and Hajji stopped all five Nigerian attempts. After one of the longest and most grueling games in World Cup history, Israel once again emerged victorious.

Outside the stadium, a full-fledged riot was underway. Fires were burning and sacrifices were being offered on the altars of malice. In addition to the usual Israeli flags, American flags, and effigies of Israeli soldiers, now Jewish books and all things Jewish were being thrown into the blaze. A mob broke into a nearby synagogue, ransacked the building, and stole a Torah scroll, which was carried off like booty plundered in battle and ceremoniously thrown into the fire. The thin line between anti-Zionism and antisemitism, if ever such a line existed, had now been blurred beyond recognition.

All of the players and fans were stuck inside the stadium, prevented from leaving by the riot blazing outside. Police, backed by soldiers, battled the rioters for several hours. Only with the arrival of an armored corps with tanks and heavy ammunition was the riot finally quelled. Three rioters were killed. Scores of rioters, police, and soldiers were injured. Hundreds of perpetrators were arrested before the flames were finally extinguished. Only then could the players safely exit the arena and leave Hamburg.

CHAPTER 71

The players received mail regularly in their hotel rooms. All packages and envelopes were screened by security for threats, of which there were many. Some were deemed serious and credible, including numerous potential bombs and one package labeled as anthrax. On several occasions, the players had to be evacuated from the hotel, and once, the entire hotel had to be evacuated. They also received an abundance of hate mail. Initially, the players were given everything to read, but they soon complained that these hateful letters were demoralizing. Thankfully, there was also a deluge of fan mail. The players relished this outpouring of support from all over the world, which included everything from children's crayon drawings to blessings of success from the faithful of many religions. But more than anything else, the players cherished personal mail from friends and family.

Hajji received a lot of mail too. Some of it was fan mail from devotees in Israel, the Palestinian territories, and numerous Arab countries, but much of it was hate mail. He was viewed by many as a traitor who was legitimizing the Zionists' crimes by wearing their uniform. He received personal threats, threatening harm to him and to his family. One group tried, unsuccessfully, to sue him in court for defaming the Palestinian people. There was also a credible attempt to bribe him: a wealthy man from Qatar offered him a million dollars for each goal he gave up in a World Cup game. Hajji referred that correspondence to FIFA officials to investigate.

During the games, he was subjected to incessant taunts and insults from angry spectators. More than any other player on the team, Hajji bore the brunt of the verbal abuse. One common sign held up at games read "Hajji Al-Salem = Hajji Uncle Tom." Hajji didn't quite understand the reference, but he knew it was unflattering.

The never-ending taunts and abuse inevitably took their toll on Hajji, and his teammates witnessed his irritability and mood swings. Avi had anticipated that the World Cup would be stressful—although he could not have predicted how stressful it would ultimately be—and he had hired a psychologist from Tel Aviv University to provide counseling for the players. The psychologist began working with all of the players before the tournament began, and he continued working with them throughout the tournament. With the psychologist's help, Hajji was able to channel all his anger and hurt into better performance on the field; the more the spectators taunted him, the more focused and effective he became as a goalkeeper.

CHAPTER 72

One night, Zar and Hajji were alone at the hotel, and it was time for evening prayers. Zar turned to one wall, facing southeast, toward Jerusalem, and silently prayed. Hajji unrolled his prayer rug in a corner, also facing southeast, toward Mecca, and prostrated himself on the rug, supporting his lean upper body with his long muscular arms. When they were done, there was an awkward silence in the room, which Zar broke, asking, "Hajji, why do Muslims prostrate themselves when they pray?"

"It's our way of showing humility before Allah."

"That's interesting. That's why Jews wear a *kippah*, actually—to show humility before God. Do you think we're praying to the same God?"

"Well, there's only one God," Hajji responded. "That's one thing Muslims and Jews agree about. So yes, we're praying to the same God."

"I suppose you're right. It's just strange that we both pray to the same God, but my people and yours can't seem to agree on anything else. Actually, even among my own people, the Jewish people, we can't agree on much. How to dress, how to pray, how to view the army and the state of Israel—there's a lot of arguments among Jews."

"There's a lot of arguments among Muslims too," Hajji said. "Sunni, Shiite, progressive, traditional —and how we view Israel. There's not much unity within the Muslim world either." While he spoke, Hajji played with his blue *shalom, salaam* wristband.

"Hey, where did you get that wristband?" Zar asked. "I've seen lots of Jews, even soldiers, wearing them, but I don't remember ever seeing an Arab wearing one. I sort of just assumed that it was more of a Jewish thing."

"Someone very special gave it to me as a gift, a sort of peace offering. It means a lot to me."

"Sorry if I'm prying. You don't have to go on if it makes you uncomfortable."

"No, it's okay. I've been keeping these feelings bottled up for a long time. Maybe it's time for me to talk about it. It could be, you know, therapeutic for me."

Zar sat opposite him, listening with empathy.

"I grew up in a Muslim village near the Green Line, close to some Palestinian villages on the other side of the border, or what *might* be the border if the Israelis and Palestinians could ever make peace. There's a checkpoint on the road outside the village. Not much happens there. It's generally pretty quiet—not too many cars drive on that road in either direction. But there was always a small group of soldiers there, maybe three or four. As a kid, I used to hang out there. I know it sounds weird, but I kind of befriended the soldiers and became the unofficial truck loader and unloader for inspections. When I was around seventeen, they stationed this one soldier there, a woman—I thought she was the most beautiful woman I'd ever seen! I started flirting with her. I don't know what I was thinking. Did I really think she'd be interested in me, that we'd have a relationship? I suppose I *did* think that—or I dreamed about it, anyway. Her name was Adin. Surprisingly, she *did* flirt with me, and more than that, she really opened up to me. She told me very personal things about herself, not the kind of things that soldiers usually talk about. She was so vulnerable, but that only made me more interested in her. I fell in love with her. And I gave her a flower once, as a gift, so she took off this wristband and gave it to me. She said it would be my lucky charm, that it would make me a great goalkeeper."

"I guess it worked," observed Zar.

"I don't know if I can really give any credit to the wristband. Maybe it just gives me more confidence. But maybe that's how all good luck charms work."

"Did she love you too?"

"I don't know. I'll never know; she's dead."

"Oh my God! What happened?"

"She was killed during a riot at the checkpoint. Some kid, a Palestinian kid—it could've been one of my cousins—threw a stone and hit her in the head. I saw the whole thing happen. She bled so much! I had flashbacks and nightmares about it for a long time. She was rushed to the hospital, but they couldn't save her. I was really crushed. It's been years, and I sort of got over it, but I still think about her a lot. And the more I think about it, the more I realize that the wristband wasn't so much a gift she gave me because she liked me; it was more like a peace offering. That whole episode had a real impact on me. It's why I continue to play for an Israeli team despite all the outside pressure to quit. I don't know if I could call myself a Zionist, but I *can* say that I'll fight for this team with all of my strength. I feel like every ball that I block is that stone, the one that killed Adin, the one that I couldn't block."

"Thank you for sharing that with me. It sounds like she was a very special person; I'm sorry for your loss."

Zar fell silent, and no one spoke for a few minutes.

"You know, I have a good luck charm too. It was given to me by a beautiful young woman, also a soldier." Zar took the shoulder tag out from his sock and showed it to Hajji. "Mine's a long story too; I won't bore you with all the details. I had a tag like this when I was a little kid—a soldier gave it to me. In my mind, the ball in the middle was a soccer ball. I thought the soldier must be in some sort of soccer battalion." Zar and Hajji both laughed. "I lost that tag when I ran away from home. Then, when I met Tikvah for the first time, she was wearing the very same shoulder tag. That's one reason she caught my eye. One day, she took this tag off her uniform and gave it to me as a present. She told me it would be my good luck charm. I've never really thought about it, but it does give me more confidence. I think it really does improve my game."

CHAPTER 73

A gainst all odds, the Israel National Team had won their first two games and advanced to the semifinals. Their next opponent was an unexpected success story in its own right; Turkey was not known as a soccer superpower. This year's team, however, was exceptional. Their most famous player was not their highest scorer or their best defender. In Turkey, he was known simply as "the Wolf" because of his reputation for violent outbursts on and off the field. He had more fouls and more red cards (expulsions from soccer matches) than any other professional player. The Wolf was a flamboyant character. An accomplished martial artist, he'd won a bronze medal in taekwondo at the 2018 Summer Olympics, and he was ranked among the top ten fighters in mixed martial arts for his weight group. He did not lead the life of a devout Muslim, but was nonetheless enormously popular at home. He lived lavishly, he had numerous girlfriends, and he gambled excessively. In the lead-up to the game, the Wolf had been talking a lot of trash on social media and in the Turkish tabloids. "Prediction: Wolf Eats Lamb!" read one headline after he declared that he'd "eat" Egel on the field. (Of course, Egel's name meant "calf" in Hebrew, not "lamb," but to the Wolf's adoring fans, that was inconsequential.)

The match was played in Frankfurt. In preparation for the match, a ten-block radius was cordoned off to traffic, and hundreds of German police and soldiers were stationed around the stadium. Fans were advised to arrive three to four hours early to accommodate the extra security. The atmosphere outside of the stadium was chaotic and portentous. As hordes of spectators squabbled, bomb-sniffing dogs barked wildly at all the entrance gates.

The game was contentious even before it started; the Turkish team refused to stand for *Hatikva*, Israel's national anthem, but the crowd drowned out the anthem with chants and boos, so this act of disrespect was barely noticed.

The game remained scoreless until minute forty-five, when Egel skillfully dribbled around the Wolf and through his legs, kicking the ball at an impossible angle across the field and into the upper right corner of the goal, just past the outstretched arms of the Turkish goalkeeper. It was an amazing performance, and Egel reveled in his accomplishment. He ran around the circumference of the field, his arms raised in victory. The Israeli fans cheered wildly; the rest of the spectators booed and taunted them. The Wolf stood there on the field, bewildered, his head lowered in shame and his hands resting tensely on his hips. "I'm going to kill the Jew," he said to his teammates, first in a whisper, then louder and louder, until he was screaming with rage, "I'm going to kill the Jew!"

When the whistle blew and play resumed, the Wolf began his attack. First jogging, then running at full throttle, he approached Egel, and with all of his strength, he kicked Egel in the back of his neck. The impact of the Wolf's foot as it collided with Egel's neck was incredible, shattering several cervical vertebrae. Egel's head snapped back, met his shoulder blades, and was thrown forward again. With no control over his limbs, Egel was unable to protect his head as he fell forward, hitting the ground face-first. His body began seizing, a pool of blood forming in the grass around his head, then went completely lifeless.

Emergency medical technicians rushed onto the field. A cervical collar was placed around Egel's flaccid neck and an endotracheal tube was inserted into his throat. His lifeless body was lifted onto a stretcher and wheeled off the field.

All the players stood in shock, watching the events unfold—except for the Wolf, who now took his own lap around the field, his arms raised, both hands held in a "V" for victory. The officials ejected the Wolf from the game, and then took the unprecedented action of disqualifying the entire Turkish team. The Wolf was escorted off the field by his coaches, and was immediately apprehended by the police and brought in for questioning. The Turkish ambassador intervened, and the Wolf was released after posting bail. He was then ushered into a limousine that took him straight to Frankfurt Airport. The Wolf had already landed in Istanbul when a warrant was issued in Germany to arrest him for murder.

CHAPTER 74

Egel was declared dead shortly after his arrival in the emergency room. He returned to Israel in a body bag, on a chartered flight, accompanied by the rest of his team. They were greeted at the airport not by adoring fans but by bereaved friends and family.

Tikvah met Zar at the airport. He was relieved to see her—he missed her terribly, now more than ever—but not even Tikvah could console him. Egel had been Zar's best friend, a pillar of strength and encouragement in the most difficult times, during basic training, on the field during team practice and during games, and through the emotional roller coaster that was the World Cup. Losing Egel under any circumstances would have been difficult enough, but losing him this way, seeing him brutally murdered, was more than Zar could handle. He'd been holding back the tears since Egel's death, mostly out of shock and disbelief, but when he saw Tikvah, the floodgates opened. His strict adherence to Jewish religious law, however, meant that he couldn't embrace her, and that made him even more inconsolable.

Tikvah didn't know how to respond. What could she say? "It's okay"? But it *isn't* okay, she thought. It's horrible and shocking and there are no words to describe this kind of grief, let alone to assuage it. All she could offer Zar was her face, where he could see her concern and her love. Then she too broke down and cried.

Technically, Egel had died while on active duty in the Israel Defense Forces, so his funeral was held at the military cemetery on Mount Herzl in Jerusalem, near the Yad Vashem Holocaust memorial. The funeral was attended by thousands: soldiers, friends, soccer fans, politicians, Jews and Arabs, secular and religious, young and old. Like all of Egel's former teammates, Zar attended the graveside service, although he felt conflicted about it. He knew that, as a *kohen*, he could have no contact with dead bodies; even entering a cemetery was forbidden. Egel had been his closest friend, though. Zar felt obligated to attend the funeral—indeed, he knew he had to attend—so he was able to rationalize it to himself. Even a *kohen*, he reasoned, could attend the funeral of his brother, and Egel was like a brother to him...

He watched as Egel's coffin, draped in an Israeli flag, was carried to the grave. A cool breeze was little consolation as the sun mercilessly beat down upon the somber crowd. As the Prayer for the Soul of the Departed was recited, there was not a dry eye to be found:

> *Oh God, full of compassion, who dwells on high, grant true rest upon the wings of the Divine Presence...to the soul of Egel the son of David who has gone to his eternal world...*
> *May his place of rest be in the Garden of Eden...*
> *May he rest in his resting-place in peace, and let us say amen.*

CHAPTER 75

As an enlisted soldier attending a military funeral, Zar was wearing his army uniform. Hajji had never seen Zar in uniform, and he hesitated before greeting him. Finally, after the funeral, Hajji approached Zar and put an arm on his shoulder.

"Can you come with me?" Hajji asked. "I'd like to visit her grave."

"Whose grave?"

"Adin's. She's buried here, somewhere."

"Are you sure you want to? I mean, are you ready for that? It might be more than you can handle. It's a lot for one day—a lot of grief."

"I have to," Hajji insisted. "Please come with me. I don't think I can do it alone."

Hajji and Zar walked slowly down the path, away from one soldier's grave and in search of another's. Hajji thought he'd remember the way there, but soon realized that he was lost. All the paths were so similar: idyllic passages lined with grassy hills and flowers, pastoral, gentle ridges flanked by row after row of simple concrete slabs:

> *Meir, son of Yitzchak, age eighteen. Died August 8, 1948, driving a convoy on the road to Jerusalem…*
>
> *Moshe, son of Shlomo, age nineteen. Died June 6, 1967, fighting bravely to liberate Jerusalem…*
>
> *Eldad, son of Michael, age twenty. Died October 8, 1973, defending the Golan Heights…*
>
> *Dvir, son of Yosef, age twenty-one. Died September 10, 1982 in the battle of Sultan Yakub, Lebanon…*

The two young men felt small as they walked along, enveloped by thousands of graves, mostly of young people—many of them younger than themselves—who had all died in the prime of life, sacrificed on the altar of Zion as they protected their homeland, in search of an elusive peace, a peace that continued to elude them.

Many of the graves had small stones resting upon them. "What are the stones for?" Hajji asked.

"Actually, this is the first time I've ever been in a cemetery, so I don't know. I think Jews put stones on top of graves as a sign of respect. I'm not really sure." So, in compliance with this strange custom, Zar and Hajji each picked up a stone to place on Adin's grave.

Finally, after wandering in silence for a while, they chanced upon her grave. Several years had passed since Hajji had last been there. In the interim, a simple flat tombstone had been erected:

Adin, daughter of Chaim and Esther.
Died May 5, 2018, protecting her country...

They stood there for a few minutes, staring at the grave, still and speechless. Finally, Hajji started crying, softly at first. He rested his head on Zar's shoulder and wept. Zar, also overwhelmed by grief, put his head on Hajji's shoulder and began to cry. Two young men, a soldier and Hasid from Jerusalem and a Muslim from an Arab village in the Galilee, stood there, in a mournful embrace, weeping.

They cried for Egel.

They cried for Adin.

They cried for the row after row of young men and women who had given up their lives in defense of their country.

They cried for *all* of the dead in this bloody conflict that seemed to have no end.

They cried because of the madness of war.

They cried because they'd been rejected by their fathers and by their communities.

They cried because of all the violence and malice directed at them and at their team during the past few weeks: the incessant taunts and curses; the stones thrown at their bus, shattering windows and spirits; the bottles and garbage hurled at them and at their fans during the matches; the fires that would forever burn in their memories.

They continued to cry for a long time until, finally, Zar put his arm around Hajji's shoulders and said, "I think it's time to go."

"I can't," Hajji protested feebly, but retreated from the grave. They walked somberly back past the gate and into the parking lot.

In the brush behind a row of cars, Hajji saw something growing: a single red wildflower, a *kalanit*, proudly displaying its blood-red petals as if to say, "I am alive! Even after death, life will go on!" Hajji picked the wildflower, ironically ending its short life. As Zar watched in puzzled wonderment, Hajji ran back to the entrance of the cemetery. The two young female guards recognized him and asked him why he was returning. "I have to go back," Hajji declared, "to leave this flower at the grave."

The guards let him back in, assuming the flower was for the grave of the recently buried soccer player. But Hajji ran past Egel's grave and found his way to the grave of Adin. He dropped the single red flower there, silently contemplated her grave for a few moments, then ran back to Zar, who was waiting for him in the parking lot. "Now we can go," Hajji said, and the two men left the cemetery arm in arm.

CHAPTER 76

Egel's family sat *shiva*, observing the traditional mourning period at their home in Kibbutz Nahal Eitan. A steady stream of visitors came; politicians from across the spectrum of Israeli politics paid their respects, as did numerous ambassadors and some heads of state, including the German chancellor. A bouquet of flowers came from an anonymous admirer in Tehran. But nothing could console the mourners. Egel had lived the life of a hero, but he hadn't died a hero's death.

A debate erupted in the Israeli media when an editorial in the daily *Haaretz* suggested that the Israel National Team should not return to play the championship match against Germany. Even *with* Egel, the team would surely have lost to the far superior German team; without him, they didn't stand a chance. Furthermore, the editorial argued, it was simply unsafe to return. The loss of Egel was a respectable pretense; they could forfeit the game and still come out as victors.

Other voices strongly objected. For the legacy of Egel and for the honor of all Israelis and all Jews, the team *had* to return and play the championship match. True, they would likely lose the game, but forfeiting meant certain defeat. This was also the unanimous decision of the players and coaches. "Throughout our long history, the Jewish people have never given up," wrote Coach Avi in another op-ed published in *Haaretz*. "Our people—and our team—have beaten all odds. Maybe we will win this game; in any case, we will return to play the championship match. This is what Egel would have wanted!"

CHAPTER 77

On university campuses throughout the United States and in Europe, the Israeli soccer team had become a cause célèbre. Anti-Israel campus groups frequently disrupted public showings of their matches in order to denounce the Israeli team. There were also some displays of support for the Israeli national team, though. Christians United For Israel paid for Israel National Team billboards in dozens of major cities. A mega-church near San Antonio, Texas held a free public showing of the final match for ten thousand faithful fans, and hundreds of smaller churches hosted similar, albeit smaller, gatherings. A grassroots organization calling itself End the Madness pleaded for "calm and reconciliation" and opened chapters on college campuses all over the United States, and another group called Swords into Plowshares preached a similar message.

Egel's murder was a turning point in the news media's coverage of the Israel National Team. The *New York Times* published a series of articles chronicling the challenges the team had faced during the tournament. The Wolf had always been the darling of the Turkish media, but now there was only shock and condemnation of his murder of Egel. *Sports Illustrated* devoted an entire issue to the Israel National Team, with a picture of Hajji, hovering completely horizontal in mid-air blocking a shot at goal, on the cover. His blue wristband was clearly visible in the picture and the caption was "Pilgrim of Peace." That image became an iconic one, and silicone blue wristbands emblazoned with the words *shalom* and *salaam* became both commonplace and highly controversial.

CHAPTER 78

The Israel National Team had already arrived in Berlin when the decision was made to move the championship match almost four hundred miles away, to a stadium near the Munich airport, to allow for better security. This was the same airport where, almost half a century earlier, Israeli Olympic athletes were massacred by members of the PLO.

The match had originally been scheduled for a Saturday, but after petitions from the chief rabbis of both Israel and Munich, the date was postponed to Sunday, to accommodate Zar and to allow Jews in Israel and worldwide to watch the match without violating the Sabbath.

Now both teams and spectators had to get to Munich somehow. The German team flew in from Berlin on a private jet. The Israelis, finding that a massive and violent crowd had assembled at the airport, awaiting their arrival, decided to travel by bus instead. It would be safer, they reasoned, and it would likely save time. The drive to Munich would take around five hours; the delays they anticipated in getting to the Berlin airport and clearing airport security, plus the flight time and further delays at the Munich airport, could wind up costing them more time.

The plan was to leave Saturday morning so they could get to the hotel in Munich in the afternoon and have time to unwind and get a good night's sleep before the championship match.

"I won't travel on Saturday," Zar informed Avi and his teammates. "We have to wait until tomorrow night, after nightfall, when *Shabbos* is over."

"You've got to be kidding, Zar. I need the guys to be well-rested for the game. This is the final game of the World Cup! No one is asking you to drive. You'll just be a passenger!"

"I'm not going on that bus. I can't! I'll rent a car or take a cab after nightfall, but I won't go on the bus on *Shabbos*! Frankly, I don't think any of us should. For God's sake, they moved the match to Sunday out of respect for our tradition, and then we go and travel to the match on Saturday?"

Many of the players sided with Avi; the rest were indifferent. Hajji was the only one to support Zar. "Zar is right. I'm not even Jewish, but I feel strongly about this. Maybe it's *because* I'm not Jewish. I don't want to get into an argument here about religion or politics. I still haven't figured out where I belong here, how I fit in. But you claim to be representing the Jewish state. What that means, I don't even know. But if the Executive Committee of FIFA granted this exception and moved the match to Sunday, I think it would be a slap in the face to them and to your people in Israel and all over the world—"

"Are you serious, Hajji?" Avi asked.

"Dead serious. If the bus leaves tomorrow before nightfall, I'll stay behind and take a taxi with Zar tomorrow night."

One by one, the players were won over to Zar and Hajji's side, until the majority ruled: they would wait until nightfall and then leave by bus for Munich. They still indicated to the media that they'd be flying early Sunday morning, however, hoping that this ruse would throw off the angry masses and allow them safe passage to Munich.

On Saturday night, as soon as Zar said the *havdalah* blessings recited at the end of *Shabbos*, their trek to Munich began. To further deceive the mobs, they left their hotel in multiple small groups in sedans and met up at a predetermined spot, the parking lot of the bus rental company. As a further precaution, their new team bus was emblazoned with the name of a Christian tour group, although their two security escorts, one traveling in front and one behind, made the deception somewhat less convincing. After everyone had boarded the bus, they immediately set out for Munich. The players were mostly silent as the bus rolled past idyllic farms and pastoral scenery. They passed Potsdam and Leipzig, and after two and a half hours, the bus pulled into a rest stop in the town of Schleifreisen to refuel. A sign on the highway pointed to an eastbound exit toward Weimar, and beyond that, Buchenwald, the infamous concentration camp.

This was a prearranged stop, and four patrol cars from the local police department were already waiting for them with blue lights flashing. The original plan was for no one to get off of the bus as it refueled. The hour was late, and they all wanted to settle into their new hotel and get some rest. Besides, they didn't want to draw attention to themselves and risk blowing their cover. The toilet on the bus, however, was clogged and overflowing.

"I've got to pee," Mizrachi informed Avi. "I want to get off the bus and use the restroom at the gas station."

"Seriously?" Avi asked. "We don't have time, and our security team told us to stay on the bus until we reach the hotel."

"But I've got to pee!"

"Can't you hold it in? We haven't even been on this bus for three hours. Just hold it in for a few more hours—then you can pee all night long for all I care!"

"Listen, Avi, I've got to go!"

Several other players also started complaining. Some had to use the bathroom; others just wanted to stretch their legs. They were fed up with being imprisoned in their hotel and on their bus. Despite Avi's vocal opposition, the bus soon emptied out, and the players staggered into the rest stop. Next to the bathrooms was a small grocery that also served as the cashier for the gas station. The owner was a middle-aged Pakistani man. He watched in puzzlement as the large group of visitors filtered into the restroom and his shop. He glanced up at a television screen; the news had been dominated by the highly anticipated upcoming World Cup championship match. He looked again at his new customers, then again up at the screen. His mouth opened as his brain processed the scene unfolding before his eyes, which now widened in disbelief.

"Israel! You're Israel!" he declared in heavily-accented German, pointing wildly at the players.

Several of their security guards perked up, realizing that their cover had been blown, and uncertain if there would be an altercation.

"I love football! I love Israel!" he screamed in near-hysteria. "My son loves football too! Go Israel National Team! Hurray for Israel National Team!"

At this unexpected show of support, some of the players started laughing, as did the shopkeeper himself, the security guards, and even the police officers. The shopkeeper took a soccer ball off the shelf and hastily removed it from its box. "You'll sign my ball, yes? It's a gift for my son. He loves football! He loves Israel National Team!"

All the players and their coach autographed the ball, then posed for a team photo with the shopkeeper in the middle grinning widely and holding his new prized possession, which he later gave to his son. He later framed the photo of himself with the Israel National Team and displayed it prominently in his shop.

A few hours later, the team reached Munich. Their hotel was only about a mile away from the Dachau concentration camp, and some road construction forced their bus to make a detour onto Alte Römerstraße, directly past the entrance to the camp. In the moonlight, the guard tower cast an ominous shadow over their bus. Zar recalled the stories he'd heard about his great-grandfather's internment in Dachau and his escape, and wondered what message, if any, God was sending him. Perhaps he had an old score to settle, and destiny had brought him back full circle. Zar and his teammates slept well that night, enjoying some much-needed and much-deserved rest.

CHAPTER 79

The night before the final game, Zar received an entire crate over-flowing with fan mail. He rummaged through it quickly, selecting a few letters to read; he didn't have time to read them all. Two envelopes stood out. Both came from Jerusalem. One of them was scented with perfume, and was covered in Xs and Os, hearts, and faint lipstick marks from kisses. Before he even opened it, Zar knew it was from Tikvah. The second letter originated from a post office somewhere in Jerusalem and offered little other indication as to its source, but the handwriting on the envelope was vaguely familiar, so Zar set it aside as well.

He opened Tikvah's letter first, brushing his sidelocks behind his ears as he read:

Dear Zar,

Why did I write a letter? Why didn't I just pick up a phone and call you? Well, I wanted to give you something that you could preserve forever, rather than a conversation, which would be fleeting, only a memory, as sweet as our memories together are. So wouldn't it have been much easier to send you an email or a text message? My grandmother told me that letter writing is a lost art. When you read a handwritten letter, you can see the penmanship, the curvature of the letters. You can almost see and feel the person writing the letter. But even more than that, when someone sits down and takes the time and effort to write a letter, she is demonstrating how much she cares, how much the recipient means to the writer.

Zar, not a minute of the day goes by that I don't think of you and dream about you. My devotion to you is so complete, so all-encompassing, that I can hardly imagine life without you. And I know that you feel the same way about me.

Words cannot express the sorrow that I feel, that you feel, that our whole nation feels, about the death—the murder—of Egel. But I don't want to dwell on that now. It's too sad, too tragic. That's not the purpose of this letter.

Dear Zar, we all know the enormous challenge facing you and your team—our team. We've all seen and heard what the "experts" say, that it would take a miracle for the Israel National Team to win tomorrow. But wasn't it Ben Gurion who said that in Israel, to be a realist, you must believe in miracles? Israel's very existence is miraculous, so why should tomorrow's game be any different? And you, Zar, of all people, have shattered stereotypes and achieved the unachievable again and again. Zar, you have been waiting for this moment your whole life! You have literally been dreaming about it since you were a little boy. And now, this moment has finally arrived. It is your destiny to win this game!

You have so many fans who will be watching and cheering you on. Practically the whole country will be rooting for you. Tens of millions of people all over the world will be praying for you. And in Jerusalem, your biggest fan will be cheering louder than anyone else.

I love you more than words can describe. I'm anxiously awaiting your return to Israel as a champion!

Love always and forever,

Tikvah

Zar closed his eyes and held Tikvah's letter close to his face for a moment, then turned his attention to the second letter, the mystery letter from a nondescript post office in Jerusalem. The letter was written in Yiddish, and Zar immediately recognized the handwriting.

Dear Luzar,

Since the day you left, not a day has gone by that I don't think about you and worry about you and pray for you. I pray for your safety. I wonder, are you in harm's way? Are you fighting in battles with tanks and guns? Are you able to pray? To eat kosher food? To keep the Shabbos? To study the holy Torah? Do you miss the family? Do you think about us?

A few days ago, one of our neighbors, whose daughter is a teacher in a school outside the community, saw an article about you in a newspaper. She cut out the article and gave it to her mother, who gave it to me. I could hardly believe what I was reading! I had heard rumors that you were famous, but they were only rumors. You know that we don't read the traif newspapers, so this was the first time I had seen anything in writing.

First of all, I learned that you are a famous soccer player. You always loved soccer, and I suppose you are pursuing your dream, so I have mixed feelings. Part of me is sad that you aren't following the path of your father and your grandfathers. You are not a Torah scholar like them. But another part of me is happy that you are pursuing your dreams and that, hopefully, you are happy with your decisions. Isn't that what every mother wants for her son, for him to be happy? (I wouldn't tell that part to your father.)

And then I kept on reading the article. It said that you still have your beard and peyos (although from the picture, I can see that you cut them and tucked them behind your ears) and that you always cover your head with a yarmulke. It said that you pray every morning (and every afternoon and evening, I hope) and that you never play on Shabbos. That made me so proud! The article said that the whole schedule for this big tournament in Europe (in Germany, of all places!) was rearranged so that you and your team wouldn't have to play on Shabbos.

I also read that your teammate was killed during one of the games. That's terrible! It made me so worried about your safety too! Please be safe! I will continue praying for your safety and for your soul.

I think that your father has finally come to terms with your decisions. I can't say that he's accepted them or that he's proud of you, but he's not angry anymore. Your departure took a lot out of him. It took a lot out of me too. He's aged a lot since you last saw him. When you come back home, will you visit us? I will speak with your father. I don't want to show him the article. I think it would upset him. But he'll be very pleased to hear that you still observe our traditions. That, I think, will be a consolation of sorts.

I love you, Luzar, and I am anxiously waiting to see you again. Soon.

With blessings for health and strength and success in all of your endeavors,

Mama

CHAPTER 80

O n the morning of the match, Zar, accompanied by a security detail, made an unscheduled and unannounced visit to a synagogue in Munich for the morning prayers. He prayed for his team, for their safety, and for their success.

To memorialize Egel, the Israel National Team had small yellow flames stitched onto the left breasts of their jerseys. They didn't realize until they saw them that the small yellow flames resembled the yellow stars that Jews had to stitch on their clothing under the Nazis.

The Germans were heavily favored to win the match. They were the reigning champions, they had already handily defeated the Israelis in the qualifying round, and they had home field advantage. Their team, featuring several of Europe's top players, was reputed to be one of the best ever to have represented Germany in the World Cup. But among all of the stellar players, one stood out. This star striker's name, amusingly enough, was Streicher. He wasn't the top scorer in the league—or even among the top five highest scorers in the league. But he was extremely fast and agile, and his shots and passes were highly accurate. He was able to draw defenders toward him, opening up gaps on the other side of the field, so for three consecutive years, he led the league in assists by a wide margin. And like Zar, he was ambidextrous, and therefore equally dangerous from either side of the field, so defenses were constantly shifting to accommodate Streicher as he moved from one side of the field to the other. In the first match against the Israel National Team during the qualifying rounds, Streicher had either scored or assisted in all six of his team's goals. More than any other player on the German team, the Israelis feared Streicher.

Streicher did have one major flaw, though. He was overconfident, even conceited; he quarreled with his teammates even as he assisted them in scoring, and he fought incessantly with his coaches. He often disregarded his coaches' instructions, certain that he was wiser than them. Confident in his value to the team, he believed he was indispensable.

He drove fancy Italian sports cars, and was often hounded by the paparazzi as he and his supermodel girlfriend enjoyed the nightlife in one European city or another. He frequently arrived late to games; he enjoyed basking in the spotlight when he showed up just before the opening whistle, always to cheers from the roaring crowd.

No one was surprised, then, that on the day of the championship match, as the pre-game rituals were underway, Streicher hadn't yet arrived at the stadium. As the two teams did their stretches and warm-up practice drills, Streicher was still in his hotel room, taking a shower and getting dressed.

The teams were introduced by the announcer, and the fans cheered and booed. The two national anthems, first Germany's, then Israel's, were played. As he sang *Hatikva*, Zar thought of *his* Tikvah, thousands of miles away.

Hajji did not sing *Hatikvah*, which declares the two-thousand-year-old hope of the Jewish people to return to their land. "The song," he had explained to the Israeli media, "does not speak to me or about me or my people." But he still stood in silence out of respect for his teammates. Looking up at the flashing billboards that adorned the stadium, an ad caught his eye. Above some German verbiage was a familiar image of a beautiful woman, laughing as she tried in vain to hold down her dress, which was being lifted up by the wind. It was an iconic image of Marilyn Monroe, the one Adin had set as the background on her cellphone. Hajji saw it as a message of sorts: Adin was no longer alive, but she was still with him in spirit. He looked at his sapphire-blue wristband, emblazoned with the words *shalom* and *salaam*, and felt a sudden boost of reassurance, as if Adin herself were whispering softly in his ear, "Hajji, you are an impenetrable wall. You can block every attempt at a goal. You can win this game!" Then Hajji looked into the stands and saw thousands of spectators sporting blue wristbands, demonstrating solidarity with Hajji and with the Israel National Team. He was overcome with emotion and infused with confidence.

Finally, only minutes before the opening whistle, Streicher showed up at the stadium. His head coach yelled frantically as Streicher pranced on the field, waving to the fans and basking in their vociferous display of affection. The game began. Streicher, eager to show his superiority, sprinted at lightning speed down the field. But the Israeli players, who had watched countless videos of Streicher and had studied his moves, clung to him closely, preventing him from finding a clean angle to pass the ball to his teammates. After several minutes of play and constant harassment by the Israelis, Streicher lost his cool and pushed Zar in the chest with both hands, screaming expletives. Zar fell to the ground and landed on his backside, sustaining no serious injuries. Meanwhile, the referee charged at Streicher and presented him with a red card, ejecting him from the game.

Zar watched with a mixture of pity and glee, trying but failing to mask his smile as he and his teammates contemplated their sudden change in fortune. Zar looked down at his leg and spied the shoulder tag Tikvah had given him peeking out of his right sock. It was as if Tikvah herself were at his side whispering, "Zar, you can do it! Your moment is here!"

The crowd was deafening; there were more fans supporting Israel than at the previous World Cup matches. Half the stadium was designated for fans of Israel, and they had arrived with unabashed pride. Somehow, the collective trauma felt by all Israelis—by all Jews—over the events of the past few weeks had brought a previously suppressed pride and courage to the surface.

The other half of the stadium was filled with fans of Germany, equally loud and equally proud, but their enthusiasm went into cheering on their own team rather than putting down their underdog opponent, so there was less blatant antisemitism and anti-Zionism than at previous matches. Nonetheless, scattered here and there throughout the stands were Palestinian flags and signs with anti-Israel slogans—"Free Gaza," "We are all Abdel," "Palestine will be free from the river to the sea"— and mock-Israeli flags with blue swastikas replacing the six-pointed Star of David. In one section of the stadium, a group of German fans displayed Nazi flags, gave Nazi salutes, and heckled the Israeli players and spectators with "*Heil Hitler!*" and other racist taunts. Within moments, police stormed that section and, after a brief scuffle, arrested them.

Once again, the Israeli team played with incredible focus and discipline. Hajji was an impenetrable wall, skillfully deflecting the few German attempts at a goal. On offense, Weisman replaced Egel as Zar's right flank, and the two were a constant menace for the German defense. But the German goalkeeper also performed perfectly, and the game remained scoreless well into the second half.

CHAPTER 81

B ack in Israel, most of the streets were deserted. Nearly every Israe-li—with the exception of the ultra-Orthodox Jews—was watching the game. The usually busy thoroughfares and highways were almost empty, as if it were the eve of Yom Kippur.

In nearly every home, Jewish or Arab, a television or computer was broadcasting the match. On every army base, the soldiers crowded around screens to watch. On Kibbutz Nahal Eitan, the mood was bittersweet, but they cheered with enthusiasm for their beloved team. In the small village of Al'ard Alhamra in the southeastern Galilee, men and boys crowded around television screens in public spaces and in private homes. Among the cheering fans was an older bearded man, wearing the traditional *thawb* robe and *keffiyeh* headdress, smoking a homemade Palestinian cigarette. He watched attentively, silently, trying but failing to hide his smile as the world's greatest goalkeeper stopped every attempted goal.

Huge screens and massive speakers were set up in prime locations in many cities. At Dizengoff Square in Tel Aviv and Jaffa Road in Jerusalem, where the light rail service had been suspended for the afternoon, tens of thousands of people congregated. Israelis from all walks of life were there, Jews and Arabs, religious and secular—even a handful of ultra-Orthodox from the nearby enclave of Mea She'arim. Hiding in the shadows toward the back of the crowd was a middle-aged man whose long white-gray beard made him look older. He had come to watch his son Elazar do what he loved to do, what he could do better than almost anyone else on earth: play soccer.

With time running out and overtime imminent, the game remained scoreless, and all the players were tiring physically and mentally. Every now and then, the crowd erupted as one team or the other snuck a shot at goal, only to be deflected by the fingertips of the goalkeeper.

As the sun set and the floodlights came on, a gentle breeze caressed the perspiring players. Zar felt transfixed, dissociated; he envisioned himself back in the alleyway where he'd practiced soccer as a child, imagining adoring fans chanting his name: "Luzar, Luzar, Luzar..." He saw himself playing in the schoolyard with the *traif* boys, imagining adoring fans chanting his name: "Zar, Zar, Zar..." He recalled the night he ran away from home and heard his father call his name: "Luzar, Luzar, Luzar..."

He was now living a dream, within a dream, within a dream. He imagined—as if the sound could carry over the thousands of miles—that he could hear the fans chanting his name in the streets of Jerusalem. He was above nature, invincible, the only man on the field; there were no opponents, no teammates, just Zar and a ball and a goal. And no force on Earth could stop Zar from reaching that goal.

As if the ball were tethered to his feet, Zar dribbled past one defender, then another, from right to left and back again, working his way forward. With only seconds left on the clock, he struck the ball at an impossible angle, with great force and precision. It soared over the heads of two German defenders, just past the goalkeeper's fingertips, and into the upper right corner of the goal.

The crowds erupted first with screams of joy, with hugs and tears, and then started chanting, "Zar, Zar, Zar..." In Munich, in Tel Aviv, and in Jerusalem, "Zar, Zar, Zar..." And one man, with a long white-gray beard and a long black frock coat, joined in the revelry, screaming, "Luzar, Luzar, Luzar..." Zar and Hajji were lifted up by their teammates and carried on their shoulders as the clock ran out with the score 1-0, and with Israel first among nations.

Acknowledgments

It all began at a meeting with Fern Reiss of The Publishing Game, in a cafe on Emek Refaim Street in Jerusalem. I had a manuscript, a rough draft, and I didn't know how to proceed. She convinced me that for my project, self-publishing would be both preferrable and achievable. But to accomplish this goal I needed to assemble a team. I then met Martha Bullen of Bullen Publishing Services who has been holding my hand (virtually) every step of the way. I can't thank her enough for her patience and expertise! I also offer my boundless praise to David Aretha, my very talented and humorous developmental editor, who guided and trained me to restructure, fine-tune and generally enhance my manuscript. I am indebted to Josh Halickman of www.sportsrabbi.com and sports columnist for the Jerusalem Post for his expert advice regarding the Israeli soccer (okay, football!) scene and the World Cup competition. Thank you, Christy Collins of Constellation Book Services, for creating the gorgeous cover and interior design and typesetting.

I also have much gratitude to my talented team of marketing specialists. Specifically, I sing the praises of Michael Boezi of Control Mouse Media for web design, podcasting, SEO and overall digital and social media marketing strategy, and Sharon Tousley of Podcast Prowess for orchestrating my podcast, and for spearheading my presence on social media. And I express much appreciation to Gail Snyder for crafting a press release, and to Eva Case-Issakov for her persistent targeted pitching and promoting of this book.

There are also many friends, acquaintances and family members whom I thank for being my beta readers, critics, fact checkers, and *pro bono* legal advisors. You know who you are! I thank Gary, Craig,

254 First Among Nations

Teri, Khaled, Rabbi G., Robert, Evy, Monica, Nachum, Sam M., Uri, Moshe, Bina, Yoni, Amir, Sam R., Aliza M., Tali, Aliza K., and Yossi. I also thank my parents and in-laws for teaching me right from wrong, instructing me how to identify my priorities, and always encouraging and appreciating me. I sincerely thank you. I would be remiss if I didn't thank all of the flight attendants and airport staff on countless flights and in countless airports spanning three continents, since the bulk of this work was done while I commuted between my home in Israel and work in the US.

Words cannot express my gratitude to my dear wife, Judy, who always has faith in me and encourages me to follow my dreams. She is both my best friend and my most valued advisor, and also an amazing proofreader! I wouldn't be where I am today, both literally and figuratively, without her.

Finally, but most importantly, I thank God who has granted me whatever skills and intellect I need to succeed in this project, and in all of my professional and personal endeavors. My goal in writing this book is to find a common ground that binds us all together, to build bridges, and to change the conversation from a contentious one to one of mutual respect and understanding. Ultimately, my goal is to help, in whatever tiny way I can, to promote peaceful coexistence. I pray every day for peace, and I thank God for His promise that peace—as elusive as it may seem—is, ultimately, attainable.

About the Author

IRA MOSEN, MD, is a physician who is also an avid reader. He was born and raised on the East Coast and received his medical training in an Ivy League institution. Once he completed his residency and fellowship, he joined a successful private medical practice in the Midwest. After working there for nearly 15 years, he fulfilled his lifelong dream and moved with his family to Israel in 2018. Dr. Mosen currently works at a health clinic in central Israel which provides high-quality medical care to Israelis of all backgrounds and religions at a low cost.

Through his interactions with a diverse population of Israelis, he has observed an Israel that is markedly different from the one often portrayed in the media, with much grassroots desire for peaceful coexistence. These experiences inspired him to write his debut novel, *First Among Nations*.

For more information on the book and accompanying podcast, please visit www.iramosen.com.

CPSIA information can be obtained
at www.ICGtesting.com
Printed in the USA
LVHW030039160321
681602LV00005B/1316

9 781735 374109